AN ICE COLD PARADISE

AN ICE COLD PARADISE

A Harry Pines Novel

Terry Holland

POINT BLANK

AN ICE COLD PARADISE

Point Blank
www.pointblankpress.com

ISBN: 0-8095-7242-7

To the Masters of Mayhem:

Dash and the Op,
Ray and Phil,
Mickey and Mike,
John D. and McGee,
and Robert B. and Spenser.

You may have been a problem but you never were a bore.

ONE

Monday, March 10
Kailua, Oahu, Hawaii

I was on my knees cursing the mealy bugs or aphids or whatever the hell was having lunch on my hibiscus kokio when a little red convertible driven by a lot of dark hair pulled through the gate and nosed up to the low wall of my front yard.

Cursing the critters is my first line of attack. I want them to get the message and just go away so I won't have to go nuclear. I hate killing them. It offends my affinity with Francis of Assisi. I said, "Fuck every one of you and all the horses you rode in on," and a few of them scuttled off. I'm not going all the way to sainthood with this and I think some of them, maybe the leaders, understood I have my limits. I hope so.

I stood up to take a look at my company. She was healthy, and nimble, too. I observed this as she took the three steps up into the yard with a quick little hop that did nice things for her legs and my imagination. She wore a yellow sundress with little straps at the top and a flouncy skirt that stopped well short of her knees. She walked right up and looked me in the eye and said, "Nice hat."

I'm not stupid. I know sarcasm when I hear it. I said, "I'm not stupid. I know sarcasm when I hear it."

"No," she said. "I really like it."

I glared at her and she smiled at me. I said, "If you knew anything about the demands of tropical gardening, you'd show more respect for this hat." It has about a three-foot brim and a high pointed crown. Straw. Think of a witch in a rice paddy.

"I'm looking for Harry Pines," she said.

"You played lucky. Who're you?"

"Valerie Sabatino."

"That a stage name?"

"Nope. That's my real name."

"And?"

"Can we talk?"

"What about?"

"A missing person. Missing here. My nephew."

"I look like a guy who looks for missing people?"

She backed up a step and looked down at my feet and came up slowly from there, slowing at my torso, and settling at my face with her head tilted a little. She said, "I don't know what a guy like that looks like."

"So, was it my ad in the Yellow Pages?"

"My nephew is Danny MacGillicuddy. His father is Packy MacGillicuddy. He sent me."

"Far out. You just earned yourself a glass of iced tea." I went up the front steps, across the lanai, and into the kitchen and she came along with me. I put the hat on a wall hook as I entered. Leanne and a girl I didn't recognize were at the counter eating sandwiches. They wore bikini tops and shorts, either just up from the beach or on the way.

"Leanne, Valerie," I said.

"Harry, Sally," Leanne said.

"Hello," Valerie and Sally said.

I washed my hands, filled two glasses from the pitcher in the refrigerator, cut a lemon into quarters, squeezed and dropped one into mine and glanced at Valerie, who nodded, so I put another into hers. "You won't need sugar," I said, handing her a glass. "Off we go."

I went out the other side of the kitchen, along the breezeway just the few steps to my apartment. I held the door for her and she went in and I followed. I sat on a stool by the door and took off my sneakers. She watched me and said, "That's a custom over here, isn't it?"

"Yes, it is. But I'm not observing the custom. I just like to go barefoot. It's up to you."

She kicked off her sandals.

I said, "Sit anywhere you like," and she slow circled the room like an old dog and plopped into the best seat in the house, a huge armchair big enough for two, swung her legs in a wide arc and put them up on the ottoman. She took a long draw on her tea and set it beside her on an odd copper thing somebody once told me is an Oriental Tea Caddy.

I took the cane rocker and cranked it to face her. I said, "You're, what, Danny MacGillicuddy's…mother's…sister?"

"Half sister. Same mother, different dad."

"And Danny is missing?"

"Yes. He's a soldier, stationed here."

"He's AWOL?"

"So it seems. Doesn't make sense. Danny was about to get out. He disappeared from some kind of exercise, went somewhere without authority ten days before he could have gone anywhere with no questions asked. When my sister got the notice, she called Packy, they talked, she said I'd be better ... said she'd get hold of me, have me call him. I did."

"Where's Packy?"

"Nevada state prison. Place called Ely."

"How'd you find me?"

"Packy said he'd heard Hawaii." The con network. "You're not hiding."

"And why... What's your sister's name? Melinda?"

"*Belinda*."

"Why did Belinda think you could handle this?"

"I think she just thought I'd be better than her. You know Belinda?"

"No. Just heard Packy talk about her. He gave her high marks."

"She deserves them. I'm a lawyer. Been one long enough to know that doesn't mean much, but Belinda thinks it makes me Wonder Woman or something. I'm probably a little short of that but I wasn't about to turn her down."

"What's Packy think happened?" I asked.

"Doesn't know. Something bad, I think he thinks."

"That's what you tend to think when you're inside."

"I'm sure."

"Has he stayed in touch with Danny? Know what's been going on with the kid?"

"They write, Packy said. And talked now and then. He said Danny visited him not long ago and Packy gave him your name in case Danny needed ... somebody like you."

"Packy indicate why he'd need somebody like me?"

"No."

"How long's Danny been here?"

"Nineteen months."

"And Packy just got around to giving him my name? What kind of kid is he? You know him well?"

"Yeah. I haven't had much contact the past few years, but I'm actually closer to his age than to Belinda's, so I had a kind of big sister thing going with Danny when he was a kid. I thought it was a good thing he joined the army, thought he needed that kind of discipline, because he had a little bit of a streak in him, wanted to be a tough guy. Sort of a loner, too, not real social. And probably not college material. But he was never in any kind of real trouble."

"That would put Danny's apple a long way from Packy's tree. How about Belinda? What's her opinion of Danny?"

"She's his mother. You remember what your mother thought of you?"

"No, but I get your point. And since he's been a soldier?"

"From what I know, what Belinda tells me, he's been a good soldier. Got his share of badges and little recognitions. Survival training. Marksmanship. Like that."

"Where's Belinda now?"

"Louisville. She's married to a college professor."

"What's his name?"

"Why?"

"I'm nosy. It'll grow on you."

"Roscoe Franklin."

"What did Packy tell you I could do?"

"He just hopes maybe you'll look into it. He said if you would, you'd find out. He said you're the toughest son of a bitch he's ever met and you don't have much backup in you. And you've got a great shit detector."

"Have you seen the paper work on this?"

"Just the letter of notification."

"Which says?"

"Nothing, really. Just a pro forma notification of his absence."

"Talked to them yet?"

"Yes. Said I'd be coming over. Asked them to assemble the record for me. Made an appointment for tomorrow morning. I got in a couple of hours ago, rented the car, checked in, came looking for you."

"And you want me to ask the Army what happened?"

"Us. I'm in. I can pay you."

"Yeah? You a woman of means?"

"I have resources. What are your rates?"

"I don't have rates."

"I want to pay for your help. May I?"

"We'll see. How long have you got for this? You took some time off from work?"

"I quit my job a few months ago."

I waited for her to say why. She didn't. I said, "Little young to be so independent."

"Easier when you're young, I'd say."

"Where're you from?"

"Here and there. Most recently San Diego. Del Mar."

"Beautiful part of the world."

"This isn't bad either."

"No. But no racetrack. What time tomorrow?"

"Just morning was all I said."

"Where're you staying?"

"The Royal Hawaiian."

"I'll meet you about 8:30. In the lobby."

I walked her to her car. She turned at the steps and looked around. "What have you got here?"

"It's five apartments, six counting mine," I said, pointing them out. "Five down there, each one with a front entrance to the lanai, which is what they call this long porch across the front, and each with a rear door to the back yard and the beach. Each apartment has a small kitchen, a room off that for whatever, plus a bedroom and bath. Lots of windows, couple of skylights. That's all. I rent four of them and keep one open for good friends or my partner when he comes over. And I put a second story on mine so I could see the sunset over the treetops, turned my bedroom into an office and library."

"Got time to show me around?"

"Sure."

I walked to the front entrance and she followed.

"This is the… I don't know what to call it…the main room."

It is vast, maybe sixty feet from front to back and half that side to side, with a vaulted ceiling that rises to thirty feet. Up front, there are enough sofas and soft chairs to accommodate a dozen people comfortably, or more if they feel like rubbing up against each other, with a huge television against one wall and a Bose setup against the other, six speakers wired to the stereo and the TV, four inside and two out back. Behind the layabout space, a dining table that will handle twelve, and to the rear, just off the back lanai, there's a pool table, an Olhausen, which doubles as a buffet table for parties.

"It's a great room," she said. "That's what you should call it. The Great Room."

"Sounds a little pretentious, but okay. Over here is the kitchen. I'm on the other side of that. As you know. Fine kitchen, if I do say so myself. A Viking range, dual fuel, eight burners, two ovens. Granite counter tops. Built-in Sub Zero."

She looked at me with a small smile, like she'd caught me at something.

"I'm bragging, I know, but I love kitchens. And this is the first one I ever built from scratch, so I put a lot of thought into it. And a lot of money. The people who live here have access to all this, of course. It's kind of like a kibbutz."

"Without the suicide bombers."

"Yeah."

We went through the main room, the Great Room, to the big back lanai where there's a jacuzzi big enough for eight, a Weber Summit grill, and a glass-topped table surrounded by six chairs beneath an umbrella.

"I'm still working on the yard," I said, as we went down the four steps.

"What's that? Tool shed?" she asked, pointing to a flat-roofed, free-standing structure with wide doors tucked off to the side.

"Yeah. And a halfass gym. I keep a set of weights and a bench in there. A heavy bag and a speed bag."

We walked along the stone path I've laid and past the hole in the ground I'm trying to turn into a pond.

"Someday this'll be a pond. Don't ask when," I said.

"Full of those fat goldfish that look like they're coming out of a coma?"

"Koi. No. No koi. They're pathetic looking. Something more exotic. That's why it's not finished. It'll have to be a lot deeper for the fish I want. Maybe I'll just forget it, fill it in. Or make it into a fountain."

"Beautiful flowers," she said. "You're the gardener?"

"Yeah. But I get help from the others. Most of these are indigenous. The palms were already here." There are six of them along the back property line, forty-feet tall and leaning in from a lifetime of bending to the wind. "I put the fence sections up between them to keep people from cutting through that way and damaging the flowers." The fence is wrought iron, a Philip Simmons design I had seen years ago in Charleston and had made over here. With Simmons' permission and my payment for the privilege. I'd have liked it more if he'd made it but the freight stunned me out of that idea.

The path led us to a wrought iron gate, the final section of the fence, that's perpendicular to a high hedge that separates me from the house next door. I unlatched it and it squeaked as it always does and we stepped on to the beach.

The Pacific Ocean, Kailua Bay actually, was in front of us across fifty yards of beige sand. Leanne and Sally sprawled on a couple of big towels, halfway down. Dark, heavy clouds roiled in the distance. The bay was dotted with sails.

"We keep this outrigger canoe," I said, pointing to the right, "and the nets,"—they were strung up along a rig of poles—"for fishing for our dinner. And this Boston Whaler." It's a seventeen-footer with a center console and a 90-horsepower Mercury. It's on a trailer that we wrestle to the water with a cable and winch rigged to one of the palms. "We fish from it, too. And day-trip to some of the smaller islands."

"Do you own the beach, too?"

"No. Nobody owns the beaches in Hawaii. They belong to all the people. The tree line is where my property ends."

"I'm impressed. Are you a man of means?"

"Men of means don't have a mortgage like I've got."

"Owning this," she said, "doesn't quite fit with what I expected."

"From an ex-con? Yeah. Especially one squared up."

"What's the history of this place?"

"The military built it sixty years ago as a retreat for the brass. It was pretty beat up when we bought it two years ago. The government was in one of those phases they go through where they want to sell obsolete assets. My partner used to live in Hawaii and knew of it and we were bucks up and flew over for the auction. We won."

"Bucks up?" she asked with a little tilt of her head.

"Yeah. It works as a business. Pays for itself with a little cushion for the landlord and gardener. I get real good rates and, even at the prices, I can be pretty picky about the people I rent to. Which is important, living like this."

"Apartments, not condos?"

"Yeah. They want to buy and if I could be sure the people here now would stay forever, I'd go for it. But things change, and it'd be hard for me to reserve the right to approve the people they might want to someday sell to. That scares me some."

"Yes. One bad apple…"

"Been lucky so far."

I walked her back through the gate and along the hedge past the herb and vegetable garden to the front and her car in the wide gravel turnaround flanked by a six-carport.

She reached for the door handle but I got there first and opened it for her.

"Thank you," she said, and smiled right at me. "Chivalry. A lost art."

"I'm old fashioned."

"You build the front wall?"

"With help." It's ivy-covered brick, seven feet tall, open only at the gate. Did it to remind me of Wrigley.

"Nice touch," she said. "Reminds me of Wrigley."

"Thanks. See you in the morning." I closed the door and she drove off with one hand in the air in a wave.

Hmm.

• • • • •

I met Packy MacGillicuddy a while back when I came up from the hole for the third and last time and found him sitting on a bunk in my cell. He was playing four hands of twenty-one against himself as the house, all the cards face-up. He put a big, full-faced smile on me and I stood there stonily as the hack slammed the self-locking door behind me and trundled down the walkway.

"Patrick Aloysius MacGillicuddy at your service. Federal Bureau of Prisons number 748, dash, 340, dash, 9922. Call me Packy. Pleased to meetcha."

"You haven't met me."

"Prob'ly will, though, sharing a cell with you. Harry Pines, right? Relax, brother. You got no worries with me. Much trouble as you go to ta keep from getting butt-fucked, I sure ain't gonna bring any more down. I do easy time. It all plays with me. I'm just getting by."

In the six months we celled together, my last six, I came to like Packy more than anybody I met inside, not that there was much competition. He was right about doing easy time. He never had a bad day or even a bad mood. He was decent, funny, and interesting, had a lot of stories to tell and he never seemed to be hiding anything as he told them. But he was. They all are.

He had grown up tough, fought professionally, as a welterweight, and when he got tired of taking punches he went to Las Vegas and got hooked on the bright lights and non-stop action. He dealt for a while, then played the tables, then cheated the tables and the slots, and then took to supplementing his income by doing favors for people, one of whom set him up with a guy who wanted to buy a silencer. The guy was an ATF undercover agent. Packy's pal gave them Packy to reduce his own pending sentence and when Packy handed over the silencer he was on his way to spend five years of his life at the Federal Correctional Institution at Terminal Island in the Los Angeles Harbor. That's where I met him.

"Silencer! Sonofabitch wasn't nothing more'n a piece a pipe, loud as shit, sounded like a atom bomb when they shot it off in court, hundred and fifty dollars I got for it." It made him laugh.

TWO
Tuesday, March 11

The next morning I drove my muddy five-year-old Range Rover across the Pali Highway to Honolulu. I had intended to wash it but Richie and I took the canoe out last night and spread the nets and brought them in at dawn with a nice catch and by the time we tidied up I was running late.

The Pali rises from sea level on my side of the island, the windward, up the Koolau mountains to a tunnel at about 2,500 feet and then descends a little less precipitously into downtown Honolulu. It would be a failure of vocabulary to call the views beautiful. They justify this superlative: God did His best work in Hawaii. If there is a God.

Oahu is my choice of the islands. Because of the city. There isn't another city out here. They think the big resort villages on Maui and the Big Island—Hilo and Kailua, Kahului and Kehei—are cities but they aren't. They're too clean and too safe, like big theme parks. Honolulu is a city, a place where you can get anything, even things you don't want.

In the city, I turned east on King Street and followed it until it hooked up to Kapiolani Boulevard and took that to Kalakaua, Waikiki's main drag, where everyone, walking or driving, blissfully presumes the right-of-way is theirs, an epidemic of *droit de seigneur* at the Pacific Rim. In self-defense, fearing imminent disaster, I always proceed with great care, timidly.

When I reached the Royal Hawaiian I gave the keys to a valet at the entrance. He looked at it like he didn't know where to grab a hold that wouldn't dirty his pink-and-white uni. I gave him a twenty and said, "If you can get it washed, I've got another one of these. I'll be back for it about the middle of the afternoon."

"I can get it detailed for a hundred," he said.

"Do it. Need it by two."

She was waiting in the lobby, dressed for success in a blue, double-breasted, pin-striped suit with a knee-length skirt, and heels. Her thick, dark mane was pulled back with a clip. She looked like a high-priced lawyer and I told her so.

"Good. That's the plan. Besides, I am one. Want coffee?"

"If you've had yours, I'll take one to go. If you'll drive. My truck's too dirty for you to ride in. Valet's having it cleaned."

"Okay," she said, "but I'll have to do it with the top up. Don't want to meet Uncle Sam looking like a wind-blown bimbo."

We took Kalakaua back to the Lunalilo Freeway, H-1. Where it crossed the Ala Wai Canal, she asked what it was.

"That's the Ala Wai Canal. It was built back in the twenties as a catch basin for three mountain streams over there…" I pointed to the right. "… that used to drain into the Pacific through the Waikiki beaches. Somebody was smart enough to see that they could turn Waikiki into one of the most perfect beaches in the world if they could divert those streams. It's sunny so often on this side it's boring, and the beach is wide and white for more than a mile. The canal made it possible." The canal cuts a hundred-yard-wide swath about a half-mile back from the beach, running east to west for two miles where, every day, it empties thirty million gallons of water into the Ala Wai Basin and Yacht Harbor. Like most solutions, it presents its own range of problems: litter, sediment, pesticides.

We hooked up with H-1 and took it west through the city to its connection with H-2, just above Pearl Harbor, and from there to Schofield.

"You can't be too careful on these interstates," I said. "The Chinese only know two speeds, pedal to the metal and sudden stop. And they use Zen to signal their intentions."

"Zen?"

"Yeah. Be as one. Share all thoughts."

"Interstates?"

• • • • •

We were in the office of Lieutenant Colonel Robert Sweet, the Commanding Officer of the 1st Battalion, 35th Infantry Division. He hadn't been easy to find, nor easy to get in to see after we found him, but once treed, he was a model of military decorum. Crisp and attentive, but guarded. He was a little guy and sat up real straight like he was stretching his frame to add a few inches.

After expressing deep concern for Valerie's nephew, he turned to me.

"And you are?" he asked.

"Her friend. A family friend." I gave him a card. It has my name on it, but no address, no phone number. "Could you tell us what happened?"

"I'll tell you what we know happened. It may leave you wondering, as we are, what actually happened.

"Spec Four Daniel MacGillicuddy and his company went on a routine exercise on…" He glanced at a document before him. "…on Wednesday, twenty-six February. It was a simulated escape and evasion drill. In the lower reaches of the East range of the Koolaus. Near the Ku Tree reservoir. They were driven to a drop-off location and marched up range for forty-five minutes to a compound, a mock prison if you will, where they were impounded. Their task was to escape, by any means possible, pair up and evade attempts to recapture them, survive by hiding in the jungle terrain overnight, and make their way the next day back to the drop-off location where they were to be picked up at fifteen hundred hours.

"The troops executed the escape by overpowering their guards. A simulated overpowering, of course. The challenge of the drill was to survive in the jungle, not to bring harm to their fellow soldiers. They disappeared into the jungle. The next day, at the appointed time, one hundred eighty-seven soldiers were picked up, all in good health and accounted for. Except for Spec Four MacGillicuddy. All those who were on hand, including those up range in the prison compound, instituted a search that continued until the light failed. At that point, a twenty-five person scout platoon took up the search and worked through the night with the benefit of tracking dogs.

"The next day, three companies of my battalion engaged the search, approximately five hundred soldiers, plus tracking dogs, three helicopters, and a number of all-terrain vehicles. It went on all day. At approximately seventeen hundred hours, the search commander was notified that Spec Four MacGillicuddy had been seen, positive identification, the previous day on the shore road near Haleiwa. The search was called off.

"The Military Police interviewed a civilian, a former soldier who was recently under my command, who had seen MacGillicuddy, and a soldier who came forward to say that he also had seen him. Their statements were accepted. Spec Four Daniel A. MacGillicuddy was then declared Absent Without Authority. The matter is now in the hands of the Military Police. That's it."

"Do you think it odd," Valerie asked, "that he would go off like this ten days before he was to be honorably discharged?"

"Somewhat. But there it is."

"How was his military record?"

"He was a good soldier."

"Are you looking for him?" I asked.

"Well, yes, of course, but there's only so much we can do. It's been almost two weeks now and there's no trail to follow."

"What did the Military Police do?" Valerie asked.

"Interviewed his acquaintances. Surveilled certain places he was known to frequent. Distributed flyers with his photo. Two soldiers who knew him were dispatched along the north shore to inquire. MacGillicuddy was a surfer, you see."

"Airport?"

"Yes. And the harbor. We distributed photos to security and examined passenger manifests. All negative."

"Is that continuing?"

"I assume so. It's in the hands of the Military Police, as I said."

"Suspect anything criminal?" I asked.

"You mean on his part?"

"That, or something that might have happened to him."

"We're not exactly in the suspicion business, Mr. Pines. We're soldiers. We deal with the facts before us. Your nephew, Ms. Sabatino, disappeared. And that's where it is."

"Are the Honolulu police involved?" I asked.

"We are the police on this military reservation."

"Does that mean no?"

"Yes, that means no."

"I'd like to interview the two who identified him, as well as read their statements," Valerie said. "And I'd like to meet with the soldiers who were on the exercise with him. And those who shared his quarters. And I'd like copies of all statements in the official record."

"And we'll need to see his personal effects," I added.

"The statements are here," he said, "along with the report. As for the interviews, you'll have to clear those with the appropriate commanding officers, see the men when they're off duty. And you'll have to contact the civilian independently of us."

"If we're going to see them when they're off duty, why do we have to clear it with their commanding officers?" Valerie asked. I was beginning to wonder how much she needed me.

"This is a military reservation, Ms. Sabatino. Not a barnyard. We have procedures."

"You said the soldiers paired up when they broke out of the compound," I said. "Can you give us the name of the soldier who paired with Spec Four MacGillicuddy?"

"I don't believe I have that," he said, riffling his file.

"Colonel Sweet," Valerie said. "I know you want to settle this matter as much as we do. Wouldn't you rather assemble the people we need to speak with rather than having us wander all over the reservation looking for them?"

"Who would that be?"

"As I said," she said, with a lawyerly edge to her voice. "His roommates. The two men who saw him on the beach road. The platoon commander. The soldier he paired with on the exercise. Those to begin with."

"As *I* said, Ms. Sabatino, one of the two who saw him is a civilian. I have no authority over him."

"Since this is an ongoing investigation into the disappearance of a soldier under your command, Colonel, and since I am both an attorney and a member of the family of the missing soldier, and since the civilian was *formerly* under your command, I'm sure you have enough *influence*, if not actual authority, to have that man come forward to speak with us. And also to assemble the others for our convenience. If the police were handling this, I'm sure they would do no less."

He sighed. She was enough to make anybody sigh. He said, "All right. I'll try to arrange that."

"Shall we say tomorrow?"

"I think that may be possible."

"What time?" Valerie asked.

"I should think mid-day."

"Noon, then," she said. "We'll be here. Perhaps you could schedule the interviews at half-hour intervals. You can reach me on my cell phone if there's any problem." She took her business card, laying it on his desk, and wrote a number on it.

We left, but politely.

• • • • •

She asked me to drive on the return so she could read the report. She took her jacket off and unclipped her hair and I lowered the top.

I was quiet while she read the report. She closed the file and said, over the wind, "This is going to take some time."

"I know. Anything in there?"

"The statements are pretty interesting. Do you have it?"

"The time? Sure. But I've got a thought about how we could save some."

"And that is?"

"We check you out of the Pink Palace and put you up in my guest apartment. Wouldn't have to drive back and forth across the Pali every time we needed to meet."

"You wouldn't be thinking of hitting on me, would you?"

"You? I've got sneakers older than you."

"You should throw them out."

"And you'd save money, too. Could use it for my fee."

"Tell me what you do."

"What I do?"

"Yeah. I know you're just jerking me around about the fee, but here I am hooking up with you on a pretty big deal and all I've got to go on is the word of a guy who can't stay out of prison."

"Not your favorite kind of reference, is it?" She said nothing. "Listen, we'll get hoarse talking over this wind. Here's a plan. I drop you off. You check out and come to my place. I'll go on ahead and make a call that's on my mind. When you get there, we'll settle you in, take our shoes off, have a drink, and talk. When we're through, if you want, we'll go forward. Or you can ... go another way. You'll probably be my captive for dinner in any case."

"I could do all that without checking out."

"True. Only reason to check out and move in is if you want to work together. So, let's just say I drop you off and you come over, with or without baggage, and we'll talk then."

She was quiet. Then, "Could you answer a couple of questions now?"

"I'll do my best."

"What did you do time for?"

"Assaulting a federal officer. It was a fight in a bar. I was trying to hit another guy. I missed and the fed caught the punch. He said he'd badged me before I hit him. I don't think so, but I was drunk. Later one charge of assault on a fellow prisoner, and later one charge of aggravated manslaughter. Also a fellow prisoner, but a different one."

"You killed a man?"

"I defended myself from a lunatic with a deadly weapon and he lost. I was cleared on the manslaughter but got an administrative set-off of eighteen months for bad behavior."

"Kind of belligerent, aren't you?"

"Not belligerent. Obstreperous. Just don't like being handled."

"How much time did you do?"

"Forty months. Could have been out in ten. One thing led to another. Finally built enough of a reputation they let me alone. Then they let me out."

"And since then?"

"I stumbled around for a while. Then I ran into a man who told me to grow up and showed me a way to do it."

"So, what do you do?"

"What I can."

"A private detective?"

"No. A private friend."

• • • • •

I called Serena's. It was eight o'clock in Chicago, the height of the evening rush at the restaurant. Muhammad answered.

"It's me," I said.

"So it is."

"I need to talk and I know you're busy. Can you find the time?"

"Can it wait 'til later?"

"If it has to, but I'd rather not."

"Okay, I'll round up Randy to fill in for me. I'll call you back from the office in a few minutes."

It took less than that.

"I celled with a guy named Packy MacGillicuddy," I began. "A good guy, by the standards of the joint."

"You mentioned him."

"His son is a soldier over here. He's gone AWOL. His aunt, a lawyer, has come over and asked me to help find him. Packy put her on me. We went out to Schofield and talked to some brass and the story is weird, doesn't make sense. He was about to get cut loose. Honorably. Hard to believe he'd just go off with only ten days left to serve. I'm going to strap it on, see what I can do."

"Okay."

"Maybe you could get Francis to dig up some background. The aunt who's a lawyer's name is Valerie Sabatino. Lives in Del Mar. Says she has resources. Late twenties, maybe. Who can tell? Her sister, half sister, the boy's mother, is named Belinda. She's remarried, surname Franklin. Husband is Roscoe, a college professor. Lives in Louisville. Packy, Patrick Aloysius MacGillicuddy, is back inside. The Nevada State Prison in Ely. The missing boy is Spec Four Daniel A. MacGillicuddy. I guess he grew up in Louisville. So, you got all that?"

"Yeah." He read it back to me. "Should I come over?"

"You getting on Serena's nerves?"

"No more than usual."

"For now, it looks like a lot of schlepping around. Talking to people. Turning over stones. Valerie's smart. She'll help. If we turn up something, I'll let you know."

"Let's see. Valerie's smart. Maybe her daddy's rich. Bet her mama's good looking, and she is too."

"Well, yeah, kind of. But you're not suggesting I'm shallow, are you?"

"If you were a pond, I could walk across you. You looking to get paid for this?"

"Expenses, at least."

"And your time?"

"I haven't decided."

"No good deed goes unpunished."

• • • • •

Muhammad hadn't exactly saved my life. Or maybe he did, just by turning me.

When I hit the bricks I had control of my more brutal impulses but not a clue about how I wanted to live. I had no home, no family, and no skills, unless kicking ass counted, and it didn't. For six months I wandered. I wasn't on paper; I had served it all. Did odd jobs, no-brain stuff, paycheck to paycheck, town to town, lived in cheap motels and boarding houses. Drank out of boredom, which put me in a lot of dark bars close to a lot of people who looked sideways at me like I had no business there. Which I didn't. I was cruising for a return to action and a ticket back inside.

One night I found myself in Chicago, just off three weeks on a lake trawler with my pay in my pocket. I checked into a low-end hotel on the north side, cleaned up and went walking in the rain. I headed south, seeking shadows, not the bright lights.

I turned a corner and a woman screamed and two men came running down the sidewalk toward me. Instinctively, I clotheslined the first one and he went down like a sack of cement. The other, still running, raised his arm from his side and pointed it at me. It held a gun. I came to a full stop just in front of him and held up my hands like he had me. He stopped, wondering, I guess, what the protocol was for taking prisoners on the sidewalk in the middle of a mugging. I shot a quick straight right into his face and grabbed his gun wrist with my left and pulled him off balance enough to get leverage to grab his nuts with my right and hoist him up on my back. I slammed him to the pavement on his back, hanging on to the gun wrist until the weapon fell. He moaned and I reached down and grabbed the front of his shirt and hauled him to his feet and put three shots into his face, finishing the last one about two feet the other side of his head, and he slithered down and stopped moaning. The other one was on his knees, holding his head with one hand and digging into his clothes with the other, so I kicked him in the stomach and he stopped digging and trying to get up.

Still pumped, I circled them, looking for another opportunity when I was lifted off my feet by a bear hug from behind. I prepared to spin or drop out of the grip or use my head as a club, wasn't sure what, when a voice, low and deep, said in my ear, "It's okay, partner. I'm on your side. Just thinking maybe you don't need to kill them."

The voice calmed me and, I don't know why, I trusted it. I relaxed. He released me.

"Here's the plan," he said. "You pick up that gun, by the barrel, and keep an eye on these assholes while I check on the lady down the street." I picked up the gun by the barrel and turned to the voice. Over his shoulder, he spoke to someone else. "Randy, call the cops. Tell them we need an ambulance, make it two."

He was a full six inches taller than me and I'm six feet. And wide enough to block out the sun. And black. Not brown, black. He wore a dark suit, a white shirt, and a black necktie. He looked at me. "You in on the plan?"

I nodded. He hurried down the sidewalk where a shape lay and knelt beside it. I heard him talking, that voice rumbling, but I couldn't make out the words. The woman said something. He stroked her head. He said something else and she whimpered and he helped her to her feet. She wobbled and the man picked her up like she was a kitten and walked her back down my way. A young man, tall and lean and beige, in a white shirt and tie but no jacket, opened the door of what I made out to be a restaurant and held it for the older man who went in with the woman in his arms. The frosted glass panel of the dark wooden door read "Serena's" in gold script.

I stood there with the gun in my hand, holding it by the barrel, trembling some. The young man said to me, "It's gonna be okay. Pop'll take care of this." I heard sirens closing in.

The black man emerged from the restaurant. "Your mother's got the woman on the sofa in the office," he said to the younger man. "She'll take care of her. You go in and run things for a while. Tell the people everything's okay, make sure they're settled. Go table to table. Take over. Go on."

A squad car arrived, then an ambulance, then another. The cops controlled the scene like they do, not asking any questions at first, just giving orders, taking command. EMTs huddled over the two men on the sidewalk.

One of the cops took the gun from me, also by the barrel, spread me over the trunk of his car and patted me down. Then he told me to stand by the window of the restaurant. I said, "The guy on his stomach's maybe got a weapon."

One cop knelt and patted him down, brought out a gun.

The big man said, "There's a woman inside, on the sofa in the office. My son'll show you where. She's the victim. Needs looking after. I think she's not hurt too badly." The EMTs from the other ambulance hurried inside.

"What happened here?" the cop who frisked me said, looking alternately at the big man and me.

The big man said, "My name is Muhammad Ali. This is my restaurant. Well, my wife's, actually. I heard the woman scream, came outside and saw this man stop the two men who were running away. After he subdued them, he kept an eye on them while I took the woman inside to have my wife look after her. My son phoned it in."

"Where'd the gun come from?"

"That one there had it in his hand. This man took it away from him."

"What'd you say your name was?"

"Muhammad Ali. I'm another one. Not that one," said the big man.

"Who attacked these men?"

"That's backwards. These two men here on the sidewalk came running toward this man here. He just defended himself. They attacked him."

"Uh-huh. And did you get in it?"

"No, sir. I did not. It wasn't necessary."

The cop gave me a long, slow look.

Things got sorted out. A second squad car arrived and the two downed men were loaded into the ambulance with one of the officers inside with them and his partner following in their car. The woman was brought out of the restaurant on a rolling stretcher, accompanied by a small Asian woman who walked alongside and held her hand.

"Muhammad," the Asian woman said, "I'm going to ride along with this lady to the hospital. I'll call you."

"All right," Muhammad said. "You got your cell phone?"

"Yes."

"I'll have mine with me," he said. He walked beside her to the ambulance, kissed her and helped her inside.

"Let me see some ID," the cop said to me.

"It's in my back pocket," I said, moving my hand slowly to my hip and bringing out a thin card case. He took it from me.

"William Harrison Pines," he read. "This license is expired."

"I know, but that's who I am. I don't use it to drive. I don't drive."

He looked at the license. "Pensacola. Pensacola's your home?"

"Not any more. But back then."

"And now?"

"Nowhere, really. I'm checked in at a hotel called the Blue Lion."

"No permanent address?"

"Don't actually have one. I'm an itinerant worker."

"All you got's an expired drivers license and a Social Security card? I want you to come down to the station with us, give us a statement."

"You arresting him?" Muhammad asked.

"No, sir. Just want a statement."

Muhammad turned to me. "I'm an attorney. If you want, I'll represent you. I'll follow you down and be there with you."

"I don't think I need a lawyer," I said. "But I appreciate your offer."

"Well, at least you'll need a ride back to your hotel."

To the policeman I said, "May I have a word alone with this man?"

He nodded. Muhammad stood between the cop and me, his size providing privacy.

"I'm an ex-con," I said. "I'm carrying pretty much cash, my pay from a job I just finished. Legitimate job."

"I'm your lawyer. I'll come along."

"I don't want to dummy up. I'm clean."

"Okay, but why don't you just drink coffee 'til I get there."

• • • • •

Valerie knocked once on the screen door and came in without my saying so.

"You got luggage?" I asked.

She had changed, shorts and a t-shirt. She kicked off sandals and went to the chair she liked.

"How'd you get the money for this place?"

"Telling you that's none of your business won't do us any good, will it?"

She shook her head. She looked serious.

"I won it."

She held my eyes.

"Well, my end of it anyway." I paused. I knew it was either come full clean or she'd walk. I didn't want her to walk and it didn't have all that much to do with Packy or his kid.

"I've got a friend in Chicago. The one I mentioned. He owns a restaurant. Well, actually, his wife owns it. I met him a few years ago. He told me I had to stop wasting time and get on with my life. Showed me how. I was there for a while, a few years, working in the restaurant. Making an honest living. Helping some people on the side who needed…the kind of things I can do. And then one day I won seven hundred sixty five thousand dollars. And two hundred twenty four. And twenty cents."

"How?"

"On the races. They call it the Pick Six. Pick six winners in a row."

"I go to the track."

"Best game of all. Del Mar had a big Pick Six carryover. I was pretty smart but ten times luckier. Short prices won the first two legs. I had them as singles. In the third, the top two finishers both got disqualified. What are the odds of that? I ran third and they moved me up to first. That one was ten-to-one. The next one was six-to-one. I had it. In the fifth, I was spread out on four horses and one of them was eight-to-one. That's the one that won. I was live in the sixth leg on two horses. One was five-to-two and the other was nineteen-to-one. Fifty yards from the wire the favorite, I didn't have him, was six in front. My five-to-two shot was running second, a length in front of my one at nineteen-to-one. The leader took a bad step, bolted, and threw his rider in the path of my five-to-two shot. He shied. Mister nineteen-to-one, his name was Dynafleet, passed him and I had the only ticket."

"You played Del Mar from Chicago?"

"Yeah. I was at the restaurant, watching on television, playing it over the phone. That's legal, you know."

"I know."

"That kind of luck… I don't know… Muhammad, that's my friend, insisted I invest it in real estate. My cash, his credit. Here I am."

"Does legal matter much to you?"

"Sure. I don't want to go back inside. And I'm happy being square. But I'm not a saint. I've cut a corner now and then when I thought it would get a good thing done. Thing is, I know the difference between good guys and bad guys and sometimes I've done what I had to do to keep the bad ones from beating up on the good ones."

"So. What's your purpose in life?"

"I just told you. Keeping the bad guys from beating up the good guys."

"Isn't that police work?"

"They do all they can, but sometimes just get too busy. Like God."

"And you made this big hit and bought this place and you retired?"

"I'm willing to help you. Is that retired?"

"I checked out."

"I'm glad. Want to know what I charge?"

"Yes."

"Expenses. And there'll be some. Could easily be a couple thousand, maybe twice that. I think a trip or two to the mainland is not out of the question and when I'm working I fly first-class. And I use a guy does Internet research and he's not cheap. But it makes a big difference and saves a lot of time."

"Okay."

"If we find Danny alive, ten thousand dollars. If we don't find him, or if we find him dead, nothing. Unless somebody did it. In that case, if you want me to find who did it and nail him, forty thousand if I do and ten thousand if I don't."

"Why nothing if we find him dead?"

"Don't have to be too smart to find a dead man. I'll help you with your luggage. Show you to the apartment. I'll read the reports while you settle in."

• • • • •

Fifteen minutes later she was back at the door, tapped once and came in.

"Let's have that drink," she said.

"Okay. I'm just about finished here. You mind tending bar? There's Boodles in the freezer and my glass is beside it. I'll have a couple ounces, no ice, a little vermouth."

When she came back she handed me my drink and raised hers to me. "To success," she said.

"Yeah," I said, and touched her glass. "To the ten thousand dollar conclusion."

She took her chair. Her chair.

"What do you think?" she asked.

"This civilian Michael Sheffield's got a strange story. He was a friend of Danny's, picked him up hitchhiking in Waialua at five o'clock the day he went off in the jungle, five hours after he disappeared, and drove him back to Schofield, just shooting the breeze. Not much chance of mistaken identity, I'd say. Make that no chance."

"Sweet said he picked him up in Haleiwa."

Not bad, I thought, catching that detail. I hadn't. I said, "Did he? Well, not according to this. Sweet maybe misspoke."

"Danny was wearing an aloha shirt. Hitchhiking to Schofield, to his barracks, for God's sake, to get a *surfboard*?" She shook her head.

"If Danny MacGillicuddy went AWOL it was not so he could catch some waves," I said.

"Unless he was taunting fate. Like his daddy."

"I know his daddy pretty well, and he was never that stupid."

"So, you can rule out mistaken identity on Sheffield's statement but you can't rule out lying. But the other one, John Osmond, his story's just thin," she said.

"Yes, it is. Passed Danny driving by the morning of day two. Two cars going in opposite directions at, what, thirty miles an hour? How often do you look into the face of an oncoming motorist?"

"You don't, unless you recognize the car. Either he recognized it or his whole story's bullshit."

"Said it was green. Didn't say what make or what year. Maybe a 'few years old.' Maybe 'a sedan.' Doesn't sound like he recognized it. Be good to talk to these two kids tomorrow."

"Do you have maps? I keep wondering how far it is from the prison compound to Schofield. And where this beach road is."

"Time you got geographically oriented," I said. "I am a man of many maps. My secret obsession." I went to the bookcase and found a Nelles map of Oahu with a scale of 1:150,000, about three miles to the inch. I brought it to the coffee table, sat on the sofa, and motioned for her to sit beside me.

Oahu is shaped sort of like a beat-up football. North-to-south, the island stretches some twenty-five miles at its extremity, Pearl Harbor at the bottom with Schofield a little less than halfway between the north-south extremes, closer to Pearl than the north shore. East-to-west, it's maybe fifty miles from a narrow point on the northwest to another on the southeast.

"Here's Waikiki," I said, pointing to the island's southern-most point, some six miles west of the southeast extremity. "Here we are now. In Kailua. Almost due north of Waikiki, across the Koolau mountains. Here's the Pali Highway, the road you've taken to cross the mountains a couple of times. The Koolaus run from here on the southeast shore," I said, drawing a finger across the map, "closer to the windward side where we are now than to the lee, to here at the northern-most point. At least that's the pattern of the crest. It peaks at about 4,000 feet which doesn't sound like much until you consider that sea level is not far away.

"There are heavy ridges on both sides, but on the lee side, the slope is more gradual and the jungle's more dense. The wind beats up the foliage on this side, the windward side, where we are.

"Here's Pearl, at the bottom, and Schofield maybe nine miles slightly north-west of that in this wide plain. Here's Waialua where Sheffield says he picked him up, maybe five miles west of Schofield. And here's Haleiwa, just a little north of Waialua, where Osmond says he passed him. The main beach road is Kamehameha. It begins at Schofield, goes to Haleiwa and if you take it north from Haleiwa, it runs along the north shore through the serious surfer zone and then wraps all the way around to here, a little south of Kailua, where we are."

"Show me the Ku Tree reservoir."

"It's here, maybe six miles due north of Pearl and three miles east of Schofield. And the prison compound would be about here, northeast of the reservoir and in the dense part of the jungle and uphill. Very rugged country. Intimidating. But nothing our boy couldn't handle."

"And Waialua's over here," she said. "On the other side of Schofield. Which means Danny came down, went through Schofield, or around it, and then Sheffield picked him up doubling back to Schofield. Would there have been enough time for that?"

"Well, getting down from the compound wouldn't have taken him any time at all. That was about noon. If he hitchhiked, he'd have to get lucky, but there's a lot of traffic heading out to the north shore, so it's possible. But he had his weapon, or at least I guess he did. We'll find that out. Who'd want to pick up a hitchhiker carrying an assault rifle? If he had a car waiting, it'd be easy. So, yes, it's possible, but pretty damn strange behavior.

"I've got a bunch of large scale maps of the island, geological surveys of the Department of the Interior. I'll get them out and we'll paper the walls of my office with them. We'll pinpoint everything."

I looked at her and she looked back. We were touching here and there from knee to shoulder, leaning over the map, our weight on the cushions bearing most of the responsibility for our closeness. The look lasted. She got up and went to her chair and I reached across the table for my drink and crawled up in a corner of the sofa, facing her, with my feet folded up under me like an Indian.

She smiled. I smiled.

"Strange," she said, "that it took these two guys almost twenty-four hours to hear that Danny was missing. The platoon comes back without him. Two dozen more soldiers look for him all night long. The next morning five hundred soldiers and three helicopters and a whole bunch of trucks and dogs head out on an all-day hunt three miles away. You'd think that would send up a pretty good buzz on the base, but Sheffield didn't report the pickup for twenty-four hours. And Osmond waited until the next day. Wonder where they were that kept them so out of touch?"

"Sheffield was maybe out of the loop, working. Better question about him is not what took him so long, but how did he even know. But Osmond? Who knows? How do you like your accommodations?"

"Very much. We have plans for dinner?"

"Yeah. I thought I'd invite the neighbors. Have them meet our new guest. We'll eat in the main room. The Great Room."

"Can I help?"

"Sure. We'll eat about seven. We caught a nice fish this morning in the nets. A mahimahi. We'll have that. I'll get on it about six."

"That's a dolphin by any other name, isn't it?"

"I don't want to sound like I know what I'm talking about, but I think it's a dolphin cousin. Some people call it a dolphinfish. I don't know. I can catch it, clean it, cut it, and cook it, though."

"How's the beach? I mean for swimming."

"We do it all the time, but it's not smart to do it alone. It's an ocean, after all. So, if you don't find anybody down there, I'd appreciate it if you'd come back and get me. But Leanne, you met her yesterday, teaches at Chaminade, music, and she manages to get off about this time so she can lay up out there, so you just might find her down there."

"Come with me," she said.

"Can't this time. I'm expecting a call."

• • • • •

I got four of the large-scale maps of the island from their bins in my office. I took down a Marian McDade watercolor of a Roman piazza, and taped the maps to the wall where it had hung, lined them up edge to edge, making a three-foot by four-foot display. Together they covered from Pearl to the north shore and from the east range of the Koolaus to the western end of

Oahu. I circled Schofield, Ku Tree, Waialua, and Haleiwa in yellow marker.

They were a 7.5 minute series, topographic, with latitudes and longitudes shown in the margins in degrees, minutes, and seconds. The scale was 1:24,000, or about 2.6 inches to the mile. Every contour of the terrain and every bend of the streams descending from the summit was displayed, the terrain in brown squiggles and the water in green. Streams, boundaries, trails, and dozens of landmarks were identified. Elevations were indicated at random intervals. I hadn't studied this series since I received them a couple of weeks after Muhammad and I closed on our investment. Seeing them again, I was once more drawn into their extraordinary detail. I wondered if they were man- or machine-made. In the digital age, almost certainly the latter, but I preferred the romantic notion of a roomful of eyeshades hunched over tables scribbling with quill pens.

I traced my finger uphill from the Ku Tree reservoir, sort of north by northeast since that would have taken Danny's platoon into the denser elevations of the jungle. I had studied this terrain from afar, with binoculars, and from up close, at the edges, on many occasions and always found it disquieting. It was said that you could walk in fifty yards, spin twice, and never find your way out. The ground was a bog that never dried. The foliage fought with itself to reach for the sun and made an impenetrable tangle of gnarled branches and leathery greenery. Deadly creatures, some large and furry, some tiny and winged, lived there and were hungry. None slithered; Hawaii has no snakes.

The phone rang.

"Dude," the caller said. "What it is."

"Francis. You're working late."

"Good hack time, late. Sinister time for sinister work."

"Whatcha got?"

"Just a little cream I skimmed. Openers. Lawyer lady's daddy's got a serious haystack. He's Rafael Sabatino, with an eff. Citizen of both Monaco and the U. S. Office in the Apple. Looks like a mogul in the money business. Got the Gulfstream, the racehorses, the yachts, shit like that. Clean as far as I've got. On wife number two. Had her a long time. Can't find a trace of wife number one. One kid, the lawyer lady, Valerie. Princeton, then Stanford Law. Top of her class both places. Lives now in Del Mar. Hired out there, San Diego, by a top firm, left four months ago. No trouble shows up. Just quit, I'd say. Madeleine Brown Scowcroft Sabatino is the name of the mother of Valerie, as well as the mother of Belinda Scowcroft MacGillicuddy Franklin. A former wild child, Belinda, some drug charges, possession, one conviction, no time served. That was twenty years ago. Now married to Roscoe Franklin who is a professor of Political Science at the University of Louisville. No negs on Roscoe. Belinda's first old man was Patrick Aloysius MacGillicuddy. Born in Chicago. Found his way to Las Vegas where he married Belinda and fathered Daniel Aloysius MacGillicuddy. Daddy MacGillicuddy got profiled in Who's Who. The wrong one. It's something in Vegas they call the Black Book, a collection of photos and shit on known and suspected cheaters of the casinos. Did fifty-five months of a five-year sentence at Terminal Island for illegal sale of a silencer. Belinda divorced him while he was inside. He was on the bricks for a year or so and then took another fall for burglary. He's at the Ely State Prison in Nevada, doing six more. The kid, Daniel MacGillicuddy, went from high school, that was in Louisville, to the army. He's now absent without authority from his army base in you-know-where, you lucky bastard. I'm good, aren't I?"

"Who knows? Maybe you make all this shit up."

"Okay, then at least I'm good at making shit up. You want I should get more?"

"Not now." He had pretty much corroborated everything Valerie had told me, except for the depth of her resources and I couldn't blame her for holding that back. "I'll get back to you if I do. I'm just doing entry-level stuff. How you doing, generally?"

"Generally, excellent. Specifically, even better than that. I can't keep my hands off a woman who does the same work I do. That's how we met. Used to be I'd have to take a lot of shit from my old lady for pounding this keyboard all night long. Now, this new one's right here with me, pounding her keyboard. When we're not poundin' each other. How lucky is that? Is this pro bono?"

"No, it's business."

"Who gets the bill? You or Muhammad?"

"Me. Email it. And attach everything you've got there so far. Copies to Muhammad. What's the name of this unfortunate woman?"

"Puddin' to you. Like Puddin' 'n' Tane, ask me again and I'll tell you the same."

"I probably should talk to her. Let her know what she's in for. Tell her to call me if you get out of line."

"You know I will. Aloha."

I went to the ice chest, removed the fifteen-pound mahimahi Richie and I had caught, and carved filets from it. At 5:30 I found Molto Mario on the Food Channel, where I was learning country Italian cooking, and got an inspiration for dinner. A risotto dish. Extra virgin olive oil and lots of chicken stock. Mario Batali said "extra virgin olive oil" every time he went for the bottle as though you'd burn in hell if you ever used anything less; he uses Frantoia, so I do, too. Zuc de Volpe Pinot Grigio and my own self-simmered chicken stock to keep it moist, canned San Marzano whole tomatoes, crush them in the pot, onions, a handful of shallots, Italian parsley, and basil from my garden, and the mahimahi, seared and slow sauteed. Put the pan juices in the risotto. Plate it with the filets on top. Serve.

While I was assembling the ingredients, Richie came in the kitchen. Richard Cosopolous lives in the end unit. He's a fugitive from a catastrophic marriage back in Indianapolis, wasn't quite a runaway but wanted to put as much distance between himself and the pain as he could. There was a son, about nine now, named Curtis, a real good kid who spends summers here with Richie.

We met when I hired a remodeling company to throw in with me on bringing the place up to snuff. Richie was the crew chief. From the first, I was impressed with his energy and competence. He was thick through the chest and shoulders, with big wrists. His hair looked like he cut it himself but not very often. He had a ratty, dense black beard and black-framed glasses with thick lenses. He reminded me of some kind of night-dwelling creature.

"A marmoset," he said one day when he caught me staring at him as he worked.

"What?"

"A marmoset. That's what I remind you of."

"Maybe."

"Harry, I'd like to live here when we finish this job."

"Would you?"

"Yeah. You could use me, too. Keep an eye on things that break, fix 'em right up."

"Where do you live now?"

"In a tree house in Tantalus."

"I don't know, Richie. You might scare people."

"I been thinkin' about that. Figure if I moved in here I might shave my beard, cut my hair, get contacts. Who knows, I might even find a chick."

"Oh, I doubt that."

We worked it out. He kept an eye on things and fixed 'em right up and charged me for his time. Without the marmoset impersonation, he was presentable, but a little short on the graces that the social swim requires. He was working on that, though, and getting better.

"You know what that fish dish needs as a first course?" he said. "Gazpacho. I kill gazpacho. I peel and seed the tomatoes and put in lots of crunchy things."

"Kill us some gazpacho. The larder's full."

"You got cilantro?"

"You don't put cilantro in gazpacho."

"You mean you don't. I do."

"Okay. It's here somewhere. Or in the garden."

Leanne and Valerie strolled in, looking showered and fresh and chuckling like sorority sisters with boy secrets. I introduced Richie to Valerie and he stammered like a high school sophomore. She smiled at his discomfort as though she was flattered by it and shook his hand graciously.

"Anything we can do?" Leanne asked.

"How many we having for dinner?"

"Sam and Teresa are on the way," she said. "There's a pair of strangers in Cindy's place, off a United crew. A nice woman named Jean and another one named Rosalie. I hate Rosalie. She makes me look like Miss Congeniality except she's more congenial than I am. I invited them. They said yes."

"Eight. Richie and I'll cook. You choose the wine."

"And we'll set the table and do the dishes," Valerie said.

"Women's work," Richie said. He tried for the light comic touch, knowing it was in there, but missed it completely.

"Harry," Leanne said, "will you make sure Richie washes his hands and doesn't pick his nose?"

• • • • •

Sam Dodson and Teresa Hanifan are lawyers. Sam moved in right after he came to the islands to take a job with a downtown Honolulu firm. He's from

Chicago and his father, also a lawyer, knew Muhammad from the restaurant. Muhammad told him to come see me about living with us. Sam was coming off a bad divorce from a childless, too-young marriage and his dad thought a few years in the islands would do his son good. Muhammad's recommendation would have been enough, but I liked him right off. He was tall and rangy and carried himself a little low in the shoulder in an unassuming sort of way. He seemed to know a lot more than he gave up. He ate the life up for a few months, bringing over a series of girls he met out running the joints. Not that there's anything wrong with that. Nor was there with them.

Then Teresa came into his life. She's five years older than Sam, and nearly as tall, and came to the islands from Kansas City. Teresa isn't pretty until you sit beside her and get into a conversation, a real conversation. Then she lights up, a glow emerges, and you want to skip whatever you had planned and go on talking with her. They met at the office—she worked there, too—and she was the only woman he ever brought home to Kailua after the first time we met her. They are so dominant at two-person volleyball, against either two men or mixed or, God help them, two women, that I was thinking about getting badminton equipment. Or maybe croquet.

We put together their wedding at a cove near Hanauma Bay on the beach where the Burt Lancaster and Deborah Kerr sex scene in "From Here to Eternity" was filmed. I had to rent it to make sure.

A treacherous walk down a steep, rocky cliff leads to a small beach dotted with big, smooth, half-buried stones. At both sides of the inlet there are wide and surf-drenched shelves, at various heights, leading out to the mouth, which is no more than fifty yards from the beach. The narrowness of the opening accelerates the speed of the surf and produces a wild churn and spray that's rare for the eastern tip of the island. I like it because you can't get down there, or up, unless you're in pretty good shape, so it draws few tourists and nobody fat.

We hauled Bob Miscavage, a good-time, hard-drinking judge with the powers of a J. P., down the rocks and he performed the ceremony. About two dozen others were assembled, from the firm and the house, and we drank champagne to their union. Richie captured the whole thing on videotape, losing focus, and even the camera, as he got drunker.

Then they flew to Chicago and Kansas City to show their folks how lucky they were. They came back and settled in between Cindy and Leanne and spent so much time alone we figured they'd soon be pregnant and wondering if this was the right place to raise a kid. Two weeks ago they told us a baby was on the way.

· · · · ·

At dinner, Valerie and Sam and Teresa talked about life in a big law firm and it seemed they all hated everything about it, except for doing the work.

Valerie said, "I don't practice any more. And I may not go back."

Teresa said, "You quit?"

"I did. Walked out one day a few months ago. Have had no regrets."

Sam said, "What do you do now?"

"Think about what I'm going to do next. School's a possibility, another degree. Maybe I'll teach."

"You're fortunate to be in a position to do that. To step back and take a fresh look at your life."

"Yes, I am."

I asked Sam and Teresa if they had any experience dealing with the military.

"Lots. It's really good business," Teresa said, "unless you want to get something done."

"So, why's it good business?"

"Well, you get to bill a lot of hours while you're getting jerked around accomplishing very little," Sam said. "Which makes it good for the firm, if not for the attorney."

"And it's not like they're protecting anything important," Teresa said. "That doesn't enter their mind. It's the procedures. You probably read Catch-22. It's still the same."

Richie was stricken stupid by Rosalie's chest and kept talking to her without taking his eyes off it. I suspected Jean, who would draw attention anywhere Rosalie wasn't, was slightly interested in Richie. Go figure. But he was too dense, or maybe too stunned by those tits, to notice. Rosalie had the good sense and manners to enjoy it, or at least to pretend she did. Jean said they would be with us for just two nights and Richie offered to build an addition on to their place if it would make Rosalie more comfortable.

It turned out Valerie had found Leanne on the beach, playing her flute, and they girl-talked for two hours before dinner, including the information that Leanne, who can make music from a wet stick and a moss-covered rock, is teaching me the clarinet. If Leanne told her she had crept into my bed one night many months ago when she was suffering from a bad romance, they didn't let on. But women are better at keeping secrets from men than we are from them. When she goes off to teach at Chaminade, a Catholic university on the other side, Leanne Fitch wears her hair in a bun and puts on blowsy clothes and glasses. But she unpins and peels back when she gets home and you couldn't pick the Chaminade Leanne from the Kailua Leanne in a lineup. She grew up Main Line Philadelphia. I'm sure her family's not as well off as Valerie's but, from the perspective of my demographic, it's a difference without a distinction.

After dinner, Sam and Richie and I shot a couple of racks of nine-ball while the women's work went on. When they finished, Teresa put on Willie Nelson's Stardust album and took her husband by the hand to dance in a wide, tile-floored space between two area rugs. I looked at Valerie and she nodded and we joined them.

As we moved, I sang quietly along with Willie, first into her ear and then into her eyes.

She had a throaty laugh, easier to feel than to hear. "Harry Pines, did you throw your sneakers out?"

"I'm just making the most of a lovely evening. It's nothing personal."

"Is that right?"

"No. Actually, that was a lie."

"Great meal. You can cook."

"Thanks. Did almost four years hard time in a restaurant kitchen. I can wash dishes, too. Wait tables. Bus 'em. Tend bar."

"That was in Chicago? With your friends?"

"Yes. The art of cooking is something I'm still struggling with, creating great food from the best available ingredients, the way a painter confronts a canvas. That's Serena's talent. Muhammad's wife. I'm not sure I have it. I tend to be a little recipe bound. But I'm getting better."

"Serena? Was that the restaurant? Serena's?"

"Yes."

"I've been there. Several times."

"Really? Maybe I waited on you."

"Nah. Cute guy like you? I'd remember."

I laughed. "Waiters are invisible, indistinguishable one from another."

"Man, there's a lot you don't know about women."

"You can say that again. Anyhow, I'm sure I wasn't there or I'd have remembered you."

"Nice life you've built over here."

"A little immature, I sometimes think. Kind of aloof from life's defining problems. But, what the hell."

"Exactly. So what if it is age-defying? I've always thought arrested development got a bad rap."

"Peter Pan forever, then?"

"For now, anyhow. Think we should feel guilty while Danny's out there somewhere?"

"No."

"You've got a useful little group here. Richie, the handyman. Sam and Teresa, the house lawyers. Leanne teaching you the clarinet. And a babe depository, to boot."

"Yeah. I hear that the era of the glamorous flight attendant is over, but you couldn't prove it by me."

"Tell me about Cindy."

"Cindy Rendell. From Michigan, the upper peninsula, the thumb. She's with United, too. She's the one on the lease. She's as pretty as they are. When she's on a flight, like now, or sometimes when she's here, she gives a key to friends."

"Must be nice."

"You're implying?"

"Yes. I am."

"I set up a little war room," I said, changing the subject. "Big maps on the wall. Want to see?"

"Sure."

We excused ourselves and made our way to my place. I put on an old Stephane Grappelli wax. It's called Vintage 1981. He ends side two with Stevie Wonder's "Isn't She Lovely," which is so perfect I play it twice.

"Get you something?"

"What you're having."

She followed me into the small kitchen, small enough that we couldn't avoid contact. I dug out a dusty old bottle of cognac and poured two.

I touched my glass to hers. I didn't have far to reach. "Let me show you the maps."

"Did you put them up securely?"

"Securely?"

"Yes. So they won't fall."

"They won't fall."

"Then later."

There didn't seem to be anything else to do but kiss her which was a good thing because I didn't want to do anything else. So I did. It was awkward, a little tentative, neither of us sure about it. We leaned back from it but kept our touch, her hands on my shoulders, mine on her waist.

She smiled. "Where do the noses go?" she asked.

"For Whom The Bell Tolls."

She held my eyes. "You read a lot in prison."

"And everywhere else I've been since then. I eat books."

She looked a little dreamy. It was a good thing to see. She said, "It's Hawaii, isn't it? That makes people feel this way."

"People?"

"Me."

"In your case I'd like to think part of it is me."

"Part of it is, I'm sure. Is it too late to see the sun go down from upstairs?"

"I'll go check. Want me to call down."

"Just in case there's not a minute to spare maybe I'd better come along."

She followed me upstairs, through the bedroom, and out to the balcony. We stood at the rail.

"Darn," I said. "Just missed it."

"Now what will we do?"

I put my hands in her hair—I'd been wanting to do that since she drove up yesterday—and I kissed her again and not tentatively. She ran her hands up my back to my neck and made a little noise. She moved back and unbuttoned my shirt and dropped it to the floor, lowered my drawstring shorts and let them fall. I slid her shirt free from her waistband and raised it over her head, reached behind her and unsnapped her bra as she slipped shorts and whatever was underneath down her hips with a wiggle I wish I could have watched. Her breasts were as full as I expected and brown-tipped. I grasped her at the rib cage like she was a Faberge egg and lifted her up and put my mouth on one of them and she wrapped her legs around me and lowered herself and I slipped inside her. I walked carefully to the bed, carrying her, and lowered her to it, staying inside her. She pulled me down and kissed me deeply, her tongue sliding around inside my lip on the surface of my teeth, then stretched her head back on the pillow and her eyes rolled up and all I could see was the eerie and exotic whites of them. She squeezed my penis with the muscles of her vagina and rocked with me in a rhythm that was not patient. We hit the peak together quickly and it lasted and lasted and lasted. Time stood still. Some time later, I came out of the coma and found I was still inside her and she looked at me with those chocolate eyes, huge and scary in their depth.

"Harry Pines," she said.

"I think so."

She squeezed me again and I stiffened and the dance renewed itself. I leaned back, sat up, extending my feet beneath her, raising her with me and she wrapped her legs behind me and we smiled and held our gazes and rocked quietly. She pushed me on my back and dragged her nails softly across my chest and her head flew back and her hair obscured her face as she rode me and her hair flew and she used me and took herself to a place she loved. Once more, we came together and she shuddered over and over and then fell face down on my chest.

• • • • •

"It's always a little awkward the first time," I said as we lay side by side, glistening with sweat, our heads at the foot of the bed. "If we're patient, we'll do better with practice."

"Okay. But I've got to tell you it was nothing special."

"We'll get past it. Trust me."

"I guess it won't hurt to give you another chance."

"You're even more fun to look at with your clothes off."

"Everything you see I owe to spaghetti."

"From the mouth of Sophia Loren."

THREE

Wednesday, March 12

Lieutenant Colonel Sweet set us up in a little conference room down the hall from his office. A metal table, two chairs on each side, one window. Our first interview was Danny's squad leader, Staff Sergeant Bruce Fensterer, a mid-twenties, square-faced, crew cut with the look of a lifer. He was sympathetic but straightforward, blunt.

"Danny—Spec Four MacGillicuddy—was damn near mutinous that day," he said. "He couldn't understand why he had to go on the exercise ten days before getting mustered out. He'd done it before, the same drill, three or four times, and he was top-notch at survival skills, so you couldn't say he needed it. But that's not the way we run things. It was scheduled and that's that. The regs say you go on drills up until five days from your last day. Not ten. Not even six. Five. He talked to me about it the day before and his attitude was so bad I was close to putting him on report. Just for the way he spoke to me.

"He kept grumbling about it all the way. In the truck. On the march up the hill. Twice I told him to shut up, but he kept mumbling. Then, when we, uh, escaped, I saw him peeling off from his partner and going solo, but before I could stop him he was in the jungle. You couldn't catch Danny in the jungle and we were maintaining silence so I couldn't call out to him. I figured, the hell with him, he'd be all right and better off alone the mood he was in."

"What time did the breakout take place," I asked.

"About thirteen hundred hours."

"So," Valerie said, "what do you think happened?"

He shrugged. "I think it's pretty clear he just came straight down and went on his way."

"Are you sure he went down?" I asked. "And not up?"

"No, I suppose not. He went in the jungle, disappeared. Except he was seen down. So, he came down pretty soon even if he went up at first."

"Why?" she asked. "Do you have any idea why?"

"No, ma'am. I mean, it's possible that he was coming down to do something and planning to, you know, get it done and then hook up with us the next day. He'd have got off clean if he did that and it wouldn't have been all that hard. Time-wise, I mean. Or maybe he just went off. Truth is, I don't have any idea."

"What kind of soldier was he?" I asked.

"Had some serious skills. At one time, he was as good as anybody. Last few months he was getting sloppier. Lot of them do that when they're time is coming up, but I was disappointed in Danny because of it. He could have been a Ranger and I told him so, but he just shrugged me off. It's not for everybody."

"Wasn't for me either."

"You turned down Ranger?"

"No, I was one. I turned down Special Forces. When Danny started to slide, did you suspect anything? Drinking, for instance."

"The good life's what I suspected. Lot of temptations over here for a single soldier. Wish I could be of more help. I'll be available if you want to talk again. Ma'am, I hope this turns out as good as it can for your sake."

· · · · ·

The soldier who was paired with Danny on the simulated escape was Corporal Herman Henderson. He said, "We busted out together and I hung with him as we ran down the hill, but halfway to the jungle he turns to me and says, 'Go on. Leave me alone. Hook up with somebody else. I'll see you tomorrow at the truck.' So, I peeled off. I went one way, he went another."

"Were you armed?" I asked. "I mean, when you broke out of the compound did you reclaim your weapons?"

"Absolutely."

"I don't actually mean you personally. I'm asking if getting the weapons back was part of the exercise and if Danny did."

"It's part of the exercise and Danny had his."

"When's your time up?"

"Out next month."

"Not planning to re-up?"

"Haven't decided."

"Did you know Danny well?" Valerie asked.

"He was in my platoon. You know all those guys a little bit. We weren't like pals, though."

"Past tense," I said.

He looked at me like he didn't understand what I'd said.

"You said he 'was' in your platoon. You 'weren't' pals. Like he's gone."

"Well, he is, ain't he?"

• • • • •

Valerie told Danny's one roommate, PFC Edgar Mason, we'd like to see where they lived, so he led us the few hundred yards to the quadrangle and showed us to the small, two-person room in their barracks. Two single bunks, two foot lockers, two chests, two desks, a closet. Bare walls, except for corkboards above the desks with notes tacked on Mason's side, nothing on Danny's. I sat on a foot locker. Valerie took the chair at the other desk.

"Danny was a good guy to bunk with. No trouble. No hassle. Not the friendliest guy I ever knew, but you don't have to be best friends just because they tell you to share a room. I like him all right."

"You hang out together?" I asked.

"No, sir. Had a couple beers once or twice. That's all. We got along."

"Who're his friends?" Valerie asked.

"Mike Sheffield and him are buddies. He's out now, but still lives around here. Danny mostly runs with civilians. You know, from off the base. Locals."

"He have a car?" I asked.

"Jeep Wrangler. Plus, he sold cars on the side, so he was always driving one around. You know, to sell?"

"He sold cars?"

"Yeah. He knew some guy, over at Pearl I think, who bought 'em, fixed 'em up. Danny helped him sell them. You know, to guys on the base."

"He have a green one recently?" I asked.

"Yeah."

"What was it?"

"Seems like it was a Toyota. Couple years old."

"Four door? Sedan?"

"Sounds about right. He'd drive them around, post them on boards around here."

"What'd he do for fun?"

"Surfed some. Disappeared mostly."

"Have a girl?"

"Nobody he told me about. One called him once or twice."

"Same one both times?"

"I don't know. I didn't take the calls. Just heard some guy holler, you know, 'Hey, MacGillicuddy, lady's on the horn.' Like that."

"Called him on the barracks line? Not on his cell?"

"Yeah."

"Did he ever talk about his plans after he was mustered out?" Valerie asked.

"Just a little. He likes it over here. Said he thought he'd do some hiking on Kauai. Surf some. You know, bum around."

"He have any money problems? Either not enough or way too much?"

"No. Enough, I guess. Not a lot. Like most of us. Far as I know. There's a lot I don't know about Danny."

• • • • •

His personal effects were in a storage facility and Valerie and I went through them in a gap between our appointments. Swim trunks. Hush puppies. Sandals. Shirts, three of the aloha style. Shorts. Jeans. Trousers. Underwear. Razor and toothbrush and stuff. A mini-cassette tape recorder with a long cord mike. A large brown envelope stuffed with paper, bills, documents, odds and ends. A bible.

"A bible?" I said. It was a big one, both Old and New Testament, not heavily used from the look. "Was he religious?"

"Not particularly," she said. "Raised Catholic like all of us. But I don't think he was especially devout."

"This is a King James edition. Not standard Catholic issue." There were three fifty dollar bills inside the front cover. I riffled the pages and found two pieces of paper tucked in different places. One was a scrap torn from a pad. There were three digits, a dash, four digits, written by hand, nothing else. I read the number aloud. I turned the pages to the other, also a torn scrap. It too had a number on it. I read it aloud and Valerie said, "Sounds familiar." Same number. I held the bible by the covers and shook it upside down. Nothing else came out.

"Is that what you call a clue?" she asked.

"Let's look in this," I said, spreading the envelope's contents out on the counter. She took the official-looking things and I took the scraps. We were quiet while we scanned them.

"Well, look at this," I said. It was a piece of paper torn from a small, spiral-bound notebook, serrations at the narrow top. It had my name on it, hand-written, and my phone number written in a different hand below the name. It was folded in quarters. "Packy said he gave him my name. Maybe he wrote it out for him."

She looked at it. "And maybe Danny looked up your phone number and wrote it down." She found the two scraps with the same phone numbers on them. "Looks like his writing, or the same writing, on the numbers here and there."

"Does, doesn't it? So, at some point he maybe took a notion to call me. But he didn't. What've you got?"

"Army records. Two bank statements. Let's take it all with us."

"Where's his surfboard?" I said. I turned to the clerk. "Is there a surf-board?"

"No."

"Soldiers keep surfboards in their room?"

"Maybe. Or in the surf shop."

"Where's the surf shop?"

"Over there in the PX." He pointed across the road.

"Where's his military gear? Fatigues?"

"Oh, you want to see that too? Just standard issue stuff."

"Yeah. We'd like to see that too."

He disappeared for a minute or two and returned with two bundles and a pair of boots.

"Is it all here?" I asked after sorting through the bundles. "I mean when he disappeared he was wearing fatigues. Does all this tally with his issue?"

"No. There's a set of fatigues missing. And a pair of boots. And helmet and helmet liner. Backpack, too."

"We'll take this bible if you don't mind. It has sentimental value. And the paperwork, this envelope."

"Have to see some ID."

Valerie dug into her purse and extracted her driver's license. "I'm his aunt," she said, handing it to him.

He looked at it. "Different last name, though, so no way to tell. Other guy at least had the same last name. But it don't matter." He began to write on a ledger.

"Other guy?" we said as one.

"Yeah. Was his uncle, I think."

"You got his name there?" I asked, pointing at the ledger.

He ran his finger up the page. "Don't think so. Don't think he took anything. Seems like he just made some notes. Nope. No name. He didn't take anything or I'd have it here."

"You remember him?"

"I just said I did."

"No. I mean what'd he look like?"

He thought. "About my size. About your age. Blond hair all messed up. Nothin' special. Just a guy." This guy was five-eight tops.

"When was it?"

He squished saliva around in his mouth. I guess it helped him think. "Last week."

"You remember his name?"

"MacGillicuddy. Sure. Not the kind of name you forget. Especially since he was here lookin' at MacGillicuddy's stuff." He chuckled at that, like he caught us there.

"First name?"

"Francis. 'Nother easy one. Francis MacGillicuddy. I said to him, 'Damn, that's a real Irish name.' You takin' the money? Didn't I see some money?"

"Yeah. Three fifties." I showed them to him.

He scribbled things and spun the ledger to Valerie and pointed to a line where she signed.

We thanked him and walked across the road toward the PX. We were quiet, puzzled.

"You carrying your phone?" I asked.

"Yes."

I stopped at a bench. "You know Belinda's number?" I asked her as I sat down, beckoning her to join me.

She said, "Yes. Want to find out if she remembered Packy's brother Francis?" I nodded.

Kind of amazes me you can plop down on a bench on an island in the middle of the Pacific and get somebody on the phone who's six thousand miles away. Makes me glad I've lived to see it.

She talked with Belinda for a few minutes, then closed the phone. "Packy's got a brother. Name is Jerry. Jerome."

"Jerome Francis, maybe? Or Francis Jerome?"

"Jerome Aloysius. Family's in a middle-name rut."

"The plot thickens."

"Yes. I know I'm new at this, but I think we've found some clues."

"You show real promise." I stood up and reached for her hand.

"Why don't I just call that number we found back there?" she said, keeping her seat and brandishing her phone. "See who answers."

"Let's find out whose number it is first. Where they are."

"My finger's itching."

"That's 'cause you're green. Us pros are careful. Know you only get one kick at the mad dog."

"I get so turned on when you talk like a convict." She rose and we went on our way.

The Schofield PX included the Kamaaina Surf Shop among a cluster of specialty stores in the concourse. A fortyish man, Chinese probably, with long straight black hair and wispy chin whiskers was at the counter.

"Are you Mr. Kamaaina?" Valerie asked. He giggled.

"Kamaaina means an old acquaintance, someone who's been here a long time," I said to her. "Like a local."

"Duh," she said. "I guess we're just looking for the boss," she said to the man.

"That be me," he said, smiling.

"I'm the aunt of one of the soldiers on the base and we think he might have kept his surfboard here. Spec Four Daniel MacGillicuddy?"

"Danny boy. Aikane. Brudda. *Kû`ai aku papa he'enalu.* Yes, ma'am."

"Danny's his friend. Like a brother. He sold him surfboards," I translated for her. To the man, I said, "*E kôkua mai ana `oe?* We surrender. Let's start over. In English."

"English? By all means, sir," he said with a big smile. Now he sounded like Prince Charles.

Valerie gave him a let's-be-friends look that would work in any language. "Does Danny keep his surfboards here?" she asked.

"Yes, ma'am. I was just engaging in a little fun. Just teasing a pretty girl. I meant no offense. Danny is your nephew? You hardly look old enough to be the aunt of a grown man." He gave "aunt" the Brahmin pronunciation, put a "w" up front. "You are *nani e makahehi `ia ai*. Which means most beautiful. I understand Danny is missing. I hope it is nothing serious, perhaps he just went *holoholo*."

"*Holoholo*?" she said.

"It means to wander around just for fun, to do nothing. It's a specialty over here," I said.

"Thank you."

"Let me check in the back. Just a moment," the man said. He went through a door to the back.

"Thank God you're here," she said.

"He would've stopped on his own. He has to speak English working on an American army base. Besides, everybody over here speaks English. They just lapse local to hassle the haoles. You're a haole."

"Haole?"

"Round-eyed intruder from the mainland. They've been suspicious of us ever since the missionaries came here and told them sex wasn't supposed to be fun."

"Right. The missionary position. What did you say to him?"

"*E kōkua mai ana `oe?* It means 'Will you help us?'"

He returned. "I'm certain Danny has two boards," he said. "At least I'm certain I sold him two boards and he kept them here. Only one is here now. You understand I'm not the only game in town? And, of course, he's entitled to keep his boards anywhere he chooses."

"Do you keep records of when they're checked in and out?" I asked.

"No. Too much trouble."

"Do you remember the last time Danny checked one out?"

"No. He was here a lot."

"You've been most helpful," Valerie said. "And most flattering."

"It ain't flattery if it's true, darlin'," he said and reached across the counter to shake her hand. "My name is Rudolph Chen and I am at your service."

"*Mahalo*," she said. He smiled and bowed. We left.

"*Mahalo*? Where'd you pick that up?" I asked her when we were outside.

"It was a long flight. I had a book."

"Now I need to make a call."

"You want privacy?"

"No. Let's sit on our bench while I do it. Use your phone?"

"Sure. You don't have one?"

"Yeah, but I don't carry it."

"Carrying's what they're for."

I peered into the bible as I called Francis. "Francis, I need two things. One now and one soon. One is a phone number that I think is here in Hawaii." I read it to him. "Whose is it and what's the address?"

I heard keystrokes.

"It's the phone number of…you got a pencil?"

"Valerie, can you write this down?" I said to her.

"Valerie? As in Sabatino?" Francis said into my ear.

"What's the number?"

"What's the number? Boy, has she got you flustered. The number *you* gave *me* is unlisted and it belongs to the Children of God."

"The Children of God?" Valerie scribbled. "What the hell's the Children of God?"

"Don't ask me. You're the sleuth," he said. "Whatever they are, they can be found at 456…fuck. I'll spell it. P-U-U-H-O-O-N-U-A Street."

"456 Puuhoonua Street," I said to Valerie. "Don't worry. I can spell it. And I know where it is." To Francis, I said, "Thanks. And the other thing. Make it two things. One, I need one of your framazoids on the Children of God. And, two, see if you can get access to the bank accounts of Daniel A. MacGillicuddy, the missing soldier. Had one over here and one back home in Louisville." I gave him the account numbers. "I want records of activity last six months or so."

"I'm on it."

"Thanks. Email me what you dig up. Copy Muhammad on everything you get."

"At your service. Let me talk to Valerie Sabatino. Tell her how to handle you when you get out of line."

I closed the phone.

"What's a framazoid?" she asked.

"It's what Francis does."

"Who's Francis?"

"Where do you keep your money? Your currency, I mean. Probably your purse, right? I keep mine in my pocket. Some people use a wallet. You ever keep any in a book?"

Michael T. Sheffield was waiting for us back in the conference room. I disliked him right off. He looked like he knew he was the toughest guy in town and didn't want you to forget it. Flashed an empty, superior smile as he shook our hands, only half rising from his seat. Sized Valerie up like he'd know what to do with her, just glanced at me, avoiding eye contact. Probably thought he knew what to do with me, too. His grip implied it. He had twenty years and twenty pounds and a couple of inches on me, so I could understand how he might come to such a ridiculously mistaken impression.

One of those kids, they run from eighteen or so to about twenty-five, who notice that all their role models are rich, famous, and arrogant, so they think, okay, I'll start with arrogant. I was once the worst of the species, so my contempt for them includes me when I was there. I can't see what their value is, other than the faint hope that someday they may get over it and become useful. For the time they're trapped in that zone, though, they're just a waste of air and water. Danny MacGillicuddy wasn't good at picking his friends. Like his father.

We were late. He looked at his watch. Didn't we know how important his time was?

"You ever go with Danny MacGillicuddy to Manoa to see the Children of God?" I asked. An expression flew in and out of his face and I knew my question had registered. But maybe he didn't know I noticed. I hoped not. Valerie gave me an uneasy glance. I knew what his next word would be.

He fooled me. I thought he'd say, "Who?" Instead, he said, "Come again?" And frowned.

"No reason to lie about it," I said. "I just wondered."

"You just call me a liar?"

"I raised the possibility. You picked him up at five o'clock on Wednesday, the 27th, just outside Waialua on, what, Kaukonahua Road?"

"Yeah. Along in there."

"What was he wearing?"

"You read the report. Aloha shirt."

"No pants?"

He sniffed. "Khakis."

"Long or short?"

"Long, I think."

"Fatigues?"

"Coulda been, maybe. I didn't scope it out."

"Shoes?"

"You think I'm his fashion consultant? I didn't notice."

"Boots, maybe?"

"Coulda been. I didn't notice."

"What color shirt?"

"A shirt of many colors."

"Such as?"

"Blue, I think. Yeah, blue."

"Just blue? Not many colors?"

"Blue and other colors."

"What'd you talk about?"

"Chicks. What else?"

"He have one?"

"Everybody's got one."

"Who was his?"

"I have no idea."

"How come? We've been told you and Danny were good friends. Seems like you'd know about his girl."

"Maybe he was the only guy who didn't have one."

"Where'd you take him?"

"To Schofield."

"Where'd you drop him off?"

"The quad."

"He say why he was going there?"

"You read the report. To pick up his surfboard."

"He said, 'Take me to the quad so I can pick up my surfboard.'?"

"I think he said please. Like you oughta."

"He kept his surfboard at the PX."

"Did he? Then I guess he had to go over there to get it."

"He say where he'd been?"

"On the shore."

"Without his surfboard?"

"How would I know?"

53

"If he was going from the shore to Schofield, why didn't he just take Kamehameha instead of going into Waialua?"

"Last time I was there, Waialua had a shore, too."

"Lot of traffic that day?"

"Always a lot of traffic."

"He have his thumb out?"

He giggled. "Out of what?"

"He carrying anything?"

"I don't remember."

"A bundle under his arm, you said. Could have been a shirt, you said."

"Then a bundle under his arm. Coulda been a shirt."

"What color was the bundle?"

"I have no idea."

"Danny had a car he was trying to sell. Do you know whose it was?"

"Nope."

"You ever ride in it?"

"Not that I can remember."

"You ask him why a guy with two cars was hitchhiking?"

"Nope."

"At the time you picked him up, he was supposed to be with his platoon up in the Koolaus. Did you know that?"

"Nope."

"He say anything about it?"

"Nope."

"He could scoot around in those mountains, couldn't he?"

"What's your point?"

"Just wondering. Here he is doing a little surfing while his platoon is up there swatting mosquitoes. You're his pal. Seems like he might have told you about it, about how smart he was, pulling it off."

He said nothing.

Valerie said, "Mr. Sheffield, I'm Danny's aunt. His mother's my sister. He's my family. My friend may be a little rough, but we're just worried sick about Danny. Please excuse us."

"Lady…What is it?" He looked at her card. "Ms. Sabatino?"

"Yes."

"Ms. Sabatino, your friend's not a little rough. He's an asshole. *I'm* a little rough. He's just an asshole."

"I'm confused about something," she went on. "You picked Danny up at five o'clock on the 27th and didn't report it to the authorities until five o'clock on the 28th. Didn't you hear anything earlier that day, or the night before, about him being missing?"

"Not a peep."

"What did you do on the night of the 27th?" I asked.

"Now, that sounds like a cop question. You a cop?"

"No."

"Then it's none of your business."

"My nephew's missing," Valerie said. "Maybe worse than missing. If it goes on, the police will get involved. I just want to know how you didn't hear Danny was missing for twenty-four hours. Just explain it, please, and we'll be on our way."

"Look. Nobody told me he was missing and I didn't hear about it until the next afternoon."

"How did you hear about it?"

He paused for a heartbeat and a breath. "Was on the radio. Base station. I still listen to it when I'm in the neighborhood."

"When was your tour up?"

"Coupla months ago."

"What do you do? Your job."

"My job's none of your business."

"Is it a secret?"

He stood up. "I'm through here. You want anything more, hire a lawyer. And I will too."

He left the room.

"Well, he's lying," Valerie said, after the door closed. "Lied up front about the Children of God and lied at the end about how he found out. And maybe a lot in the middle, like the car."

"Talk about shit detectors. Mine pales."

"Now that's an awkward expression. But is he lying about even seeing Danny? What do you think?"

"Possibility."

"He told the truth about one thing, Harry. You really were an asshole. Thanks."

"Just making an omelet."

• • • • •

Corporal John Osmond was a little taller than me, a little thinner, and a lot more polite than Mike Sheffield. So I was, too. The Golden Rule.

He said, "Sure, I recognized the car. I'd driven it. Danny was trying to sell it and he let me take it for a spin. I saw it coming, thought it might be him. I honked and waved. He didn't see me. Or maybe he ignored me. Breezed on by."

"No doubt it was him?" I asked.

"No doubt."

"Where was this exactly?"

"You know the area? Around here?"

"Pretty much."

"You know Kawailoa Beach?"

"Just down from Waimea?"

"Yeah. I'd been at Kawailoa. Just left. There he came."

"You were heading south?"

"Yeah. Yes, sir."

"Which means he was heading to the point?"

"That direction, anyway."

"What time of day?"

"Early morning. Eight or so."

"And it was Thursday, the 27th?"

"Yeah."

"Notice a surfboard?"

"No, sir."

"Could you tell what he was wearing? What kind of shirt?"

He thought. "It was white. Might have been a t-shirt."

"Not an aloha shirt?"

"No. Solid color. White."

"Anything on his head?"

"No, sir."

"Was he alone?"

"No, sir. There was a girl with him."

"Did you recognize her?"

"I don't think so. I didn't exactly check her out. You know, bang, bang, they're gone."

"Long hair or short? What color?"

"Long. Light brown."

"Would you say local? I mean Oriental or Caucasian?"

"Couldn't say."

"You said you don't think you recognized her. Does that mean you might have seen her before?"

"Yes, sir. I might have. I mean, I've seen Danny before with a girl with hair like that, but there's a lot of girls with hair like that."

"The girl you'd seen him with before with hair like that, was she a local?"

"You mean Asian?"

"Yes."

"No. She was white. Caucasian."

"Do you know her name? This girl you'd seen him with?"

"Betty, Betsy. Betsy, I think."

"Last name?"

"Never got it."

"Where and when did you meet her?"

"There's a bar around the point on Kamehameha. An open air spot. Locals playing country. It's called the Texas Paniolo Bar. There one night. A while back."

"Danny introduced you?"

"No, we met her together. At the same time. He took a shine to her. They danced."

"He leave with her?"

"I don't know. They were still there when I left. Listen, I might be leading you on without meaning to. I don't know that's the same girl I saw him with that morning. I'm just going on about a girl I saw him with."

"I understand. You're not leading us on. But tell us about her, this girl that night. She made an impression on you?"

"Yeah. She did. She was pretty."

"And you're pretty sure her name was Betsy?"

"Yes, sir. Betsy was her name. I was talking with Danny, checking out the action. She was at the bar with another girl. She smiled at us. We went over. Turned out she was smiling at him, I guess, they hooked up so fast. All of a sudden, they're dancing. I turned to the other girl, some guy's got her dancing.

Wasn't my night, I guess."

"What was the other girl's name?"

"Esther, I think."

"I've passed Texas Paniolo before. It's pretty much out of the way. Where do the people who go there usually come from?"

"Well, a lot of us go there. Brigham Young has a campus not far from there. It's not that out of the way. People come from around, I guess."

"Tell us about your relationship with Danny," Valerie put in.

"My relationship?"

"Yes. How well did you know him? Did you hang out together? That sort of thing."

"Danny had a lot of loner in him. He could be friendly enough, but he didn't go out of his way to do it. I've known him…well, since he got here, I guess. But I don't know all that much about him. Seems he told me his dad was in prison. Mentioned his mom once or twice, just, you know, he'd be reading a letter, I'd say something like, 'Letter from home?' and he'd say, 'Yeah. From my mom.' We got along. We drank a beer now and then, not a lot. I don't know. We were friends, but there's lots of guys I'm closer to than Danny."

"He tried to sell you the car, though?" she said.

"Well, he didn't single me out. He posted it. I saw it. I looked into it."

"What'd you think of it? The car?" I asked.

"It was all right. Just not the kind of ride I'd want. Not hot enough."

"Corporal," Valerie said, "you've been very forthcoming and we appreciate it. Just one more thing. In your statement, you were vague about the car. I got the impression you hadn't seen it before. Now you're saying you not only had seen it, you had driven it. Why didn't you make that clear in your original statement?"

"I don't know. I guess it was maybe the way the question was asked. I don't know."

"And I'm confused about why it took you until the next morning, twenty-fours later, to come forward with your statement. All that day they were looking for him, didn't you hear about it?"

"No, ma'am. It wasn't 'til the next day I heard it on the base radio. Even then, I didn't put it together. 'Til I heard some guys talking about how Mike Sheffield had picked him up hitchhiking. All of a sudden I just snapped to it. Like, 'Hey, I saw him too.' And told them."

"What kind of car did you buy?"

"Little ragtop."

"Danny surfed, didn't he?"

"Yeah."

"You too?"

"I body surf. Can't stay up regular."

"Know of any other hobbies Danny had?"

"Gambling. Is that a hobby?"

"You mean like… No, you don't mean like poker in the barracks, do you?"

"No."

"Where do guys gamble around here?"

"If you can afford it, there's a boat. Offshore. The Princess something. Mike Sheffield's like the … the guy to see. He gets enlisteds on it."

"You ever go?"

"No. I can't afford it. Or maybe I can and don't want to."

"But Danny went?"

"He talked about it a couple of times. Said it was hot, said it was a lotta fun."

• • • • •

We left Schofield and took Kaukonahua west to Waialua. I found the intersection where Sheffield said he'd picked Danny up and told Valerie of it when we got there. Then I turned north on the two-lane road that headed into Haleiwa.

"I'm thinking while we're out here," I said, "maybe we'll grab dinner and then go by the Texas Paniolo Bar on the way home. I know a place around the point does great grilled lobster. That suit you?"

"Sure. How many green Toyotas you think there are on Oahu? Say between two and five years old? With four doors?"

"He thinks it was a Toyota. We'll ask the police. I've got a friend down there. We'll pay him a visit tomorrow. And maybe go by the Children of God on the way."

We picked up Kamehameha in Haleiwa. It carried us north hard by the shore.

"Osmond says he passed Danny along in here," I said. "Danny was heading the same direction we are. Somebody along in here, somewhere around here, knew Danny and saw him that day, was with him."

"Maybe. If he was really here."

"I don't think Osmond's smart enough to make all of that up. The girl and everything."

"Okay. So he was here in a green car with a girl. How sure can we be Osmond's got the day right?"

"Less sure."

There were small cottages on both sides of the road. On the right, away from the sea, they were interspersed with farmland; on the ocean side, more closely together, clusters of them hidden by unattended foliage. Surfer huts.

"Danny's been in one of these houses," Valerie said.

"Maybe."

At Sunset Beach I parked and we walked to the beach so I could show her the Banzai Pipeline where the ocean, unimpeded from the North Pacific, meets the submerged reaches of beach and erupts in its legendary thirty- and forty-foot waves.

Back in the car, driving as slowly as the traffic would permit, we came to Kahuku Point, the northern tip of Oahu, and the Turtle Bay Resort, where Kamehameha turns southeast towards Kailua. A couple miles farther along we passed the Texas Paniolo on our right, set back from the road, its parking lot empty at this too-early hour. Five minutes later, we came to Ahi's, parked and entered. It's a small hacienda-style building, long ago a truck stop for cane haulers.

After we ordered dinner and a couple of drinks, Valerie said, "Harry, did we make a mistake last night?"

"You noticed that? Too much garlic in the risotto, wasn't it?"

"We didn't, did we?"

"No, we didn't," I said quickly. If she'd been anyone else, just another woman, I might have been chewing on the same thought. Usually, I wake up the morning after the first night thinking I've led them on. It's my ego lying to me about what a great catch I am. I know better. All I am is thirty seconds of ecstasy, and not always that. Not many women dumb enough to think I'd be worth staying with. And this one, in particular, needed me like persistent dandruff. No, her concern wasn't romance. It was business.

She said, "The work comes first, right?"

I wiggled my eyebrows. "I wouldn't go that far." She gave me an unfeminine tap on the arm just above the elbow. For the second time—last night in bed and now with the tease tap—I took note of her strength. I guessed her to be maybe five-seven and about 130 pounds but her voluptuousness—a dramatic word, but the right one in her case—concealed a very fit and powerful woman. She rubbed my arm like she thought she'd hurt it. How silly. She said, "I feel a little guilty. Enjoying myself so much while Danny's out there somewhere."

"You sure you're not Jewish?"

"Don't you?"

"We're doing all we can. And we're picking up speed. The gambling. The Children of God. Him having my name and phone number. Uncle Francis. That sleazeball Sheffield. We find Betsy on the way home, it'd be a hell of a day. At some point… We need to talk about this. If this gets rough, I won't want you exposed. I can't do that."

"That's in the manual, isn't it?"

I looked confused. It comes naturally to me.

"The Private Eye's Handbook? Get the women and children off the street. Got to be one of the ten commandments."

"Are you trying to piss me off?"

She sighed. "Just having a reaction to being patronized. Put all that off for now. I've already thought about it, thought about how you'd feel if things got dangerous. But we're not there yet. We'll talk about it when we get there."

"So you'll understand?"

"I said put it off for now. That's all I said."

"Okay. Just so you know."

"Put it off!"

"Okay."

She laid her hand on mine and smiled at me. "So, you were a Ranger. That's a big deal I didn't know about."

"It's not that big a deal." I was a little grumpy.

"Don't pout. Tell me about it. Tell me about your life. Start with your mother. You didn't know her, did you?"

"No, I didn't. My father came home from Vietnam in a body bag when I was still in diapers. He was one of the early ones. My mother went crazy.

Turned into a sad, drunken, roadhouse floozy and, one day, just disappeared. I never really knew either one of them, little snatches of little boy memory is all. My uncle, my mother's brother, raised me, filled in the details when I got old enough to understand. He never married. Took good care of me, though. He was a plumber. I can also do plumbing. Did I tell you that?"

"Plumbing's a big plus in a man. Where'd you grow up?"

"Baton Rouge. I was a jock and a jerk, a bad student. Got a football scholarship to a small college you never heard of. Enjoyed the football, but not the class work. Left after two years and joined the army, stayed at it and became a Ranger. Learned my primary skill there. Thing I'm best at."

"Being a Ranger?"

"More like being a weapon. Packy told you. I can kick most anybody's ass. And I'm not bragging. If you can do it, it's not bragging."

"Were you ever married?"

"Once. Sicilian girl. With all that passion. She challenged me, said I might be the toughest guy at Fort Bragg, but I'd never break her. She was right. And jealous? God. One night," I smiled at the memory, "I walked in the front door a little later than she thought was proper and she came across the room like a banshee and hit me on the head with a bottle of Dry Sack, you know, the one wrapped in a burlap bag? Put me in the hospital. Somehow I found that attractive. It turned me on."

"How long did it last?"

"Not quite four years."

The lobsters came. I asked for a bottle of Pinot Grigio and they had a pretty good one. We were quiet, attacking the lobsters, getting messy. Girl could eat.

She broke the silence. "What was her name?"

"Elizabeth. Liz."

"Must be tough being married to a weapon," she said.

"It is for most women. Lot of Ranger and Special Forces marriages come apart over it. Guys can't get out of character when they get home for dinner. In our case, as it turned out, it bothered me more than her."

"Really?"

"Yeah. I loved the physical part of the Ranger life. Jumping out of airplanes, swinging on ropes. But I never could get into that 'hoo-ah' shit, couldn't rah-rah like the rest of them. Seemed pretty stupid to me. And I couldn't lay down to an authority I thought had its head up its ass. Like going to Grenada just because we fucked up in Beirut. I'm not much of a team player when you get right down to it, and Rangers have to be."

"You were in Grenada?"

"Yeah. I thought it was kind of embarrassing. Like dueling with an un-armed man. But whenever I could stop thinking big picture and just rock and roll, I loved it. I looked for action, for violence. I could be scary, scared my-self. Nothing else scared me. Just myself. I wasn't always under control. And that's a very bad sign. Plus, I was kind of split, and I knew it. This other side of me wanted to be another kind of person entirely." I paused, not completely comfortable, yet knowing I wanted to tell her all this. Previously, I had only discussed this with Liz and Muhammad and I had known each of them much longer before I came to it.

"What was that? What kind of person?"

"A good guy. Civilized. Educated. Decent. Respectful."

"Those sound like things we expect to find in good soldiers."

"And a lot of them are like that. Most of them, probably. But I couldn't get the balance worked out."

"Get in trouble over it?"

"Once or twice." Plus five or six. "Anyhow, I confused what I wanted for myself with what I thought Liz wanted. I wanted the marriage to work and I thought the better side of me would be better for us. Now I know she didn't want me to change and I was really doing it for myself. She liked my mean streak. Liked tangling with me."

"You ever hit her?"

"No, but I came close." There was a white lie in that. I hadn't hit her, but I grabbed her from behind once to restrain her and broke four of her ribs. "When I was accepted for Special Forces, I decided dealing with my dark side and being as good for Liz as I could was worth more than my career. I left the Army. Thought civilian life would give me more time to work on myself and the marriage. Big mistake. Hard enough to work on yourself, but working on a marriage … I don't know about that. I'm not sure I believe in that. Now."

"Well, some people cherish the pure idea of marriage. So, for them, I don't think working on it's a mistake. At the same time, I don't think *I'm* one of those people."

"Seems to me marriage is the enemy of romance. And I prefer romance."

"Katherine Hepburn said her mother told her marriage was a way of trading the admiration of many men for the criticism of one. Then what? Did you do?"

"I got a job. Selling advertising for a TV station. Hated it. How could I not hate selling commercials after being a Ranger? I should have gone to school. Got my degree. And maybe a couple of others. Instead I became a professional bullshit artist. I was not impressed with myself. And Liz wasn't either. She didn't think being married to a civilian bullshitter was as cool as being married to a Ranger. Or as hot. I drank too much. So did she. Drinking's a real bad thing to do when you're unhappy. It makes you unhappier. We broke up. Slowly but surely. Any of this make sense?"

"All of it. And I can't tell you how honored I am that you're telling me. I know it isn't easy."

"Not all that hard. Must mean I trust you."

"Yes, it does. Trust is harder than love, don't you think?"

"Much."

"So, you and Liz got divorced and there you were working at a job you hated."

"Yeah. I was…making a fool of myself pretty much every night. One night in a bar I broke the jaw of a law enforcement officer. You know the rest."

"Where's Liz now?"

"In Los Angeles. She moved there to make it easier to visit me when I was in prison. We keep in touch."

"Is she remarried?"

"No. At least she wasn't the last time I saw her."

"When was that? The last time you saw her?"

"About six months ago. We had dinner."

"What's between you?"

"Just shared experiences. But I'll be there for her if she ever needs me."

"Tell me about prison. About all those fights. Was it all about rape?"

"It was about control. Inside, sex is just a by-product of control."

"Yes," she said. "Even out here, rape's not about sex. It's about dominion."

"Yeah. I spent a lot of time in the hole, solitary confinement. It's the penalty for making trouble. To me, though, it was the reward for making trouble. I preferred solitary to being in population."

"How did Packy handle the rape thing?"

"I … I don't know." I knew. Packy did easy time. "It starts when you first get locked down. I didn't meet Packy until a long time after he went in."

"Does everybody have to … ? Does it happen to everybody? Even old people?"

"Yes. Everybody. When you don't have anything, don't own anything, you'll settle for owning another person if it's the only available commodity. Sometimes the ownership doesn't involve sex. Just … ownership."

"I'm sort of proud of you for the way you handled it."

"Nothing to be proud of. I had no choice."

"And then Chicago. How'd you meet your friend Muhammad?"

"On the street outside the restaurant. I broke up a mugging. He saw something in me. Took me in, put me to work in the restaurant. He had these other responsibilities, too. Muhammad is sort of a universal father. Some of it's his size. He's huge. And it's his presence, too. You'd have to be pretty stupid to cross him. So, some of his neighbors were having trouble with gangs, paying protection or getting their businesses broken up if they didn't and, with me, he was doubled up."

"Vigilantes?"

"Sort of. Never shot anybody. Hurt some, though. And enjoyed it. And we kept the police informed, stayed on their side."

"And that's how you started feeling good about yourself. You became Batman."

"Robin, maybe."

• • • • •

We went to the Texas Paniolo Bar after dinner, chasing a wild goose named Betsy.

You could hear it before you saw it. The parking lot was filling up. The building is wrapped by a low wall on the front and both sides with posts supporting a roof with a wide overhang. Open air, in fact. The band was up front, their backs to the parking lot. Inside, there was a counter along both walls with high stools, no tables, just all dance floor, raised a foot or two with a rail around it, and mingle room. A big bar in the back. The crowd was good-sized and happy, early enough there were no ugly drunks.

We walked around the room separately, looking for pretty Betsy with long, light-brown hair.

"I found five of them," she said when we met back at the bar.

"I found twenty, but I grade on the curve."

We ordered beers. I said to the bartender, "We're looking for somebody. A missing soldier. Few weeks ago he was in here dancing with a pretty girl named Betsy. Long hair. Light brown. Know anybody like that?" I laid a hundred on the bar.

"Man, I'd like to pick that up, but I can't earn it," he said. "Look at this place."

I wrote my number on my card and put it on the bill. "Consider it an advance. There's more where that came from. Ask around. Maybe you'll get lucky. Betsy's got a friend named Esther."

He looked at the card and pocketed it along with the bill and said, "I'm on the job. Just pretty Betsy with light brown hair? And a pal named Esther?"

"White. Not Oriental. And young."

"They're all young. Guy on the door won't let 'em in if they're over twenty-five."

"He let me in," Valerie said.

"Your card's a fake." He winked at her and went back to work.

We turned on our stools and took in the scene.

"Nice joint," Valerie said.

"Yeah. If a guy didn't have a girl, this'd be the place to find one."

"I'm cramping your style?"

"Sure. I rule in places like this."

She smiled. "You know how to dance to this stuff? The Texas two-step?"

"Used to. But I'm at the age where I like to get a snug hold on the girl when I'm dancing."

"Get up by her ear and sing to her?"

"Yeah. Let's go home. I'll sing to you."

A storm hit suddenly, the rain coming straight down like a waterfall, and about that hard. Thunder followed lightning within seconds. The wide overhang of the roof kept the storm away from the open interior and there was nowhere to go and it felt good being trapped there, watching and listening to the storm.

"No," she said. "Let's dance."

So we did.

FOUR
Thursday, March 13

We were up early, had stuff to do. I was in my robe in the office at my Mac, drinking coffee, downloading pdf files from Francis and filing them on my hard drive. Valerie was across the room, studying the edges of the maps with a magnifying glass, wearing one of my t-shirts. The phone rang.

"Good morning." Muhammad. "Hope I didn't wake you."

"No, we're ... I'm up."

"Slip of the tongue there."

"Yeah. Valerie's here. I'll put you on speaker phone." I punched the button and said, "Got your email?"

"Yes. Tell me what you've learned."

"Couple of leads. Some bad feelings." I told him of the bible, the three fifties, the two phone numbers of the Children of God, finding my name and phone number in Danny's papers, the gambling, Uncle Francis, a thin lead on a girlfriend. I told him we'd been lied to at least once, maybe more, and didn't know why. I asked him to put Osmond and Sheffield in play with Francis.

I said, "Packy told Valerie he gave Danny my name not long ago when he visited him. And I think with a purpose. And Danny looked up my number and wrote it down but didn't call it. You've got something in your email from Francis about the Children of God. And we've both got stuff on Danny's bank accounts."

I was looking at my monitor. "Danny MacGillicuddy had a savings account and a checking account in Kentucky and a checking account over here," I said. Valerie pulled a chair up beside the computer as I talked. "He's withdrawn close to $10,000 from his savings, pretty much all he had. $2,000 in December, $2,500 in January, $4,000 more on February 14th, small stuff in between. Each time an electronic transfer from Kentucky to his bank here followed by a matching withdrawal. Maybe gambling money. If it was, he was losing. Unless he kept his winnings under his mattress, because he didn't put them back in the bank.

"Other stuff in his local account looks like mostly his paycheck until February when he made a couple of deposits that don't match his pattern. One for $600 and one for $800. A little odd. But he had a sideline selling used cars, so maybe that's where it came from.

"Then on February 23rd, three days before he disappeared, he withdrew $1,700 from his bank account. And the day before he disappeared, the 25th, $3,000 more, taking his balance down to less than $500. So, about to get out…well, about two weeks from getting out, he had his hands on a lot of cash.

"His roommate said he said when he got out he thought he'd go hiking and camping on Kauai. Wouldn't need a lot of cash for that, I don't think. Be better to have it in the bank than in your pocket. But add it all up, it's not enough money for…well, it's…"

"Not enough money to get killed for," Valerie said.

Muhammad, hearing her, said, "It's close though. Hello, Ms. Sabatino."

"Hello, Muhammad. Please call me Valerie."

"Valerie. Pick up the phone for a moment, please. I want to speak with you in private."

She did. Their conversation was brief. Once or twice she chuckled, glancing at me as she did. Then, "Thank you," she said. "I'll look forward to that. Very much. Good to talk with you." She punched the button and we went back to the speaker.

"I've got my copies of Francis's work," Muhammad said. "Have you digested the Children of God stuff?"

"No. Have you?"

"Yes. The Children of God is a non-profit organization under the IRS's 501-c-3 designation. Three years old. Vaguely noble goals, like making the world a better place, improving the lives of the impoverished. They have five of what they call 'way stations' around the country. One is in Hawaii. There's a primary office in Manhattan and a 'hostel' in Boundary County, Idaho, wherever that is. They have been fully funded by their founder, a man named Orrin Massey, to the tune of about two point five million annually. I'll ask Francis to take a look at him.

"Money goes for salaries, office support, and what they call 'communications tools.' But they don't have a web site, which I find odd these days. Payroll is rising.

"What's it mean? I don't know. You can run a pretty good scam with a non-profit and get away with it for a long time as long as you stay square with the IRS. File timely returns. Do the paperwork. Or, you can do good things for the impoverished. Make the world a better place. So, I'm not impugning these people, you understand? No way to know from here. Could be a confederacy of angels."

"Muhammad, is this a religious organization?" Valerie asked. "Their charter, I mean?"

"No. Charitable."

"I have, uh, contacts in Manhattan," she said. "Maybe I can get someone to take a closer look."

"Someone associated with your father?" Muhammad said.

"How … ?" She looked at me. "You ran a framazoid on me."

I shrugged. "Little one. Due diligence. I told you I was a pro." She was not amused. I didn't care.

"Yes. My father. I'll call him. He'll have someone pay a courtesy call on the Children of God. My father's emissary can get in to see most anybody. Especially a charitable foundation."

"I think that's an excellent idea," Muhammad said. "What's next?"

"Osmond said Sheffield's sort of the Schofield rep for this gambling boat. The guy to see for enlisteds looking for action. We'll look into that."

"Okay."

"We're going to see Dick Wong today. He's the top detective with the HPD. When we're over there, we'll go to Manoa, see the Children of God. What do you make of the bible?"

"Hard to say. Guess first thing I'd do is find out if he got it from home. Mom or Dad. That would make it pretty innocent. There'll be a chaplain's office at Schofield. Maybe they could tell you if Danny was showing an interest in religion. And you should ask his daddy why he gave him your name."

"It's on my list."

"Long list. I'll pick up any part of it you want."

We hung up. Valerie called Belinda about the bible, which she hadn't sent, and her father, who agreed to have someone visit the Manhattan headquarters of the Children of God. She said she'd forward to him the report we had.

• • • • •

Manoa is a neighborhood close enough to the university to have a bohemian feel, students, mostly, and some teachers, hippies of various ages. The peak called Tantalus dominates the skyline. The streets were damp from the rain they get almost every night.

In my shiny Range Rover I exited Lunalilo at Punahou and headed up the hill. As we passed Punahou School, I said, "See that school? That's the oldest high school in America west of the Mississippi. Little known fact."

"I've got a head full of little known facts. I'd like to trade some of them in."

"So, knowing history and stuff like that's not as impressive as plumbing? That the kind of girl you are?"

"Not much as impressive as plumbing. Muhammad told me you're the best man he's ever known. Said he hopes his son turns out half as good. He said you were absolutely trustworthy."

"Muhammad drinks. Really ought to be in rehab. Tells a lot of lies."

Punahou became Manoa Road and then it forked and I took the left branch and then, two blocks later, a left on Awapuhi. A hundred yards more and I turned into Puuhoonua which, I remembered from my early days of driving around chasing rainbows and getting familiar with neighborhoods, dead-ended after two blocks of old bungalows along the narrow street.

I slowed to a crawl. 456 was the last one on the left in the last block. Nicely isolated. Privacy on two sides from a meadow behind and beside it that sloped down from a hill, the edge of park land. A high privacy fence ran the length of the driveway, blocking the view from that side. A two-car garage with a high roof. The house was two stories plus an attic, bigger than most of its neighbors, with a widow's walk that wrapped the crest of the attic on all four sides. The widow's walk looked like an add-on. A small front yard, a little neglected looking, was enclosed with a waist-high chain link fence with a "Beware of Dog" sign on it. No mailbox outside the fence. Hazardous duty for the mailman. A van in the driveway, kind of beat up, plastered with bumper stickers. Nobody to be seen. No sign that said "Children of God." I eased on by, turned in the driveway of the house across the street, backed out, and went back down and nosed into the driveway of 456.

"That van's not as old and broken down as it looks," I said. "As it's been made to look."

"Front door or side door?" she asked.

"I don't see the dog out front."

We unlatched the front gate. No dog barked. Walked to the door and knocked. A teen-aged girl wearing a denim mini-skirt and nothing else opened it. She was brushing her hair.

"Yeah?" she said.

She was a little thin for my tastes, but naked enough for me to struggle with words. Valerie filled in for me, said, "Is this the Children of God?"

A man appeared behind the girl. He looked a little wasted. About five-eight and sort of stooped on top of it, my age, maybe a little younger. Mean, shifty eyes. He had a surfer-do, bleached and stylishly unkempt, but his complexion didn't look like he caught a lot of waves. Reminded me of those people who wear jogging outfits to drive to the store. When he saw me something odd flashed across his face; maybe recognition or something more. Respect? Nah. My ego again. I recognized him, though. He was Uncle Francis.

"I got it, baby," he said and the girl scurried off. "Help you?"

"Yes, sir," I said, going for respectful. "We're looking for the Children of God. Are we at the right place?"

He stared at us.

Valerie said, "We're actually looking for a missing soldier. My nephew. His name's Danny MacGillicuddy and we found your phone number among his things. Do you know him?"

"No."

"You sure?" I said. "You look just like his Uncle Francis."

He sneered.

"May we come in?" Valerie asked, trying to get us somewhere. Unlike me.

"No."

"We'll come back later," I said.

He closed the door. We walked through the front yard and out to the driveway. I circled the van, looking it over, thinking it would probably piss Uncle Francis off and maybe I'd learn something. I was half right. The side door opened and a Samoan about the size of an industrial refrigerator stepped out. He came down the steps, carrying himself with his ham-sized arms out from his side, his legs spread wide like he had too much equipment down there to get them together. He walked with his butt settled back for balance.

"This is the dog," I said softly to Valerie.

"Beat it, brudda," he said with a flat smile that was used to being obeyed.

"Don't mean any harm, friend," I said. "We're just looking for a guy who might be in trouble. Just trying to do some good work for our fellow man.

Just like you guys do."

He came to me, stopped a few feet away. "I said, 'Beat it.' Motherfucker."

"Look," I said, spreading my arms wide. "We …"

He drew back his right to launch it and I hit him in the nose with a quick straight left and blood erupted. He put his hand to his face with a look that couldn't believe what had happened and I bent and buried a right in his stomach trying to reach his backbone. He went whoosh and leaned forward and I swung my foot into his crotch like I was punting for the Raiders. He went "Unh" and fell to his knees and I heard a shotgun ratchet a shell. Uncle Francis stood at the side door.

"You're trespassing, asshole, and if you don't get in that car and disappear, I'll put holes in you. And the cunt."

I saw his point and we drove off.

"Now that, little Miss Crimestopper, was a clue," I said.

"Jesus."

"They never think you'll come with a left. I don't know why that is. I mean, you got two hands. But, no, they only expect the right. Listen, we need to have that talk about backing you out of this a little."

"Jesus."

• • • • •

I had met Honolulu PD Captain of Detectives Richard Wong when I first settled in, showed him a letter of reference from a Chicago detective named Reggie Thompson I'd worked with back there, just to get acquainted.

Later, Sam Dodson asked me to track the daughter of an important client who wanted the search kept quiet. I found her in a Korean bar, hustling drinks and turning tricks, strung out on the needle. I got her back to her family but had my doubts she'd stick. Anyway, after it was over, I met with Dick Wong and told him the story, left out the girl's family name but told him where I'd found her and who she was with. I wanted him to believe he could trust me, that I wouldn't be a rogue problem. He said he appreciated my coming by.

He had a pumpkin face with a wide, happy mouth on an oversized head, but eyes that narrowed quickly. He wore a dark suit, white shirt, and his tie pulled up snug to the top button, uncommon attire in Honolulu, except for serious cops. His eyes were narrow today.

"I've got a hell of a lot going on, Harry," he said, "without playing 'my favorite cop' for you. I hope you appreciate that. And you, young lady, who are you and what are you doing with this thug? Just trying to ruin my day?"

"We've spoken before, Captain Wong." I turned to look at her. "I'm Valerie Sabatino, the aunt of the missing soldier who called you to inquire about Mr. Pines."

I looked at her. She looked at me and said, "Due diligence."

"Yes, I remember, Ms. Sabatino. Should I apologize for telling you he's not too bad a guy for an ex-con and a busybody?"

"Can you stay open on that? I've hired Mr. Pines to help me find my nephew."

"Have you? A couple of amateur sleuths messing around in my city. How nice. And what have you *discovered*, if that's not too strong a word for it?"

I opened with a little overview, a picture of the oddness of Danny's disappearance, and he raised a hand for me to stop and he picked up the phone, punched a button, said, "Bobby. Come in here."

A guy about thirty in street clothes came in. Wong said, "Detective Bobby Bentley, this is Harry Pines and Valerie Sabatino." We shook hands. Bentley was tall and lean and his grip was strong. Horn-rimmed glasses made him look smart and the eyes behind them reinforced the impression. Wong pointed to an empty chair and Bentley took it.

Wong said, "This lady's nephew's gone missing from Schofield. She's hired Harry on my recommendation which I am certain to regret. They've been looking into it. It strikes me as interesting. I want you to open a file on this. On the clock but off the record. You fit that in?"

"Yes, sir."

He said to me, "Start over."

I did. I got to our day, yesterday, at Schofield, said we'd found the phone number and traced it back to the Children of God. I told them about the Uncle Francis Danny didn't have who'd gone to Schofield to look through his things. I didn't say I thought I'd found the guy at the Children of God because I knew Dick would tell me if conclusion-jumping was an Olympic event, I was a medalist. I said Danny was gambling on an offshore boat and apparently losing badly, making big withdrawals from his savings, and that the former soldier who was the link to the boat was one of the two guys who saw

Danny and got the search called off. I told them as much as we knew about the green car. I left out the discovery of my name among Danny's papers and the lead on Betsy. I said it smelled like anything but a routine AWOL.

"Okay," Dick said. "I'll give you a little help. But I'm going to expect a lot in return. Double pay-back. That's my goal here. We'll run the DMV report on this green Toyota. Get back to you on that.

"There's a fancy ocean-going ship named the Princess Leilani that leaves Honolulu Harbor four or five times a week. Been here for a little more than a year. Goes out into international waters and turns into a casino. Does real good business, they tell me. Legal operation because of where it goes, but I'm in a bad mood about it because it's run by bad guys. And if you've got a boat full of criminals—prostitutes, gun hands, shylocks, folks like that—where are they going to go when the ship gets to the dock? My fair city is where. Local businesses aren't too happy about it, either, all the money it drains.

"The Children of God? It's a joke. Take a guess how many runaways and flower children show up here every year. Don't bother. Question's rhetorical. The right answer is zillions. And the pretty ones've always got a way to get by, don't they? One place they go to get by is the Children of God in Manoa. It's like an intake unit for bar bimbos and hookers. I hear the real pretty ones get trained in the fine arts of high-priced escort services. Not exactly a cat house, because the girls don't ply their trade right there, so I can't bust them. Unless I catch them holding them against their will, or having sex with the underage ones. And so far, no luck on that. Guy named Eric Fox is head pimp. We've also got him connected with the boat, provides hostesses, escorts, refers customers, maybe a little loan sharking.

"Pretty picture, huh? And your nephew, Ms. Sabatino, maybe found these people. Or they found him. Now, what does a high rolling operation like the Princess Leilani want with twenty-year-old soldiers? Just their life savings? Or something else? We hear from what you might call back channels that the military has a problem with missing ordnance. Small arms. Medical supplies. They haven't asked us to look into it, so what do I know? Could there be a connection? One wonders.

"And finally, that massacre of those homeless people in Pearl City a couple of weeks ago? It was done with an organized precision that was, well, military."

I said, "What are you saying?"

"Just what I said. No more, no less. I've got a heightened interest in my military neighbors as a result of a couple of things lately."

Valerie said, "A massacre of homeless people?"

I said, "Yeah. Seven of them. Four men, two women, one child. Under a bridge. Eric Fox," I said to Dick. "Describe him."

"About your size. Maybe thirty-five. Dark curly hair, mustache. Kind of Mexican looking."

"How 'bout a little guy with a surfer-do works for Fox? Kind of pale and shifty looking? Know him?"

"No."

"How about a big Samoan maybe does heavy lifting for Fox?"

"All Samoans are big. You could be talking about Manu Tsiasopo. You probably are. He's mean. You're not going to put this lovely lady in harm's way, are you, Harry?"

"See?" I said, turning to Valerie.

He eyed me closely. "You've been to the Children of God, haven't you? You didn't tell me that. Why didn't you tell me that?"

"It was just a social call. I thought you'd be bored. Could we go through some mug shots?"

"Why?"

"Surfer-do guy."

"Why?"

"Because we saw him and the Samoan at the Children of God this morning and he fits the description of Uncle Francis."

"Okay. Bobby'll set that up."

"Now?"

Bentley looked at his watch and said, "Let's say after lunch, about two. That work?"

I nodded. Valerie said, "That'll be fine and I really appreciate it. Don't you, Harry?"

"Yes. I do."

"Okay," Wong said. "That's it. I'm going back to work. I expect cooperation from you on this, Harry. Feed me good information and do it often and we'll be friends. Don't and we won't."

• • • • •

Outside the police station, on the sidewalk, I said, "If I take you on a cruise and it's business, can I put it on my expense account?"

"Only your end of it. I go with full date privileges. Or I pout."

"How about my action at the tables?"

"Your losses are yours. Your winnings are mine."

"Those're date privileges, all right. We're not far from the harbor. Let's walk."

It was another perfect day in paradise in a long procession of them. What clouds there were scurried off to sea on the trade winds that brought them over the mountains. Palms, bent to the sea, shed their oldest fronds in the breeze and they fluttered to the pavement and mingled with the fallen petals of nearby flowers. The rustle and the chatter and the wind made music. After a week or two of this magnificence, when it finally rains, people feel cheated and become sour. Such is humankind's willingness to whine.

Here, in downtown, there was a higher percentage of suits among the pedestrians than in Waikiki, but still far fewer than in any business district on the mainland. And of the suits, the jackets seldom matched the trousers and rarely were accompanied by neckties. Every day is casual Friday in the islands. We walked down Nuuanu past the French Consulate to the many busy lanes of Ala Moana Boulevard and crossed it, surprisingly, without dying in a horrible accident.

Three blocks more and we reached the Aloha Tower Marketplace at Honolulu Harbor where there was entirely too much happiness and too many people for me.

A local custom called Aloha Boat Days insists that every cruise ship be met as it docks. Every one. And a big white one was here today. Hundreds of locals gathered on the pier. They serenaded the arrivals with the languid rhythms of slack key guitars that always make me want to smoke a joint and lie down. Lovely hula girls swayed their hips and air-swam their arms and smiled and kissed every passenger, draping leis upon them. Those without musical skills or good hips just grinned and called out "Aloha" to the disembarking hordes.

I'd stay on the boat.

The dozens of shops of the marketplace at the harbor were the equivalent of the slot machines in the Las Vegas airport, an immediate reminder of why you came and what you're expected to do while you're here.

In the shadow of the Tower itself we found the Visitors Information Bureau and I said, to the pretty brown girl at the central desk, "We're interested in a cruise on the Princess Leilani."

She looked at me with an expression that said she'd heard that one before and didn't like it then. But smiling was her job so she found her smile and said, "Let me see," and hit the keys of the computer before her.

"I'm sorry, I don't show that here. Is it a cruise ship?"

"Yes, ma'am."

"Umm. I don't show anything about the Princess Leilani. I'm sorry."

Kapono's, an outdoor place, was right there, almost in our way, so we took a table overlooking the Pacific for an early lunch.

"The powers that be seem not to be embracing the Princess Leilani," I said.

"Yes. Still, I think we might enjoy it."

"I could ask Mike Sheffield to get us a couple of tickets."

"He could do it. But probably not for you. Suppose I just phone the Princess and request permission to come aboard."

"Do that."

"May I use your phone?" she asked.

"Starting tomorrow."

She used hers. I ordered a couple of fish sandwiches and grapefruit-and-mango slurpees while she had a brief conversation and closed her phone.

"One is referred to the Princess Leilani by one's concierge or bell captain," she said. "Or, alternatively, for such as those residing here, a representative of the Princess will phone the interested party and conduct an interview. I may expect to be graced with such a call on this here phone. Do you think we should go incognito? Fictitious names, maybe. We have been making something of a spectacle of ourselves."

"You don't have incognito potential."

"Why not?"

"We'd have to put a bag over your head. Down to your knees."

"How sweet."

As we were eating, her phone chirped. She engaged the caller with a few questions and a few answers. And made a few notes on a pad she withdrew from her purse. She closed the phone.

"Here's the deal. There are three levels of participation aboard the Princess based upon one's credit line. $5,000, $15,000, and $30,000. Or cash in hand will also serve."

"Is that apiece? Or may one who qualifies bring a friend less qualified?"

"You would think. Be awfully rude to the bimbo set, otherwise."

"You have first class in mind?"

"Sure. Nothing's too good for my bimbo, baby."

"So, we won't be surrounded by the hoi polloi. I like that. They tend to be smelly."

• • • • •

We sat at a computer console beside a plump, pretty, and fiftyish Asian woman Bobby Bentley introduced to us as Orchid. We described the guy at the door at the Children of God and she came up with a pretty-good facial likeness. She stored my guess on height and weight in a companion file.

"Now," I said to her, "let's assume that he didn't get that ridiculous haircut until he came to the islands and that he hasn't been arrested since then so you won't have that picture on hand."

"Consider that assumed," Orchid said.

"Okay."

"Okay what?"

"Give him another haircut."

"From among all the other haircuts known to humankind?"

"I see your point. Can you just run for matches on the face and forget the hair?"

"I can. Against what database?"

"I bet you've got a lot of them, don't you?"

"You have no idea."

"Okay. Let's take a stab. Run it…with that hair…against arrests here since…" I paused, remembering the way he looked at me at the door. Cautiously. Warily. And I remembered where I'd seen that look before on many faces, if not his. In the joint. "No," I said, "I got a hunch. Can you run it against inmates at a federal prison?"

"Which one?"

"The Federal Correctional Institution at Terminal Island, California."

She hit a few keys, said, "What time frame?" I gave her the months I was there.

She got four hundred fifty-four possibles, allowing for variations in weight and a fudge factor on height.

Valerie said, "Would you consider that to have been a good hunch or a bad hunch?"

"He's in there," I said, fingers crossed and pondering the efficacy of prayer. I really wasn't too surprised at the number. The population at TI averages about a thousand, with lots of turnover. Times almost four years. And the place is full of low-rent weenies like Uncle Francis. People think the joint is full of tough guys but not more than one in ten could hurt anybody but himself. Of course, one in ten out of a thousand is enough to keep you on your toes.

Orchid put us side-by-side at two monitors with keyboards and we each entered the file, Valerie up from the Z's, I down from the A's.

"You know, this reminds me," I said as we began. "I think we should go through the bible one page at a time looking for any notations Danny may have made in it."

"This *reminds* you? You say that in case I might be thinking that after we finish this, life will be good again? To keep me from having any hope of a better day tomorrow?"

"Yeah. I've been spoiling you. It's not all glamour. This kind of work is the real thing when you're a sleuth. This is why we get the big bucks."

"Tell me exactly how many times you've done this before. By which I mean *exactly* and if you lie I will disembowel you in your sleep."

"Okay. No times."

"Let me explain something," she said, turning to the task. "Shut up."

"Ring Lardner."

"Yeah, but you don't know what it's from."

"Yes, I do. It's from Ring Lardner."

"That's who. I said 'what.'" She small-smiled and I knew I'd get a good night's sleep.

I leaned over and kissed her on the cheek and whispered, "You don't know either."

Twenty minutes later, staring at faces, I said, "Ha! Gotcha! Looky here, Valerie. This particular piece of shit named Wilton Randolph Crandall is in reality..."

She leaned over and looked. "Uncle Francis!"

"I betcha. Wilton was incarcerated at TI when I was there and when Packy was."

"And now he's gainfully employed at the Children of God. A non-profit charitable organization. Doing God's work. Learned his lesson, didn't he? No recidivist, he."

Orchid aged Crandall and put the surfer-do on him and printed out a couple of color copies for us. I told Bobby Bentley that Crandall was the doorman at the Children of God and I thought we'd drive out to Schofield and ask the custodian of the personal effects of missing soldiers if he was also Danny's Uncle Francis.

And he was.

· · · · ·

I went black tie on the cruise. Valerie also wore black, a filmy thing, not quite knee-length, nicely low-cut, with thin security straps, set off by a strand of black pearls, and sheer black stockings. Not those abominable panty hose either, but thigh-highs, which I knew through special privilege. Her three-inch heels were attached to her feet with an intricate arrangement of thin black straps that made no sense at all. Every man with a pulse would be staring at her. Standing beside her, I'd be invisible. So maybe we were semi-incognito.

It seemed inappropriate for a couple with a big line of credit to arrive in an old Range Rover or a tiny Miata. Looking good mattered above all. So we arranged to repair to the Princess Leilani in a limousine.

The Princess wasn't particularly lovely, more a creature of function than grace. She was twin-hulled, 300 feet in length, and sported two stacks aft of the wheelhouse. Her apertures, even the ones well above the water line, were portholes, not windows. They were not only small, but scarce, and the promenade decks were narrow and uninviting. Clearly, both strolling around and stargazing were considered inimical to the point of it all.

There were, both in fact and in policy, three patron levels to the ship. Everyone arrived at the first and then ascended, as their means permitted, to the slightly smaller and more exclusive floors above. The tables were covered until international waters were reached, the guests amusing themselves during this period with food and drink and the performances of pathetic impersonators of Elvis and Marilyn.

We rose to our lofty station on the third deck and then wandered around getting familiar with the surroundings. It didn't take long. Every casino's the same. All glitter and no gold.

I went through the motions of playing $25 blackjack for the first thirty minutes, losing $200, while Valerie played $10 chips on numbers at roulette. Then we made a spectacle of ourselves at craps as she made six straight passes and I let my first $200 ride, backing off on the seventh just before she crapped out. Dumb luck. I tipped lavishly. We drew a crowd with that run and the floor manager introduced himself as Ramon and asked if there was anything he could do to make our stay even more enjoyable.

"I'd like to meet the captain," Valerie said. "Just to pay my respects."

"He'll be down shortly and I'll be pleased to introduce you," he said.

"Oh. No. I meant I'd like to see him at work. In the pilothouse. And then come down and play dice again."

The last part did it. Getting her to "play dice again" was Ramon's goal. He summoned a mate to take us up.

The captain, to his credit, didn't try to dazzle us with the complexity of his challenge. "There's not too much to it, you see. We just come out to international waters and cruise. When the seas are calm, we drop anchor and just hold our position."

The foredeck included a helipad. I asked, "Do you have your own helicopter?"

"Our owners do. They sometimes use it to deliver special guests who have been unable to make our launch schedule."

"Where does it leave from?"

"I ... I don't know." Or couldn't say.

"How many men under your command?" Valerie asked, batting her eyes.

"Twenty-seven. The casino personnel are, of course, not my responsibility."

"Are there quarters on board for your crew?"

"Yes, but most of us live in the city. Only a few are necessary on board when we're in port. We rotate those responsibilities."

"Where are the cabins? May I see them?"

"Well, they're on the lower decks, but I can't imagine why you'd want to.

They're just, you know, cabins."

"Well, yours then. Perhaps just yours."

"I don't actually have a cabin in the way you mean. We have a suite which we maintain for private parties while we are performing our current ... duties. It is referred to as the Captain's Cabin. When we are on a serious voyage I reside there, but not under the current circumstances."

"I'm sure it's lovely. May I see it?"

He glanced at me.

"You go on ahead, dear," I said. "I'll wait here."

They were back in twenty minutes. The captain glowed from within.

"What is your range?" I asked, just to snap him out of it. I wasn't thinking of a charter.

"Oh, she's ocean-worthy in all respects. We're licensed in Hong Kong."

Valerie flirted with him for a few more minutes and then the mate returned us to the gambling floor and handed us off to Ramon. I asked him, "Can we play whatever stakes we want on the other floors? Or are the limits lower down there?"

"I can arrange your limits anywhere on the boat if you'd like."

We made our way to the first level and ordered a drink at the bar. I said, "Cappy have a cozy little bunk, did he?"

"There was a lovely sofa. When I tried it out, I gave him a little looksee."

"Tramp. More as a sleuth than a cuckold, may I ask where it was?"

"Where *what* was?" She affected shock. "Oh. Just aft of the helipad. Is the aft the behind part?"

I saw, over Valerie's shoulder, a dark, Mexican-looking guy about my size with curly hair and a mustache, wearing a tux. "There's our boy Eric Fox, I betcha," I said, telling her where. She made a casual sweep of the room with her gaze and turned back to me.

"Fine looking specimen for a pimp," she said. "Got his bling under control, too."

He sat on a high stool against a wall. A floor man brought him a piece of paper that may have been a check and he examined it and made a notation on its back and handed it back. Then he made a notation on a pad he withdrew from his coat.

A waitress in a short grass skirt came up and waited beside us to place her order with the bartender. If the skirt's grass why bother with short? Valerie dropped a $25 chip on her tray and said, "Excuse me, but do you know the name of the man sitting on the high stool against the wall? Dark and very attractive? Mustache. Curly hair."

"Eric Fox," the waitress said.

"What does he do?"

"Different things. Brings special customers. Some of the hostesses are with his company."

"Does he cash checks?"

"I think he approves them."

She gave her another chip. "Please don't tell him I asked about him."

"Usually I get tips for telling him. My lips are sealed." She went on her way.

A little ruckus erupted at one of the tables. A soldier slammed his fist on the 21 table and did an angry spin. "Goddammit," he said, too loud for refined company. A man in a tuxedo came to him and chatted with him for a moment with his hand on his upper arm. Together, they walked over to Fox who spoke with the soldier for a moment, then summoned another man dressed all in black, a man who had pointed a shotgun at us that very morning and had posed last week as Danny's uncle. Wilton Crandall passed the soldier through a door just beside Fox, said something to whomever was inside, and went on his way. Ten minutes later, the soldier emerged, looking flushed. He went to Fox who spoke to him. The soldier turned on his heel, flashing anger, and started to walk away. Fox barked something to him and the soldier came back to him. He spoke to him again and the soldier nodded obsequiously and walked to the bar looking sullen and subdued. Another soldier came away from the table where the outburst had occurred and joined him. They talked for a moment and the first soldier calmed down and, after a moment, laughed a little too loudly.

Crandall returned and spoke into Fox's ear and, as he listened to Fox's response, he turned his eyes to us and found me. I held his gaze for a moment and then winked.

"We've been made," I said to Valerie.

"Really? Was it as bad for you as it was for me?"

We gambled aimlessly with house money. I kept an eye on the door beside Eric Fox. In a little while the Samoan emerged from it. He had a bandage on his nose and a bluish cast above it. He walked over to Fox who directed his gaze at us. When he saw me, I grabbed the bridge of my nose and wiggled it.

"I've seen all I need to see," I said to Valerie. "And now here I am trapped in a lousy casino. You think you could get your friend the captain to summon the helicopter for us so I can get a good night's sleep?"

"I think I could pull that off. I'd need maybe twenty minutes alone with him."

I think she was kidding.

• • • • •

We disembarked in the first wave and waited in the limousine. A few minutes later, the two soldiers came down the gangplank, the one who'd lost and been lectured looking pretty drunk. "Wait here," I asked of Valerie, and got out and followed them in the crowd as they crossed Ala Moana and entered a multi-level parking garage. Ten minutes later, as I skulked inconspicuously, I watched them drive out, the sober one at the wheel of a Geo Metro. I observed and memorized the license number and rejoined Valerie in the limousine.

On the way home, I explained the stupidity of casino gambling to Valerie. I helped her understand that each bet in each game is played against odds that favor the house, insuring the player's inevitable defeat. I contrasted this with pari-mutuel betting, like horseracing and poker, where the players compete against each other and the house takes a cut of their bets for putting on the game.

"The difference is that losing isn't guaranteed. It's a meritocracy. The smart eat the dumb. In a casino, everybody's dumb."

She patted my hand and said, "Honey, you're so smart. When we get home I'm going to give you a prize."

FIVE
Friday, March 14

Sifting and sorting; making lists.

If Danny had gotten religion, he hadn't shared it with any of the clergy at Schofield. Francis wasn't able to unearth any negs on Osmond or Sheffield. Sheffield wasn't employed anywhere, best Francis could tell. The bartender didn't call. Valerie's father called her to say the Manhattan "office" of the Children of God was a mail drop and one button on a phone console answered by a cranky redhead. We took turns going through the bible one page at a time, looking for notes in the margin. Or something. It was a lot of fun. Only 2,000 pages. If the Toyota assumption was correct, thirty-six cars matched the parameters we'd given to Dick Wong. Fifteen were licensed in Oahu and owned by men under thirty-five, a cut I made on a guess.

Packy and I got together on the phone. He called collect after I left a message. Something in his voice said he wasn't the same guy I knew, more nervous, more guarded, but I made an allowance for the circumstances of his call, probably ten guys lined up behind him waiting their turn. He said he'd given Danny my name for no particular reason. "Just, you know, hey, I've got a pal over there. Give him a call." I didn't believe him but didn't say so. Prison phone calls weren't good for heavy talk. He said he didn't know anything about the bible. He pressed me to pay him a visit so we could talk. I agreed and he said he'd put me on the visitor list. I didn't tell him about Wilton Crandall posing as Uncle Francis. I wanted to see his face when I told him that.

Francis produced a profile of Orrin Massey.

He was a never-married forty year-old, born in Colorado City, Arizona. He had spent six years in the Army, leaving at the age of twenty-five with a dishonorable discharge. He'd faced a court martial on an assault charge but the charge was dismissed. He had risen to sergeant before the incident. Something less than a poster boy.

His "resume" had a twelve-year hole in it at that point, which I was sure annoyed Francis. You can do that, though, if you deal only in cash and live in one of the world's many places that ask few questions of their residents.

He surfaced again in the states when he set up the Children of God. He owned a 20,000-acre game preserve in Boundary County, Idaho, and showed a mailing address at a post office box in the county seat, Bonners Ferry. So, there was evidence of Massey's wealth, but none as to its source.

Valerie had emptied the guest apartment and moved into mine. I had told Muhammad to come anytime he felt like it, that I'd appreciate having him to talk with, but I didn't want to waste his time. "You decide," I said. "And, yes, your apartment's empty."

About noon, chafing a little, I drove to 456 Puuhoonua to sit outside and be a nuisance. I took my cell phone, but not Valerie, which severely pissed her off. I told her it wasn't to keep her out of danger, but to cover both our bases. "Nobody calls me on my cell phone," I said. "So if somebody's looking for me with stuff we need to hear, why not have you here to handle it?" It had the virtue of being true, so she agreed.

She settled for calling the fifteen possible car owners, working the addresses from west, out by Schofield, to east to inquire about a car she'd heard was for sale.

The Samoan came across the street a few minutes after I took up my position. He wore shorts and a tank top. When he got to the car window, I lowered it and said, "You should put on a sweater, Manny. If you take a chill and sneeze, you'll lose a lot of blood. It'll hurt, too."

"Either get the fuck outta here or get outta the fuckin' car, asshole," he said in a tone I took to be unkind.

"Thanks, but I'll just sit right here. How's things between your legs, by the way? You seemed to be steppin' a little lightly comin' across the street. You might try epsom salts on that, a little sitz bath, maybe. Crushed nuts tend to be slow healin."

"I got a date comin' up with you, motherfucker."

"Oh, no. You've made a mistake. I prefer girls." I smiled and there wasn't much he could do except get violent and end up in jail. It didn't get me anywhere either. He went back inside. And I sat there. If Danny was inside they wouldn't let him walk out while I was there. I was left with hoping he'd arrive unsuspecting of my presence. He didn't. Quite a few attractive young women came and went. And a few young men with military haircuts in civilian clothes.

We'd been on it for four days, which didn't seem all that long in some ways, but I didn't think we were getting closer to finding Danny.

My phone chirped.

It was Valerie. "Captain Wong just called. He wants to talk with you."

"What about?"

"I asked. He wouldn't say. He was patronizing. But he said it was important for you to call."

"I'll call him and call you right back."

He picked up on the first ring. "Harry, we've got a guy over here who showed up with a skull he found on a hike in the Koolaus. And a military belt. And he says he saw a fatigue shirt among some bones and other stuff and the shirt had the name 'MacGillicuddy' on it. He's here now, giving a statement."

"Walked in with a skull in his hand?"

"Had it wrapped in newspaper."

"Can you hold him 'til I get there?"

"Yeah. I didn't tell this to Ms. Sabatino."

"I know and it pissed her off. She thinks she's got some rights because the kid's her nephew. I'll bring her with me. Figure about a half-hour."

I told her exactly what I'd been told and she said she was on her way, would meet me there. I said I'd wait outside the main entrance for her, wouldn't go in without her.

• • • • •

"The skull's intact, except for the lower jaw," Dick Wong said. Bentley stood behind him. "Which means we may get a dental match on the upper teeth. Some skin left around one ear. Damage looks like carnivores, maybe mongooses or wild pigs. No evident fracture, but everything's preliminary."

"Where'd he find it?"

"Up range and east from where the boy went missing. He's got GPS coordinates. Carried a little notebook, recorded everything. Came into a clearing with what looked to him like a makeshift lean-to. A t-shirt spread on the top, like to dry it. He went down the slope to the stream to refill his canteen. Said it was a treacherous descent, he almost lost it. Down there, he found the skull, some other scattered bones. The fatigue shirt turned inside out, still buttoned. A pair of trousers with what he thinks was the leg bone in a boot. He slipped the belt through… I'm sorry, Ms. Sabatino. This is sort of grisly."

She looked coldly at him and said, "I'm a grown woman, Captain, and I've decided to forgive you for being condescending earlier if you don't do it again."

"Okay, I'll remember. Hiker slipped the belt through the skull, through the eye socket, and carried it that way on the way down. He got down, wrapped the skull in newspaper he found in a trash can by the roadside. Hitchhiked to Haleiwa. Called his wife to pick him up. That was last night. This morning he just walked in here with the skull."

"Is the location within your jurisdiction?"

"Yes."

"So, you're on this?"

"Yes. But we won't cowboy it. We'll work with the military. I've put them on notice. They're going to arrange for a helicopter. I'm expecting a call any time."

"I want to go," I said.

"No way."

"I'm a Ranger, Dick. Was. I can handle that terrain. I can help."

"No. We may get up there yet today if the light holds. I'll get a copy of the hiker's statement for you. You wait someplace where we can reach you. I'll call as soon as I know something."

"Dick, dammit. Let me go."

"Forget it."

Valerie hadn't yet spoken. She said, "Captain, may we speak with the hiker?"

"He'll be going up with us, so I don't see how that's possible. At least not today. But I'll see that you have the chance, probably tomorrow."

His phone rang. He listened, said, "We'll be there in thirty minutes," and hung up.

• • • • •

We went home. I paced. Valerie sat in her chair with her legs tucked beneath her, reading the hiker's statement. I said, "I feel like a kid who's been sent to his room."

"It's him," she said. "I know it."

"Wish I could say, 'Don't be silly.'"

The phone rang. I hit the speaker button and said hello.

"Dry run," said Wong. "We couldn't get down. Too much wind, ugly terrain. Tried to lower a couple of soldiers, but couldn't pull it off."

"Now what?"

"Tomorrow we go back. With a bigger helicopter. I'll reserve a seat for you, Harry. It's a big favor."

"I know. And you're keeping score."

"Damn right."

"You see anything?"

"The clearing. That's about all."

"What time tomorrow?"

"Meet me at my office at 8:00. I'm sorry, Ms. Sabatino. I know the waiting isn't easy for you. I'm sorry."

"You did the best you could."

"Well, no, I didn't. I always underestimate how rugged it is up there. You're welcome to come with us tomorrow. Wait at Schofield for the helicopter to get back."

"Thank you. I will."

I broke the connection. She seemed a little dazed. She said, "Francis emailed you the name of the soldier the Geo Metro's licensed to. He's at Schofield. Think we should go out there tonight?"

"No. He won't go anywhere."

"Okay. I got blanks on seven of the Toyotas. Why don't I keep calling?"

"That'll keep, too. Let's take a walk on the beach." I extended my hand and she took it.

"Okay," she said in a small voice.

It was raining so we put on shorts, short slickers, and ball caps and went barefoot. We walked at the water's edge beneath the weather system that had stopped the copter mission on the other side. Gulls and terns hovered above us, flying hard into the wind, going nowhere, playing. A Hobie Cat flew through the surf, one hull in and one up high, a blonde with her butt in a sling hanging over the side working the lines, her mouth open wide, probably screaming with delight.

"Your turn," I said.

She gave me a sideways glance.

"The story of your life."

"Not very interesting. Not as much as yours."

"So, everybody wants to be filthy rich and you're telling me it's just a bore."

She stifled a false yawn. "Fighting vainly the old ennui."

"And I suddenly turn and see your fabulous face."

"I get a kick out of you, Harry. You know the difference between fun and excitement?"

"Tell me."

"Fun is everything I did before I pulled up in front of your house. Excitement is since then."

"So tell me about the fun."

"But you can just imagine what it's like to live like that. And talking about it always makes me sound shallow. It was, is, great fun." She ran her hand down the inside of my arm to take my hand in hers and tucked the two of them in the pocket of her jacket, pulling me close as we walked.

"It's everywhere and everything. All the laughs, all the parties, all the games. Golf, tennis, polo. I can ride, I can shoot—arrows or bullets, crossbows or long bows, handguns or rifles. I sail, I ski, drive fast cars and fast boats, dance all the dances. I can defend myself with my hands empty. Or full. I speak four languages, and read three more. Had cute boyfriends by the dozen. Made all the glamorous events. All the premieres. La Scala. The Old Vic. The Met. It's a wonder I didn't get nosebleed from the sheer altitude of it.

"At Princeton, I masqueraded as an ordinary girl just to see how it would feel. I got the hang of it and liked it. A few people knew, people I'd take home with me on weekends in the city, but I swore them to silence. Kept the act up at Stanford, too. After I graduated I took the bar, passed it, and then took a year off and traveled the world, a graduation present from Daddy.

"Afterwards, I asked him to cut me loose for a while, not to send me any money even if I begged for it, told him I needed to find out how to make my own way. We compromised. He said he wouldn't send me any unless I did beg for it. I worked with a law firm in Chicago for about a year. Then I got found out. Revealed as not just wealthy, but staggeringly so. So I went to San Francisco and did the same thing until the same thing happened there. Then San Diego and you know the rest."

"You kept running away from people who found out you were rich?"

"Pretty much. That's why I left Chicago. I was seeing someone and when he found out, his reaction just repulsed me. So I split. By the time I left San Francisco it was as much a reaction to the law … no, to the lawyers, as the rich girl thing. In San Diego, some of both. But by then, I was fully disenchanted with the kind of people who become lawyers. I mean, Christ, is a little nobility too much to ask, a little respect for the part the profession is supposed to play in holding things together? Yes, it's too much to ask. In fact, ask it and be thought a fool."

"How do people act when they find out you've already got everything their dreams are made of?"

"Everything changes. At first, they don't know how to act. They're sort of off stride about it. Stumble around. Then they go from being the person I liked for who they were to being an even better person. Or trying to. More sophisticated. Cleverer. Like snappy repartee is required. Like they're afraid to fart or reveal that there's something they don't know or someplace they haven't been that everybody who hasn't been there thinks is fabulous but they've been there—in season, too, by God—and they know it's overrated. It makes me want to wrap my hands around their throat and squeeze until their eyes pop out."

"So this is why a moderately attractive woman like you showed up over here without one of those significant others?"

"Of course. I mean, how can I even go to dinner, much less bed, with someone whose eyes I want to squeeze out of his head?" She stopped and turned to me. "I need exercise."

"Ever handled an outrigger canoe?"

"No. Ever known a woman who knows how to hit a heavy bag?"

"Two firsts. One for you and one for me. Let's start with the bags and the weights. Work up a sweat and then rinse it off in the canoe."

We jogged back up the beach and went in to put on shoes, sweat tops, and swim bottoms. I latched open the wide front and back doors of the tool shed to let the breezes in. She did light weight work with lots of reps while I worked first the speed bag and then the heavy. She said, "Switch?" after maybe ten minutes and I gave her a spare pair of bag gloves of unknown provenance which were smaller than mine but still too big for her. She said she'd make do. I lowered the speed bag platform to suit her height and watched while she rattled it inexpertly.

"Show me," she said.

"It's not about power," I said, as I tapped it a few times. "It's about hand-eye coordination. Tap it forward, hold your follow-through and then backhand it as it bounces off the platform and comes back in range. Then the other hand the same way. It's more like dancing than fighting. Rhythm. It's easy once you get the hang of it and hard 'til you do."

"Okay. Don't watch me. Get on the bench. You need me to spot for you?"

"No. Thanks."

I listened to her work it as I bench-pressed in reps of twelve-by-three, working my way up from one-fifty to three hundred, backing down at that point to twelve-by-one. She got better but not much. Then she said, "Fuck!" and laughed. "I'm not relieving my aggressions. I'm developing them. I want this big dude." She knew how to hit the heavy bag, square on, wrist locked, and from the belly. I did squats and dead-lifts and kept my eye on her. She worked first in two-punch combinations, hard left, harder right, and then went the other way, right-left. After five minutes, which is a long time, she backed off and took a few deep breaths.

"Had enough?" I asked.

"Not quite." She went back at it in three-punch combos with good foot-work, moving in, slipping to the side, circling it. After a couple of minutes of that, she backed off, stepped in, and drove a big one in and stood there as it came back and slammed into her torso. She hugged it and giggled and slid to the cement slab floor and lay on her back. "Count me out, ref," she said.

"Skip the canoe?"

"Kiss my ass, cowboy. Let's paddle."

An outrigger canoe is pretty much unchanged since the first one was built centuries ago. The hull is narrow and shallow, with very little draft. Two long arms curve up and out from the left side and then down to a narrow float the length of the hull, giving it some of the two-hulled stability of a catamaran but none of the comfort. Mine has three seats, just flat panels, fore, aft, and middle, and single-blade paddles.

We were drenched as soon as we pushed off from the beach and climbed in ten yards out. The sea was up and we paddled hard to get through the surf to a calmer place. Valerie was up front. The rain had passed but the clouds on the horizon were agitated and weather didn't take a long time to arrive on this side. I guessed she wouldn't be bored.

I heard her shouting and laughing over the roar of the waves. We took maybe a dozen of them head on, paddling fast, rising up in the bow nearly to vertical and then crashing down the other side like an amusement park ride. Slow going. Finally, it leveled out and I shouted, "Having fun?"

"And worn out."

We went out about a thousand yards and the calm passed. We were in three-foot swells and they were growing. Small-craft-warning weather.

"Let's turn back," I shouted. "It's picking up."

"Don't baby me," she said over her shoulder.

"Baby, you're in for a rude surprise. We're turning back."

We picked up speed on the way in. I spent as much of my time steering as paddling. I wasn't needed for power; the Pacific was giving us that. We took a couple of big ones over the stern and the canoe took on water. The person in the center seat bails when that happens, but the center seat was empty. A really big one hit me in the back still a hundred yards out and suddenly we were just sitting in a boat full of water. You can't paddle a sunken canoe, but it won't sink, just settles right below the surface. The natural buoyancy of the koa wood takes care of that.

"Now what?" she shouted, laughing.

"I forgot to ask if you can swim. Can you swim?"

She grinned at me.

"Put your oar in the canoe. Slip it under your seat. Get out on the left side, stay behind the arm, hold on to the oar with your right hand and pull with your left. Kick with your legs." It's awkward, but there's no other way. "Drop your legs every now and then and pretty soon you'll feel sand. Just keep going. We'll get there. The surf'll take care of that."

Ten minutes later we stumbled ashore, overturned the canoe to empty it, and dragged it up to the tree line.

"Damn," she said. "That was a workout. How'd I do?"

"You did good."

The long, hot shower's always my favorite part after coming in, and taking it with Valerie made it even better. We had a little time before dinner and then we had to take another shower.

SIX
Saturday, March 15

The day was sunny and unusually calm. The helicopter seated eight, plus two pilots. The eight included an HPD SWAT team cop named Akaka who looked like he'd had broken glass for breakfast and it went down fine, the hiker whose name was William Runner, Bobby Bentley, four soldiers, and me. Dick Wong had stayed at his office saying he'd leave for Schofield when the copter headed back. He made it clear that on the ground we'd be in what he was treating as a crime scene and that Bentley would be in charge. They told me to run a still camera, a Nikon digital with a voice recorder, shoot everything and then shoot it again.

Runner was about thirty, quiet and very much within himself. He was tiny, and as lean as you'd expect of someone who hiked the Koolaus for fun.

About ten minutes into the flight we hovered over an opening in the trees. The co-pilot verified the coordinates and Runner said, "That's it, I think."

Bentley told us to land soft and stand still, said he wanted to look it over before we walked all over it. And he wanted me to land first, stand still and shoot it. "Go three-sixty," he said. "Swinging left. Lots of shots. We'll start down when we see you've made the full circumference." He gave us blue rubberish gloves with long cuffs and said, "Put these on as soon as you get down. Before you do anything else."

Six of us would go down. Bentley behind me with Akaka, then two of the soldiers, and finally Runner. Two soldiers stayed with the copter crew and ran the hoist.

The clearing was larger than it looked from the air, maybe thirty feet on each side, kind of square. It sloped severely; I felt myself leaning. It began at the foot of a hill at the upper end and ended at a precipice at the other where the sound of a fast-moving stream could be heard below. For the thousand or so square feet of it, it was barren. The dirt was smoother than seemed natural, and dry. There were a few footprints and a little disturbance here and there, and I guessed that was Runner's passage. All this I noticed as I shot. The others landed.

The lean-to was a construction of intriguing intricacy, about three feet high, made with two branches, their ends buried in the soft earth, and above them three others that formed a frame that reached back to the hillside. Leafy branches were spread across the top of the frame. The supporting poles had been narrowed by a knife at their lower ends where they entered the ground and the framing members were notched where they were joined. It was created by someone who knew what he was doing.

But I wondered to what purpose. It wouldn't give much protection from the rain and the sun couldn't easily get through the cover above. One person would fit in it seated, his back against the hillside. Lying down, his feet would stick out. The earth inside it and for ten feet in front appeared to have been swept with what may have been another leafy branch.

The t-shirt was army brown and hung with its tail down at the front opening of the structure and the upper part, chest and sleeves, across the leafy roof. Akaka bagged it.

One of the soldiers bent low at the clearing's edge and picked something up. "Detective," he said, and showed Bentley a cigarette butt and then bagged it.

Bentley said to Runner, "Where did you enter this clearing?"

"There," he said, indicating a spot a few feet from the lean-to where there was a gap in the brush.

"What did you touch?"

He thought for a long minute. "Nothing. Nothing up here."

"Did you make entries in your notebook up here?"

"No. Wait. I did. I checked the coordinates on my GPS and wrote those down."

"Do you smoke?"

"No."

"You didn't build that lean-to?"

"No."

"Or go in it?"

"No."

"Do anything to smooth out this dirt?"

"No."

We stood at the precipice, the drop-off to the stream, and Runner said, "I nearly lost it going down there. I was holding on to roots and branches and they wouldn't support me, kept coming loose." It was fifty feet straight down, widening at the bottom on both sides of the stream.

Akaka said, "We'll rappel." We tied ropes to two trees and tossed them over the side, went down in pairs.

What appeared to be a fully-buttoned fatigue shirt turned inside out was on the narrow bank, stretched out as if to dry and held in its place by a good-sized rock in the center of it.

"Did you put that there?" Bentley asked Runner. "And that rock?"

He nodded.

Akaka picked it up it as if to bag it and I said, "Can we verify the name on the patch?"

"Detective?" he asked.

"Let's take a look."

Akaka struggled to get to the buttons, working his way up from the tail of the shirt, revealing and then opening them one at a time. I looked at Bentley and his eyes met mine. When it was done, Akaka, annoyed with the tedium of the effort, flared the shirt open dramatically and we saw the patch on the breast: MACGILLICUDDY, D. A., and a small cluster of maggots chewing on it.

"When you found this, was it inside out?" Bentley asked Runner.

"Yes."

"And you turned it outside in to read the name?"

"Yes."

"And then turned it back again?"

"Yes."

"Didn't use the buttons?"

"No."

There were bones on the edge of the bank and they were clean of flesh, with striations criss-crossing them, likely teethmarks of predators. An ilia and ulna were still connected, and the carpal and phalanges were just inches away. A piece of a rib cage. I wondered that the water level hadn't risen to them and carried them off since they had fallen where they lay, but then thought perhaps the animals that had fed on them had something to do with where they were now.

We made our way downstream and found more. I came upon the trousers. They were lowered upon themselves in a little two-legged pile as though the wearer had dropped them and walked away. But he'd left behind his lower bones—pelvis, sacrum, two femurs, two fibulas—in a disorganized pile to the side. The predators had nudged the trouser legs farther and farther down to get to the meat and then left them looking abandoned. I found a canteen, still covered in canvas but with its top off, dangling from the chain. It was half full, but whether of stream water or what it had been filled with in a happier place I didn't know. I bagged it. A soldier found a boot stuck in the crevice of two rocks. There were no bones inside it and no strings in its lacings.

Bentley's two-way radio crackled and the copter captain said, "Detective Bentley, we can remain here for another thirty minutes. Another crew can replace us. Just giving you a heads up."

"We'll find more the farther down we go, sir," Akaka said. "But what's the point?"

Bentley said. "We'll use up our time. Keep going down a little longer." He spoke over the two-way, "We'll meet you at the clearing in twenty minutes. Call Captain Dick Wong at HPD and tell him what time we'll be back at Schofield. Tell him we have remains and a positive on the shirt."

We found more bones, ribs, vertebrae. The bones of a hand, still connected, submerged and trapped by a rock. Extricated, they revealed puckered flesh on the tips of two of the fingers. A few yards away, long thin bones, as if metatarsals. An inexpensive analog watch, black plastic strap, stopped at 4:47 pm, Friday, March 7.

Bentley waved us off, said, "Back up top." I toyed with staying, going for more, walking out, then reconsidered and hustled on ahead back upstream.

I was the first back up to the clearing. I stared at the little shelter, tried to imagine its purpose. I took a full knee bend and duck-walked around it, shooting into it with the Nikon from the level of one who would be within, then wedged myself inside and shot from the point of view of an occupant. Something sharp poked my butt and I scrambled out and crawled back in face forward. It was a tiny bone, a small cluster of tiny bones, similar in size to chicken. I bagged them.

I went to the place where Runner said he'd entered the clearing and climbed the hill. The slope was severe and the ground was covered with wide, slippery leaves. I struggled, lost it, and slid back down on my belly, halting my slide with purchase from the toes of my boots. As I stood up, I saw a reddish-brownness in the dirt at my feet. I bent to it and thought it might have been blood. I shot it with the camera.

The others, except for Runner, were up. Apparently, he lacked the upper body strength for the ascent. Akaka called to him. "Wrap the rope around your arm two or three times and take a good hold. Got it?" And with a soldier's help pulled him up in one great tug that carried him well above the crest.

I beckoned Bentley over and, as he approached, my eye caught an out-of-place color on the trunk of a tree behind him.

"Bobby," I said, passing him as he came to me and keeping my sight locked on the tree. "I think I found something that might be blood back there and now I think I see more on this tree." He followed me and we stared at it together and he said, "Shoot it," and put a piece of yellow tape above it. "Where's the other?"

"In the dirt at the bottom of the slope Runner came down. I scraped it accidentally with my boot and there it was, like somebody had covered it up."

"Sergeant Akaka," he said over his shoulder, "Mr. Pines has found something on that tree that may be blood. Take a scraping, please. And there's another one over here that I'll get. Then, let's give this area one more close look for anything that may be blood. It will be brown by now, but redder than the dirt. Trees, ground, inside the lean-to, all over. Got it?"

"Yes sir," Akaka said. But we found no more.

The helicopter hovered above us, drowning us with the roar of its rotors.

• • • • •

Valerie ran to meet me as I jogged from the copter to the low building where we had left her. She waved her cell phone, said, "Harry, I've found the car! I've found it!"

My expression must not have matched her excitement and she knew why and went to a lower key. "I found the car," she said almost in a whisper. "Is it his shirt?"

"It says MacGillicuddy, D. A. Tell me about the car."

"Give me a minute."

I put my arm around her and walked with her to Dick Wong who had trailed her from the building and handed him the camera.

"The shirt said MacGillicuddy?" he asked.

"Yes."

"Let me meet with my guys back downtown. I'll get to you. Real soon. Call you at your place?"

"Yeah." He touched Valerie's arm affectionately and went past us, joined Bentley and Akaka. I turned, waved to them, and called out, "Thanks." I needed a shower.

• • • • •

I came down from the shower, wearing only shorts, still drying my hair. Valerie was in her chair. "Get up," I said, taking her hand. "Sit on my lap." I sat and held her and she buried her head in my chest. All that glorious hair spread across me.

On the drive back I had told her everything we'd done and observed, left nothing out. I said unless she felt like talking we could discuss the green car later. She said she'd wait.

"Want to talk?" I said now.

She nodded.

"Two ways to go. We can wait to hear from the police, and maybe it's not Danny. And then we go back to work looking for him. Or we can assume the worst and proceed now on that basis."

"Let's do that," she said. She sat up a little bit and turned to look at me. She held my face in her hands and kissed me softly. She said, "I think I'm in love with you."

"I've had thoughts like that, too. I tell myself it could be what we're going through, just the two of us. Or maybe not. Maybe I really am. But, it doesn't matter whether we are or not. We've still got this other thing that's more important right now."

"He was killed, wasn't he?"

"I'm sure of it."

"Consider your contract extended."

"Okay."

"So." She sat up a little straighter, wiggled around to face me, put her legs around me and dug them in. It's a great chair. "We've… I've got to think about a funeral. I've got people to call."

"So do I."

"How long do you think before they'll release the remains?"

"Pretty soon, I would think. They won't let weekend hours slow them down. Good chance they'll release them tomorrow. Maybe not all of them, though. I mean..."

"I know what you mean. So, I'll fly back with them. With him."

"To Louisville?"

She nodded.

"I'll go see Packy. Then meet you in Louisville."

"Will you? I'd like that."

Death makes us all hungry for sex, for affirming life in the face of its end. We spent the afternoon affirming our lives.

SEVEN
Sunday, March 16
Ely, Nevada. Chicago.

To make my schedule work, I took a Saturday night flight. Valerie arranged a charter and left Sunday morning with barely enough of Danny for a funeral.

I took a twin-prop commuter flight from Salt Lake City to Ely and rented a car at the airport.

The Ely State Prison, at 6,500 feet above sea level, is closer to heaven than any place else you ever heard of. The prison was squat and ugly, the terrain barren and baked.

Every con I ever knew preferred the hardest federal pen to the easiest of the state version. The feds build them better and run them better. The states go cheap; they're too close to the people to get away with anything else. The same logic would make county jails the worst. And they are.

Packy's first fall was federal. This one was state. TI had likely spoiled him for Ely.

I identified myself four times against checklists as I proceeded through the gates, was wand-searched at the first one and the third one, emptied my pockets, except for a handful of change for the vending machines, at the last one. A long, stern corridor of echoes led to the visiting room, tables with steel, folding chairs pulled up to them, clusters of softer chairs here and there against the gray columns that reached to the gray ceiling. The visitors were mostly women. Some children. Some old people. Uniforms sat against the wall in elevated chairs.

I saw Packy as he entered, before he saw me. When he did, that same wide smile filled his face and he hurried to me, brushed away my extended hand and wrapped his arms around me, pounded my back.

"Long enough, MacGillicuddy," called out a guard. We sat down.

"Harry! Goddamn! Good to see you, brother."

"Good to see you, Packy. I'm real sorry for what happened."

"I know, Harry. I know you are. Tell me everything I don't know. Start talking."

I told him all of it, except for Wilton Crandall posing as Uncle Francis, thought I'd save that. Talked for ten minutes, maybe more. He held my eyes for most of it, looked down at the parts where anyone would. When I was finished he reached across and grabbed both of my hands with both of his and looked down and we were quiet for a long moment. I think we both did our version of praying. I know I did.

He looked up, smiled. "Let's get a Coke." And we walked to the machine against the wall, waited our turn, got our drinks, and walked back, silent all the while.

"Change the subject?" I asked. "Get caught up?"

"Sure. Goddamn, it's good to see you. You look great. Hawaii, huh? Must be nice. How'd you end up there?"

I gave him the story of my months of wandering, of landing in Muhammad's arms in Chicago, of working there, of finding the place on Oahu and moving there.

I didn't tell him about the Pick Six hit, left the impression, implicitly, that it was all Muhammad's money and I just lived and worked there. For two reasons. I didn't want to give him any more cause for envy than he already had, locked down. And the other one I was a little ashamed of, but it didn't seem wise to leave a convict and his friends to ponder a distant pot of gold. They have so little to occupy their minds with.

"And you're working for the man, too," he said. "Is that right?"

"Well, not exactly. They don't hire ex-cons. But in Chicago, when I got there, there were some friends of my friend having some trouble with gangs and I got in on that a little. One thing led to another, and from time to time, well, I just did the best I could. And made sure the man saw me, knew my fingers never left my hand. So, yeah, I do have some friends in law enforcement. What are the odds of that?" I laughed. "Now you tell me. Last time I saw you, you were sitting on a bunk counting down the days to walking around free as the breeze. What happened?"

He looked down, then up with a sheepish little smile. "You know, Harry, I been thinkin' about this since you said you'd come see me, about what I'd say, what I'd want to say when you asked me. And I decided I just don't want to talk about it. I mean, look at me in here. What kinda dumb fuck's it take to end up here? And twice? And now in this state joint? There's no such thing as respect in this pisshole. Not from nobody. But, fuck it. No snivelin' allowed, right, Harry? That was your mantra. What you always said. No snivelin' allowed.

"So, let's just say I stuck my head up my ass. But I want to tell you this much. I want to tell you about the first stupid step I took to end up here. Okay?"

I nodded.

"When I got cut loose, well, my story don't sound all that much different from yours. I mean not knowing what the hell I was gonna do. Except I had a family. Mom and Dad in Chicago. Danny in Louisville with Belinda, and even though she was hooked up with what's-his-name, Roscoe, Belinda don't hate me, never did. Got a brother, too, ended up dealin' in Vegas, but I sure as hell wasn't goin' there 'cause I was on paper and the man wasn't havin' any of that.

"So I went to Chicago, moved in with my folks. Got a job sellin' cemetery lots, graves and vaults. Went down to see Danny a bunch of times. You know, took up one of those square john lives like all the guys in here ran away from." He chuckled.

"So, it's goin' along all right, but I gotta tell you it was borin' the shit out of me. And I ain't got any fuckin' money. At least, not like the money I used to have.

"Guys from Vegas and TI are checkin' in now and then, talkin' about … well, you know what they're talkin' about. And I gotta say they sounded like they was havin' more fun than me. But I was determined to make it on the square. I just knew I was smart enough and I didn't go for that bullshit that a con can't get the first leg up on the square ladder, so it's either go back to the old life or suffer, sucker. Look at you. You're proof that's bullshit."

"I got lucky, Packy. Real lucky."

"Yeah? I'm kinda sorry to hear you say that." He paused while he thought about that.

"Well, here's where I'm goin' with this. I'm strugglin'. I'm still readin' all that spiritual stuff. You remember how I went for all that. All them gurus in beards and robes and shit. Ram Dass. The Baghwan. Meditation. You musta thought I was loony, sittin' on my bunk sayin' my mantra. *Om mani padme sum.* I thought it was just right on. George! Great way to live a life. We should all do it. But we ain't gonna.

"So, I win this contest, you know, sellin' my line? And they send me to New York for our convention, I'm off paper by now, they're gonna make a big deal outta my success. Ex-con makes good. Which was george. I had it comin'. But it didn't put shit in my pocket. I mean, they gimme a grand, a thousand fuckin' dollars, and they withheld from that.

"So, I'm in my hotel room in New York and I'm readin' Krishnamurti and he says … I mean it just jumped off the page at me, I seen it a hundred times before, but this time it just jumped at me. He says, 'Be who you are.' And I snapped right to it. Just sat up in bed and said out loud, wasn't nobody there, 'I'm a thief! That's who I am! I'm a fuckin' thief!'

"Packed my bag, checked out, went to the airport, flew to Vegas, and hooked up with my old friends. And the rest is history. How 'bout that?"

"So what's the moral of the story?"

"The moral of the story is that all that spiritual bullshit is bullshit. An' I ain't read a word of it since I got put back in here. Now I read detective stories. You ever read Robert Parker? Spenser? You oughta. Great shit. Just great. An' there's a bunch of 'em."

"Packy, why did you tell Danny to call me?"

"Like I told ya'…"

"Don't say that again. Don't lie to me. Either tell me or tell me you won't tell me."

He was silent and he smiled at me.

I said, "You remember a guy from TI named Wilton Crandall? Skinny little fuck?"

He looked down and smirked. "Yeah. Now that you mention it, I think I do." Yes, he did. I gave him a moment to ask me why I'd brought the name up, like anybody would, but he didn't.

I said, "He went through Danny's things last week. Went to the base and told the guy he was Danny's uncle Francis MacGillicuddy."

"Did he? Wonder why he'd do that?"

"Time you stopped fuckin' with me, Packy. Time you started helping."

"I take care of my own problems, Harry."

"Yeah? Well, take care of this problem, Packy. You need to grow up. And you ain't gettin' any younger."

• • • • •

I landed at O'Hare late in the afternoon, took the train to Division and walked the six blocks to Serena's. Mid-March was still cold in Chicago and I was suffering from a case of South Pacific thin blood. I huddled and shivered in the inadequate Aquascutum I'd brought.

I was expected, but you would have thought I'd been on the moon for a year the way Serena and Randy greeted me.

"My God, Randy, you're damn near the size of your dad," I said when he released me.

"Only vertically," he said.

"And a lot better looking."

"Thank God for Mom."

I picked Serena up and hugged her. It saved my back, all the bending over I'd have had to do. She kissed me about twenty times.

"Oh, Harry! Oh, Harry! I love you so much. And now someone you care for has lost someone she loved. How awful for her. For you."

"Yes, it is."

"How long will you be with us?"

"Just tonight. I'm going to Louisville in the morning. For the funeral."

Muhammad pumped my hand, put his huge paws on my shoulders, raised me to my toes, and shook me. "You'll be staying with us," he said.

"I thought maybe I'd bunk on the sofa in the office like I did the first month I worked here. And I want to work a kitchen shift if that's all right. Or the front room. Wherever I won't get in the way."

"My bartender asked for the night off. I gave it to him figuring you might do that."

"You just assumed you could put me to work?"

"Everybody in my family works here."

"Listen to him giving orders," Serena said. "And he's no more than hired help himself. You can work anywhere you want, Harry. Or nowhere at all."

"I… I'll tend bar."

The bar's small, only six stools, more than a service bar, but less than one that invites a drinking crowd. Serena's is mostly a restaurant. Twenty four-tops, eight booths against two walls. Not a big place.

They'd been running it for more than twenty years. When it became apparent that Serena's cooking could draw a crowd Muhammad thought about moving to a bigger location. He ran the numbers and said they looked great, but Serena told him to forget about it. She liked things just fine where they were and it made them more than enough money. "You want to spend money, buy the building we're in." So they did. I lived in the apartment on the second floor until I moved to Hawaii; Randy was there now.

Their life together had been all about food. They met in Hawaii, on Oahu, twenty-five years ago. Muhammad, a top sergeant, ran the food service at the Fort DeRussy Military Reservation on the Waikiki beach, and fit in law classes at the university. He hired a pretty woman from Singapore as a cook one day and married her thirty days later. He said he knew from the first she'd make them enough money from her cooking that he wouldn't need to practice law, but he finished his degree at Northwestern after he brought her home to Chicago.

Muhammad handled the phone, the front desk, and the bar and showed customers to their tables. And handled the money. Randy waited tables and ran the serving crew and the bussers. Serena ran the kitchen, but as an executive chef these days, shopping the markets, creating the recipes, planning the menus, and then wandering the floor, making a fuss over the customers, mostly regulars by now, asking about their families.

I was rusty at my chores and Muhammad growled at me as I struggled with Blood Orange Bellinis and Ramos Gin Fizzes. "Guess we ought to cut the list to bourbon on the rocks tonight."

"And martinis. I do martinis."

Serena brought me one dish after another, which only complicated my life so I started sharing them with the people waiting at the bar for a table to clear.

"Quit giving my food away," Muhammad told me in a quiet moment. "We're not running a mission for the homeless here. This is a business."

"Yes, sir."

It was pretty much all a homecoming can be.

Late in the evening, the bar empty and the restaurant quiet, Serena came over and took a stool across from me.

"We've missed you," she said.

"Me, too. But when they finally grow up, you gotta send 'em out there to fend for themselves. Buy you a drink?"

"No, thanks. But Muhammad wants one, wants to talk with you soon as he can get away."

Behind her I saw Muhammad say goodnight to the last departing customers. He bolted the door but left the exterior lights on, then came to the bar and sat beside Serena, put his arm around her and kissed the top of her head.

She leaned into him and patted his big arm.

"Get that bottle of Woodford Reserve down," he said to me. "And three glasses."

"Two," she said. "I'll wrap things up here and go on home. You boys take your time. You mind taking a cab?"

"That's a good idea," Muhammad said. "I'm glad I thought of it. You just go on now if you want. Randy'll wrap things up." He called Randy over, said, "I'm taking the rest of the night off to talk with Harry and your mother's going home. You take over. Clean up. Tally the receipts. Square things with the crew. Can you handle it?"

"Pop, I can run this place from top to bottom. And when I do, the chef don't give as much crap to the front man as when you do it."

"Doesn't," Muhammad said. "Doesn't give as much crap. And don't say crap in front of your mother."

"Yes, sir." And saluted and walked off with mock military precision.

Serena said, "Randy's got a bigger sofa than the one in the office, Harry. If you want to stay upstairs."

"Thanks, but I've got a real early flight. I'll be fine down here."

She leaned across the bar and I did, too, and we kissed. She put her palm to my face. "I love you, Harry. I don't want anything bad to happen to you."

"I'll be careful, Serena. And I love you, too."

She said, "How 'bout you, Muhammad? Do you love me?"

"More every day, darlin'. More every day." He got her coat from the tree by the door, helped her in to it, and walked her to the car.

While I waited, I poured two drinks, straight, no ice.

Back inside he reached into the podium where he did business and extracted a book, came to the bar and sat down, took a sip, and said, "So, this Valerie Sabatino. She's special, isn't she?"

"Off the charts. Pretty damn good lookin', too."

"Time you settled down."

"Whoa. Pull up, big boy."

"When you goin' back?"

"Right after the funeral."

"How're the police treating this?"

"If it's suicide, it's the strangest one in history. They know it's homicide, but they're keeping their powder dry 'til they get everything sorted out. Still...

No good suspects, no obvious motive. Lot depends on the blood samples. If it *was* blood, human blood."

"This Crandall guy made himself a suspect, didn't he? And these bad boys at the Children of God?"

"I guess. But Crandall didn't do it. He's not physically capable of it, of dealing with that jungle. And I can't see the ten-ton Samoan up there, either. But there're other possibles."

"What do you make of the stories of missing ordnance? And the massacre of those homeless people? See any connections."

"No, but you'd have to be brain dead to brush it off the table."

"If it walks like a duck. I'm going back with you. Why don't you come back up here? We'll fly out together."

"That'd be good."

"Valerie going back?"

"Not if I can help it. But she's hard to turn."

"What can I do while you're at the funeral?"

"Look at Packy MacGillicuddy. He wouldn't tell me about this last fall he took. Probably just embarrassed. But I think it's good to know what people don't want you to know. And he's holding out on why he told Danny to get hold of me. Take a look at him."

"Okay."

"You know anything I don't know?"

He grinned. "What do you mean?"

"You know what I mean. You been thinking hard about this."

"Yeah, I have. And done a little research of my own." He turned the book so I could read its cover. It was "Under The Banner of Heaven" by Jon Krakauer. "You read this?" he asked.

"No. I read his one on Everest. 'Into Thin Air.' He's good."

"Yes, he is. Between what Francis has dug up and what I've learned about the Mormons I know Orrin Massey was born in the strangest town in America and now he lives about twenty miles from the strangest town in Canada."

"Yeah?"

"Uh-huh. Lot of signs point to the possibility Orrin's dangerous and maybe bad. What do you know about the Mormons?"

"Let's see… They're all white. Which I don't think is a bad thing. They do missionary work. They used to be polygamists but they gave it up and I bet that chapped their asses. They live in Utah, but I don't think that's a requirement. That's about it."

"They're the youngest and fastest growing religion in the world. There's ten million Mormons, more than Methodists or Episcopalians. There's sixty thousand Mormon missionaries out there every day and they average two converts a year apiece. Plus they're big breeders. I've seen projections that there'll be close to a hundred million Mormons world-wide by the end of this century. All the members are called saints, by the way, thought of as saints. It's officially the Church of Jesus Christ of the Latter-day Saints. They try to discourage being called Mormons these days.

"A guy from Vermont started it… You sure you want to hear all this? Been travelling all day."

"The next time you waste my time'll be the first time."

Like me, Muhammad is an agnostic, if you want to put a fine point on it. We both have trouble with the concept of faith. Thinking always seems better to us than not thinking, throwing up your hands and saying, "Okay, I don't get it, but it feels good, so count me in." We believe what we can prove and keep thinking about what we can't. It's not that we don't believe in God, but that we don't believe we can know for sure. We think maybe, maybe even probably, but not for sure. I think that's an agnostic.

I was raised as kind of an off-hand Baptist. That's where Uncle Ralph went when he felt like it, which wasn't all that often, but when he did feel like it, he took me along. Uncle Ralph's religion was respect for other people. I think he went to the Baptist church because it was close to home and he thought I ought to see what the inside of a church looked like. Since then, I've given a fair amount of thought to the big cosmic questions, what this whole thing is all about and who's behind it, and the best I can come up with is it's the Republicans. As for churches, I pretty much pass them by. Not that I think there's anything wrong with them. Unless you get carried away.

Unlike me, Muhammad is a serious student of religion and religions, sort of a religious hobbyist. He was born and raised Muslim, but his skepticism and independence ate away at that and he gave it up many moons ago, pre-Serena. Now, he goes to church whenever and wherever Serena asks him to and he always enjoys it, wears the little caps, sings and claps and says his Amens and Hallelujahs, smiles and shakes hands with strangers, goes to the altar when Serena elbows him to get whatever's up there. He's got a long shelf at home full of texts on the subject. He knows enough about it to think we all should be really afraid of the true believers, wherever they are. And they're pretty much everywhere.

He continued. "If Orrin Massey fits like I think he might, I believe it'll be helpful to understand some of the history of Mormonism. So, I've been reading up on it. I don't think Orrin's a Mormon. I think he's a Mormon Fundamentalist. The Mormon church disowned these guys a long time ago, wants nothing to do with them. They're real throwbacks. Still polygamists, too. Polygs. Polyg is a word they use, by the way."

"Polyg. I like it. Be good for Scrabble. Lots of points."

"That mention of Colorado City, Arizona as Massey's birthplace in Francis's report triggered something in my head. That's the town that was established by the Mormon Fundamentalists when they broke away from the main church a long time ago, early part of the last century. Right on the Utah border in the strip of Arizona that's blocked off from the rest of the state by the Grand Canyon. Pretty much everybody in Colorado City's a Fundamentalist. Top to bottom. Maybe ten thousand of them. And they operate a sister city colony in Bountiful, British Columbia, just across the border from Boundary County, Idaho where Orrin Massey has his ranch. Remember Ruby Ridge?"

"Sure."

"Boundary County, Idaho."

"Really? But those people weren't . . . That wasn't about Mormon Fundamentalism, was it?"

"No. It was about guns. And wanting to be left alone. ATF undercover guy sold a couple of shotguns to Randy Weaver, kind of forced 'em on him according to Weaver. They got an indictment but he wouldn't come in for the trial, so the feds set up the siege to bring him in. You know that story. They killed his son and his wife. Weaver surrendered and was tried on the original charge and acquitted. Entrapment carried the day. Having a Boundary County jury of his peers probably helped him, too, but that's the way it works. Weaver was apparently a white supremacist, so not one of my favorite people on those grounds, but really just a guy who wanted to be left alone. And ran into the mad dog of government. He's no longer even up there, lives somewhere in Iowa now off a three million dollar settlement he got in a civil suit. My point has more to do with northern Idaho than Randy Weaver. It's remote. And its people are remote, too.

"Back to the Mormon Fundamentalists. They're all either bad or potentially bad, because they are unrestrained and unrestrainable."

"So's the FBI and the ATF," I said.

"Which means there's considerable tension between them.

"Mormonism was started not all that long ago. Eighteen twenties. Vermont guy's name was Joseph Smith. How 'bout that for the name of a guy started a religion? A spirit named Moroni appeared to him and led him to a hill in Palmyra, New York, and showed him a set of golden plates buried there. They were three-ring bound, if you can believe that, and a lot of people do. There's a picture of Joe turning the pages of the plates on the church's web site. An illustration, I should say. And they're sure enough hole-punched. Inscribed on the plates was the story of an ancient Hebrew tribe that believed in strict obedience to the Lord's every commandment.

"Six hundred years before the birth of Christ, the tribe came to North America by boat."

I must have raised an eyebrow at that because he said, "If you suspend disbelief for a while, it'll help you along.

"The leader died and bequeathed control to one of his two sons because he was good, and this pissed off the other son, who wasn't good. Was bad. It split the tribe in two and the tribe led by the bad son—the golden plates said they were idle and full of 'mischief and subtlety'—they were all cursed by God. He darkened the skin of every one of them."

"See?" I said.

"No, they eventually became America's Indians, not your Negroes. Moving along, the resurrected Christ visited them over here and patched things up for a while, but it didn't hold."

"The resurrected *Jesus* Christ?"

"Uh-uh. War broke out and in 400 A. D., after what I calculate to be a thousand years of bitchin' back and forth, the darkies slaughtered the whole lot of the whiteys, all 250,000 of them. Almost all. The leader of the defeated tribe was named Mormon. He died in the battle, but his son, Moroni, survived and went on to write the story on the golden plates."

"And then punched and bound it."

"Yeah. And fourteen hundred years later came to Joseph Smith in a vision and led him to them."

"Where're the plates now?"

"Joe Smith gave them back to Moroni when he was through with them and he still has them."

"Oh. In a secret hiding place, probably."

He nodded. He took another sip. "Damn, that's good.

"Joseph Smith translated the plates and printed the whole thing up in what he called the Book of Mormon."

"Translated them?"

"Yeah. Then he hustled it and one thing led to another and 'fore long he had himself a religion and a fair number of followers. Joe kept hearing the voice of God as he went along and every time he did he wrote down what God said in another book that he called the Doctrine and Covenants. One of the things God told him was that anyone who obeyed the word of God could hear his voice and I'll bet Joe rued the day he heard and wrote that one down because it was, and is, at the heart of one of the biggest problems Mormonism has."

"All Mormons believe they can hear the voice of God?"

"Was one of the first sections of the Doctrine and Covenants. And not just that they *can* hear it, but that when they do, they must do what the voice tells them to do."

"It's like encouraging the lunatics to run the asylum."

"Yeah. Not long after Joe passed this along to the flock, he heard God tell him to take charge, probably as a way of saying to the troops, 'You might think you heard what God said, but you need to come to me to make sure 'cause sometimes he speaks in riddles.'

"The boss, the guy at the top, is called the President, Prophet, Seer, and Revelator and Joe Smith declared himself the first one. One they got now lives in Salt Lake City and wears a suit and tie six days a week. As 'seer and revelator' he breaks ties on what's true and what's false, in case you heard God wrong. If you want to be a Mormon, you are going to be obedient. In all things. At all times. Period.

"Over the years not everybody has bought into that, some of them think they heard God different. It's one of the reasons there are more than two hundred religions that have spun off from the original."

"I'll bet polygamy was another one."

"Yes, it was. We'll get to polygamy in a minute, but now I want to tell you about the one mighty and strong."

"Okay. Want me to raise my hand when I have a question?"

"Or write it down." He opened the book to a marked page. He said, "Section 85 of the Doctrine and Covenants, the D and C they call it, says that,"and he read, "'it shall come to pass that the Lord God will one day send one mighty and strong, holding the scepter of power in his hand, clothed with light for a covering, whose mouth shall utter eternal words, while his bowels shall be a fountain of truth, to set in order the house of God.' So, God's anointed one is coming. Some say he's here among us now. Today. Some have said that since back when Joseph first wrote it. Some have heard and written..." He looked at the book again and read. "...that the Lord said that the 'one mighty and strong shall grind in pieces all those who would oppose My work, for the prayer of the righteous shall not go unheeded.' One of Smith's successors went so far as to specify that the one mighty and strong would come in the time of the seventh president, prophet, seer, and revelator. But evidently he didn't, because they're on their thirteenth right now.

"So, now we've got everybody hearing God's voice and most everybody eligible to be his terrible swift sword.

"Let's turn to polygamy. That was Joseph Smith's D and C number 132, the revelation that got him killed. Section 132 declares the sacred principle of plural marriage, not as a right but as an obligation. For men only. Women go that way and it's called adultery. The unvarnished history makes it pretty clear that Joe's problem was he just couldn't get enough, just couldn't pass a lady by, so he decided... Excuse me, he *heard from God* that he was supposed to be that way, was supposed to be polygamous and, what the hell, so were the rest of us.

"Joe got locked up for advocating polygamy, this was in Illinois, town called Nauvoo where the Mormons had settled after they were driven out of Missouri. And while he was locked up, a mob broke in and shot him dead. After Joe got killed, the widow Smith went off and started a splinter church of her own. One that didn't approve of polygamy.

"Guy named Brigham Young took over then and led them from the Midwest to, eventually, Utah. He also transformed them from pacifists to warriors. He heard God tell them to fight and, over the years, they have shown themselves to be merciless when they're offended. And they're easily offended.

"In 1890—they were long since established in Utah by then—they officially abandoned polygamy. It was costing them too much. The government was hunting them down, locking them up. They wanted to go mainstream, increase market share. So, the big guy at the time heard from God that they'd been wrong all along about polygamy. Said it was a bad thing."

"Well, sure. Besides, there's always sneakin' around."

"Yeah. And most of 'em went on sneakin' for another twenty or thirty years, but slowly the idea that monogamy was just good business took hold.

"With most of them. But not with the Fundamentalists.

"There's gold in all this, by the way. Couple zillion dollars worth. The Fundamentalists believe it's hidden away in a mountain in Utah at a place called the Dream Mine, hidden there until the whole world's shit hits the fan and then God will hand it off to the one mighty and strong who will use the gold to save the red asses of everybody on board. And nobody else.

"So, there's a pretty good job opening for the right guy. Whole bunch have staked a claim to it at one time or another over the years, lots of them still out there, waiting for Armageddon. They were real disappointed when that Y2K thing laid an egg."

"The one mighty and strong could be anybody?"

"Anybody white and male. The Mormon church gave up racial discrimination in 1978. Sort of. Said your coloreds could be in the church, could be saints. Didn't go all the way to mixed marriage, though. My opinion, they're still racists. Just too smart to act like it in public.

"The MF's didn't buy into that one, either. Much prefer your kind to my kind and don't mind saying so. The Fundamentalists don't hesitate to kill if God insists. Been known to kill their own families, even children. Many have. Kidnap little girls, too. For wives. Homosexuals are always in season. Also guys like me. Lots of them doing time for it. Say, 'Don't blame me. God told me to.' And lots of these bad boys are still on the bricks because important material witnesses have just disappeared.

"They tend to cluster as you can imagine. I mean, here they are believing something so strongly and so heretical that their former friends threw them into the outer darkness for it. Might as well move, go hang with like-minded fruitcakes."

"What do you know? Small world, after all. There's got to be some chance that Orrin Massey is a Mormon Fundamentalist, doesn't there? So... Take me to your conclusion."

"Too soon for a conclusion. I'm just shooting the shit with an old friend."

We clinked glasses and took a couple of healthy swallows.

"How about a theory? Too soon for a theory?"

"Too soon for that, too. But I've got one. My theory is that Orrin Massey believes he's the one mighty and strong and is getting good and ready to be discovered."

"Your theory have anything to do with Danny MacGillicuddy?"

"I can dream it from here to there but when I do, it doesn't even deserve to be called a theory. Still, as you said, hard to brush it off the table."

EIGHT
Monday, March 17
Louisville

Valerie met my plane in her father's car and with his driver and we rode downtown to the Seelbach to unpack. I was pleased to see that her things were in the closet and the bathroom.

"Mother and Daddy are here, too. Upstairs. The Presidential Suite. They're looking forward to meeting you. Visitation this afternoon and tonight. The funeral's tomorrow. Then we'll head back."

"Can I talk you out of that?"

"Not with a gun at my head."

"Muhammad's coming. I told him I'd go back through Chicago, we'd fly out together."

"Good. I'm looking forward to meeting him. And Serena. Let's layover, have dinner at the restaurant."

"Unless you change your mind."

She came to me, took my hands and eyeballed me. "Listen, tough guy, get a few things straight. I'm not the kind of girl hangs out at boutiques chatting with pals on her cell phone. On the other hand, I don't have a death wish. I'm not reckless and I'm not stupid. I know when I'm in over my head and when I'm not. I live my life on my terms. I'm involved in this and I intend to stay involved. I'm going back. And there's that other thing, too."

"The nice weather?"

"Right."

"I'll keep an eye on you."

"Of course you will. You can't help it. But if you don't treat me like a grown woman, I'll cut your balls off. Got that?"

"Yes, ma'am."

$$\cdots\cdots$$

I'd never been in the company of the very rich and very powerful. If I had, I might not have been surprised at how they fill the room with their presence without doing anything. If you could take away the impeccable tailoring and style of their clothes, their perfect accessories, the cut of their hair, and the glow of their complexions, then Rafael and Madeleine Sabatino might have been just any two people with perfect manners and grace.

Roscoe Franklin carried a sweet and befuddled air with a perpetual smile and a bad haircut. He was as rumpled as Rafael was crisp, but they chatted like old friends even as they looked like the alpha and omega of style. Belinda was pretty but no more than that. She wore a simple gray dress that was off-the-rack, but still fit well on her trim body. She scurried about nervously as though she was afraid to slow down for fear she'd collapse. Among them all, her grief was the most palpable. Roscoe had his arm around her shoulder as often as her busyness would allow.

Each of the four of them, Danny MacGillicuddy's family, treated me with far more honor and respect than I had ever before experienced from strangers. In fact, I'd never before been treated with anything other than caution by strangers. After we had passed the first stage of our acquaintance, they settled me on a sofa at the funeral home.

"You won't know a soul who comes here, Harry," Belinda said. "So just relax and be here. Don't feel like you've got to work the room."

They took turns coming over to sit with me and chat and I enjoyed the company of each of them. I noticed none of them asked a lot of questions about my past, probably because they were aware of it and were too polite.

Madeleine did get a little personal.

"Harry, you seem to have taken on great importance in my daughter's life."

"As she has in mine, Madeleine."

"So, I look forward to all the time you and I can spend together while we're here. You understand that, don't you?"

"Yes. I want that, too."

Valerie took a break and came over smiling, sat down beside me.

"You're making a fine impression, Mr. Pines. Nobody'd ever know you're a hard-case ex-con with a great shit detector."

"I feel obliged to make a good impression, Ms. Sabatino. I am consciously on my best behavior. And it's very comfortable. I like them all. And they treat me so well I suspect you may have lied to them about my past. Whatever happened to your mother's first husband, Belinda's father? Scowcroft? Wasn't that his name?"

"I bet Francis told you that."

"You'd win the bet."

"So how come Francis didn't tell you what happened to him?"

"He just did a quick little skim. Just to make sure you weren't a complete impostor."

"Maurice Scowcroft was killed in an automobile accident. Mother got a big settlement out of it and used some of it on a grand tour of the continent. That's how she met Daddy."

"They must have been unhappy when Belinda married Packy."

"I don't remember much of that, but I know they weren't pleased when he got locked up. They encouraged the divorce. They can be very…encouraging. Back then Belinda went through what we call a phase."

"Who was Rafael's first wife? Where's she now?"

"One of those teen-aged things. Early marriage, early divorce. She's… somewhere."

"You know, it's funny Packy never told me about Rafael. You know, how Belinda's stepfather was one of the richest men in the world. We had a lot of time for chit-chat."

"Now that you mention it, that is odd. I just figured out what you're doing while you're sitting here. You're working."

"Is that so wrong?"

She squeezed my hand and smiled. "These things are dreadful, aren't they?"

"It's my second. The first was when my uncle died. It wasn't any fun. All these young people. Probably friends of Danny's?"

"I think so. I don't know many of them. Any of them, really. Did mother grill you?"

"Not at all. But I bet she could."

"Wait for Daddy's turn. That's the big leagues."

Daddy's turn wasn't long in coming, but he didn't spend it on his daughter's love life.

"Harry, the event that has brought us together is most strange, is it not?"

"Yes. Very."

"Homicide, do you think?"

"Unquestionably. Though for the moment the Honolulu police are more equivocal. I think that will change, though. We found blood up there where

Danny died. At least, I think it's blood. Two separate locations. If they get positives on those, that would make suicide pretty unlikely. Impossible if the samples are different. And the place appeared to have been swept, sort of tidied up. He was killed, I'm certain. And left there as food for the predators."

"Are the Honolulu police good? Competent, I mean."

"The one I know pretty well strikes me as very competent. And he's their top detective. And the guy assigned to Danny's case is very solid."

"And it is now in their hands, is it not? And not a matter for the military?"

"Yes. I don't know everything about how they handle turf issues, but Danny was found on land that is within the jurisdiction of the HPD."

"I know of your arrangement with Valerie. I refer to your business arrangement. You understand that I stand behind her commitment to you?"

"It's very...cordial of you to say that, Rafael, but the security of my fee is not topmost on my mind."

"Good. Valerie is impressed with your competence."

"I've never thought of it as competence. It's more like pigheaded."

He patted my knee. I don't remember a man ever patting my knee before. I was picking up a lot of firsts. "We will talk again before we part. And beyond that, I'm sure. Valerie is an extraordinary judge of character. Did you know that?"

"I don't know anything about Valerie that isn't extraordinary."

"I believe that you are well chosen."

"Thank you. Thank you very much."

He patted my knee again. I kind of liked it.

NINE
Tuesday, March 18
Louisville. Chicago.

The funeral Mass was at St. James, a huge Catholic church set back from a grand lawn. I sat with the family at Valerie's side and rode with them to Calvary Cemetery.

The day was heavy and the sky low. It wasn't raining, but the air was wet. A bagpiper in full regalia—kilt, sporran, waistcoat, cap, cape, all of it—appeared on a hillside fifty yards above the gravesite and played "Amazing Grace" and then "Taps." It gave me chills. Seven soldiers fired their rifles three times each and four others lowered a flag, folded it, and presented it to Belinda.

Roscoe and Belinda lived on Douglass Boulevard in a big, old four-columned house that needed painting, and that's where we adjourned for the wake, dozens of friends coming back to the family's home to stare down enough food for a battalion. It was a good release, a good way to end a tiring time.

My Belinda moment came. She took me by the hand and walked me up to a sitting room at the top of the stairs, patted a seat on a sofa for me, and chose a chair for herself.

"I know you were in prison with Danny's father," she opened.

"Yes. Not only in prison, but his cellmate for a good while. I know Packy well. That's the source of my involvement in this. As you know."

"And you've just come from seeing him."

"Yes. And I'm sure you know exactly how he felt."

"Yes. Packy loved Danny. Really loved him. And Danny adored his father. All the more, it seemed, when Packy made mistakes. Packy made such big mistakes. He's… Can I say a good man? Yes, I believe I can. His problem is of two parts in conflict. He has much charisma, that powerful combination of confidence and energy. And at the same time, he is incapable of effective discrimination. So, he's like Pinocchio, always falling in with evil companions who are charmed by his songs. His life went wrong when he went to Las Vegas. If he'd gone to…oh, Pittsburgh instead, or here, he'd likely have ended up running a nice neighborhood bar. But, of course, if he'd gone to Pittsburgh he wouldn't have met me and there'd be no Danny to mourn.

Roads not taken."

She paused and I could think of nothing to put in. I could have told her that in the last thirty seconds my opinion of her depth and intelligence had soared, but I didn't.

Finally, I said, "Tell me a few things about Danny, please. Things that may help me."

"All right."

I thought about where to begin. At the hard spot, I decided. "If Danny was in trouble, who would he go to?"

"Packy."

"Really? If it was big trouble, maybe something about money, a lot of money... Not Rafael?"

"No. Rafael would have done anything in the world for Danny. Without a moment's hesitation. As he would for any of us. But Danny wouldn't have gone there unless Packy told him to."

"Ego issues?"

"Yes. Packy's ego and Danny's devotion to him."

"Was Danny...easily manipulated?"

"Danny wasn't real smart. Certainly not college material. That's not a fun thing to admit but it doesn't mean he wasn't wonderful or that I didn't love him deeply. He knew it and he was insecure about it. He was also very immature. Unworldly. Very sweet and gentle. Quiet."

"Goals?"

"He wanted to...wanted to make his father proud of him by...by making up for Packy's failures. That was his goal."

"Thank you. I hope you haven't minded my asking. Or been annoyed."

"Not at all, not at all. My sister tells me that both of you are going to return to Hawaii and try to find out how Danny died."

"Yes. Although I wish she wasn't coming."

"Because it may be dangerous?"

"Yes."

"You have come into our lives in a strange way, Harry. But I'm sure we're the better for it."

"You and your family have been very kind to me. I'm grateful."

"You're very welcome. It is we who are grateful. One more thing." She leaned forward and her face contorted into a small, angry fist. "Get them,

Harry. Get them good. Make them pay."

"I will, Belinda. I'll make them pay a terrible price. Sleep well on that."

• • • • •

The wake was ending, the crowd dispersing. Rafael approached me.

"Harry, a moment of your time before we go?"

"Certainly."

"Let's sit in my car."

We walked to it and the driver held the door for us. Rafael said to him, "See that we are not disturbed."

Inside, he said, "Two topics are on my mind. First is Valerie. You don't strike me as the kind of man who would foolishly expose her to danger."

"I'm not."

"And yet you are taking her back to Hawaii."

"Hardly. If I could think of any way to keep her from coming, I'd do it. Nobody takes Valerie anywhere, best I can tell. I can't talk her out of it."

"You have tried?"

"Tried hard. Struck out. Three pitches."

"Yes. Me, too. Girl's got a fastball, doesn't she?"

I smiled.

"So. That's that. She's going. You will do all you can to protect her?"

"With my life."

"It won't come to that. You will accomplish this, Harry."

"Yes. I will."

"Proceed with an aspect of purposeful aggression."

"Okay."

"And the other thing. It would be disingenuous of me to suggest that you may not know the extent of my…resources. So I will just say that they are vast. In reach. In breadth. In potency. I know that you are not permitted a license to carry a weapon. And I know that there is perhaps no weapon you have not used with effect. In your past, I mean. In the army." He handed me a small piece of folded paper. "There are two phone numbers on here. The first is mine, where I can be reached at any time. The other is a number in Honolulu. If you call it at any time of any day and use my name and your name in the first sentence, any weapons or equipment or personnel or money you desire will be made quickly available to you. And they will be secure as to source. Keep this and tell me now that you will not let any concerns of legality interfere with my daughter's safety. And yours."

"Count on it." I put it in my pocket, inside my money.

• • • • •

On the flight from Louisville, Valerie said it'd be hard for her to really get to know Muhammad and Serena while they were working at the restaurant, so why didn't we drag them out and feed them as our guests. So I called Randy from the plane and asked him if he'd back us up on it and he said he was happy to.

"Take them to Gibson's," he said. "Put a little whiskey in 'em. Feed 'em some meat. A big ol' sirloin. We never have that here and Pop loves it."

"Will they go?"

"They'll whine a little, but they'll go. No reason not to. Tuesday's are slow. Time you get here, Mom'll be through in the kitchen, won't have anything left to do but her earth mother routine. And I'll cover for Dad. They need to eat out more. It's good for business in this business to eat at other spots, gets that cross-reference thing going. Make sure they make their presence known. Spend a lot of money."

We all got a little drunk at Gibson's. Valerie suggested we give up work for the evening, not say a word about it. We drank to that. We talked Iraq, Cubs, racehorses, terrorists, shopping, weather, shoes, March Madness, politics, food, wine, tropical gardening, Randy, Randy's girlfriend, and a couple other things. But not Danny MacGillicuddy.

When the plates were cleared, I found an ancient and excellent cognac on the menu and asked for four. As the waiter walked away Muhammad said, "Valerie, I think there's one piece of business we really should discuss. May I?"

"Of course."

"Harry asked me to look into the circumstances of Packy's last crime while he was in Louisville. Packy was unwilling to discuss it with him on their visit. I have. And it may... Well, I don't know what it may, but here's the story."

He said Packy had burglarized a condo in Las Vegas with two other guys. Furs and jewelry. Paintings. And a safe.

"They bypassed the alarm system on the way in. Probably felt kind of smug at that point. Occupants were in Europe. Probably took their time. The safe was a floor model. They couldn't bust it so they decided to take it with them. It must have been a load. They went down the freight elevator with their haul, got a dolly from down there somehow and hauled everything out to their van. But the safe fell off the loading dock and hit the pavement and kind of exploded in this screaming honk when it popped open. It had its own built-in alarm. Just went on and on, honking its head off. Two cops were having coffee a block away and came on the run. Two of them were caught on the spot. Packy got away but was caught in less than an hour boarding a plane at McCarran."

"Sounds like the Three Stooges," Valerie said. "Why was there even a trial?"

"Wasn't much of a trial. Prosecution made its case and the defendants pled right after. Deprived me a chance to read their defense. That would have been a hoot. Packy got six to ten. He's done three. Five each for the others."

"What was in the safe?" I asked.

"Documents. Bonds. Some cash. But there's a twist.

"Francis looked into the victim, name is Colin Winslow, and came up with some interesting newspaper stories.

"It seems Mr. Winslow said the safe contained a very valuable sapphire. Something called the Sultan's Star. Valued at $750,000. Insured for that. It wasn't found.

"Two of the boys barely got off the dock before the jig was up, so if they took it, it doesn't seem like they could have done much but swallow it. And I imagine that possibility was, uh, looked into. Packy didn't have it when they caught him. The jewel wasn't mentioned at trial, was not part of the state's case. I guess they didn't need it.

"Winslow filed a claim and the insurance company denied it. They took the position since the government didn't prosecute the stooges for stealing it, it wasn't stolen. 'Well, what happened to it?' Winslow asked. Not our problem, the company answered. Case went to trial. The insurance company won. Mr. Winslow was either lying or…who knows?"

"Packy knows," I said. I looked at Muhammad. I looked at Valerie. "I need to go back to Ely."

"That's why I brought it up," Muhammad said.

TEN
Wednesday, March 19
Salt Lake City. Ely, Nevada.

We flew to Salt Lake City. Muhammad and Valerie went to the Mormon Temple and Library of Family History to see what they could find on Orrin Massey's genealogy. Muhammad said the Mormons were compulsive record keepers, but he had some doubts their databases would include Fundamentalists.

I chartered a Beechcraft Bonanza, a quick single-engine, and flew on—was flown—to Ely.

Packy didn't greet me with the same big smile. I spoke very softly and he had to lean in close to hear me. "I looked into what put you back in here, Packy. You had an hour with that jewel, didn't you?"

"Goddamn! You too? I didn't take that fuckin' jewel. Prob'ly would have if I'd seen it, but I didn't see it, so I didn't take it." He spoke even more softly than I had.

"What do you mean, me too?"

"I mean you ain't the only one thinks I took it. But I didn't."

I stared at him. He stared back. "Hmm. I believe you. I should, shouldn't I?"

"Yeah, you should. 'Cause it's the truth."

"I've been thinking you stole it and somehow Danny got killed for it. Got a little ahead of myself, didn't I?"

He leaned in even closer, spoke even more softly. "I didn't steal it, but that don't mean he didn't get killed for it."

"What?"

He put his palms together, patted them gently, folded his arms, lowered his head to his chest, shook it slowly. He was trying to make up his mind. I decided to help him with it.

"I know you, Packy. I know you're not going to let what happened to Danny go down the way it stands. You've been thinking when you get out of here, you'll square it. But let's not wait for that. I'll take care of it for you. You show me how."

"I take care of my own problems."

"You said that before. Stop feeling sorry for yourself. You're not the only one who loved Danny. You're not the only one with a stake in this."

"Harry, this ain't your beef."

"Oh, yes it is. I'm in this to the dead fuckin' end, Packy. It's business. And it's a lot more than that, too. A lot of people are depending on me. People who matter to me. They're like this team standing behind me, the Danny MacGillicuddy team, ready to help me in any way they can. I want you to get on that team. I'll settle this long before you get out of here and a lot sooner if you help me."

He expelled a breath, smiled a small smile. "You gotta gimme a chance to pay you back."

"Okay."

"Okay. A little while back I'm walkin' the yard and this guy's been here since before I got here comes up to me and starts walkin' along beside me and starts talkin' outta the side of his mouth. Say's, 'Packy, some people we both know asked me to let you know they're hooked up with your kid in Hawaii.' Says, 'His name's Danny, ain't it? A soldier?' I'm not sayin' nothin'. This guy says, 'Yeah, that's his name. Danny.' Says, 'These guys say the kid looks like a million dollars, so you prob'ly wouldn't mind swappin' him for a lot less than that. Say seven hundred and fifty thousand.'

"I stopped walkin' and took a good look at this guy. He wasn't noth-in'. Scrawny little motherfucker. Which was the point. He was, you know, Western Union. I said, 'Seven hundred and fifty thousand, huh? These guys take a check?' He says, 'Oh, they don't want your money. They want some-thin' you got that's worth that much. They'll take it from there.'

"'Lemme guess,' I said. 'Your friends are some idiot motherfuckers who think I stole the Sultan's Star, right? An' if I tell 'em where it is, my kid'll be safe and if I don't they're gonna hurt him. Is that where this is?' 'Yeah,' he says. 'That's where this is.'

"'Well,' I says, 'you tell your friends I ain't got the jewel, I never saw the fuckin' thing, an' since I don't have it, I guess I can't go along with what they want.' An' I said, 'You tell 'em if they fuck with my kid I'll hurt 'em so bad they'll beg me to kill 'em.'

"An' then I called Danny and told him to get over here soon as he could. He sat right over there and I told him the story, told him as soon as he got back to get hold of you, told him you'd handle it one way or the other.

"Then he tells me he's in some other shit. He's been gamblin' on this boat over there. Been losin', big fuckin' surprise. Like anybody don't. This guy, some kinda shylock, gives him more credit than he can handle an' when he loses that, too, they come down on him. Three choices, take one. Pay up. Turn into a cripple. Or steal it off. He goes for that last one, throws in with this gang that steals guns and grenades and drugs and shit like that from the army, just walk off with it a crate at a time, the security guys, the guards, are in on it, too. Army's got so much of that shit, I guess they don't miss it a box at a time.

"Danny wanted out, said he was thinkin' about goin' to the police. I said absolutely not. I said go to you, you'd get him hooked up with a good lawyer and then all of you could go to the police. Made him promise to do it that way. He promised. I guess he never called, did he?"

I shook my head. "Belinda's stepfather is one of the richest men in the world, Packy, so why didn't Danny go to him for help?"

"Because Danny's old man's a idiot macho dumb fuck and wouldn't let him. Sold him a bill o' goods from th' beginnin' that him and me were gonna be a team and make millions on our own. On the square. 'Fuck that rich dago,' I said." He shook his head. "I got a lot to make up for. I just hope I get the chance."

"You got any names? Western Union give you one?"

"Nah. He dummied up. I'll beat it outta him some day just for fun. But Danny said Wilton Crandall asked him if he was my kid. Crandall works with this guy does the loan sharkin' on the boat. And he was on the street in Vegas when I took this last fall. Ever' low rider in Vegas thinks I took the jewel, so prob'ly Crandall fits as the guy was in on threatenin' Danny. And he was prob'ly lookin' through Danny's stuff for...whatever... Fuck, for the jewel! These idiot motherfuckers start thinkin' there's a jewel an' ain't nothin' gonna pull 'em up on it. Ain't no way they're gonna pull up. You prove to 'em there ain't no jewel, *prove it to 'em,* an' they just think you're lyin'. They get that fuckin' thing in their heads an' it ain't comin' out! They smell it! It's a fuckin' rock an' it ain't even there an' they can actually smell it."

"Danny say anything about a guy named Orrin Massey?"

"No."

"How about Eric Fox?"

"No."

"Anybody else?"

"He mentioned his girlfriend. Name was Betsy. Said they were tight, said he loved her and trusted her."

· · · · ·

Muhammad and Valerie were at Harmon General, the charter company, when I landed. I had expected to hook up with them at the gate for the flight to Honolulu and said so.

Valerie said, "We think we should talk first, maybe consider a detour."

We went to a snack bar and got drinks and sat at a small table.

Muhammad said, "They have records of every wagon trainload of Mormons who came west to Utah beginning with Brigham Young's first wagon train in 1846. With passenger manifests. Alphabetized. Man named Eben Massey was shown coming on one in 1850. I traced his descendants all the way up to 1942 when the last of them, Randall Massey, was excommunicated for apostasy. No records of the family after that. There's some records of more recent Masseys, of course, but Orrin's not among them. On a guess, I'll say Randall was Orrin's ancestor, maybe his grandfather. Or maybe his father if Randall's apostasy had to do with polygamy because those guys go on having kids up to nine months after they die, at very advanced ages. Young wives'll do that for a man, and that's the kind they go for. I found a Massey woman, Randall's sister Irma, who married a Jesse Sheffield in 1939. He was excommunicated in 1950.

"That got me to thinking about your boy Sheffield in Hawaii, so I called Francis and he came up with Michael Sheffield's place of birth in St. George, Utah about thirty miles from Colorado City. You could guess him to be from Jesse's family if you wanted to and that would relate him to Orrin Massey. Cousin, maybe."

"Hmm. What else?"

"Other stuff, but I'll hold it. Your turn now."

I took them through my conversation with Packy, the threat to Danny, the jewel, Crandall, Betsy. I said, "Packy says these guys believe in that jewel. Once they get a notion of a payday like that, they hold on tight."

Muhammad said, "So, we've got confirmation of Danny in big trouble on the jewel and also stealing to pay off a gambling debt."

"And wanting to get out of it," Valerie said. "And maybe sharing his thoughts on everything with Betsy. Pillow talk. And if he did try to get out, or if somebody who knew he wanted to, somebody like Betsy, spilled the beans…" She let that hang in the air.

I said, "Snitched it off, Valerie. Not spilled the beans."

She ignored me and said, "They wouldn't kill him for the jewel, would they? What good would that do? Then they wouldn't have the jewel and they wouldn't have any leverage with Packy."

"True," I said. "They'd maybe snatch him, but they wouldn't kill him. But he'd get killed if they thought he'd spill the beans on the other thing, the stealing."

Valerie said, "I told Muhammad there's something about all this crate-by-crate stealing I don't get. What happens to it? I mean, I don't know a whole lot about international arms dealing, but I don't think they work in odd lots. Crates is what … Well, what would you use crates for? And he said …"

"For a gang," Muhammad said. "Or a small army. And it got me to thinking."

"The one mighty and strong could use a small army," I said. "Muhammad tell you about that?" I asked Valerie. She nodded. I said, "Something about all these other guys makes me think they're, I don't know, just bureaucrats with guns. And Eric Fox is no more than a regional vice president. Plus, Crandall and the Samoan didn't stalk and kill Danny in that jungle. Wouldn't be up to it. Not Fox, either. Not his style. He's too…silky. So … somebody else. Did it."

"Which returns us to Orrin Massey and what we wanted to talk about before we got on the plane to Hawaii," Muhammad said. "I don't see him, whatever his big plan is, losing sight of it over the rumor of a stolen jewel. I asked Francis where the other locations of the Children of God are and they're in Savannah, Myrtle Beach, New Orleans, and San Diego. Then, he did a little research and came up with this. Those four, and the one in Hawaii, have in common access to casinos and significant nearby military populations. And warm climates. Which attract vagabonds and runaways."

"Casinos in San Diego?"

"An Indian casino about fifteen miles north."

"Where you going with this?"

"Speculating. Maybe daydreaming. My theory is that Orrin Massey runs all his way stations the same way he runs the one in Hawaii. As a place for runaway girls to come for what seems like a safe haven. Big surprise they get, don't they? He sorts 'em out. Some become basic hookers, some a little fancier, some probably get thrown out or leave or get hurt or worse, and maybe some become wives. His wives, maybe. And wives of his friends in faith.

"He uses the access to gambling as a way to hook soldiers with more credit than they can handle and turns them into thieves. The girls help keep the soldiers happy.

"And, here's the big jump. I think he may be building himself a little army with some of the soldiers for the day when the Lord calls him to action."

"How's he do that?"

"I don't know. He's already got the hook in. He knows they're capable of crime. All he's got to do next is cull them. Find out which ones are gullible enough to sign up. He's got plenty of money, so paying them a lot more than they're likely to make either by staying in the military or coming out as civilians wouldn't be out of his reach. He probably goes for the ones about to get out, ones who like the soldier life and can buy into his philosophy. They'd have plenty of women, get to stomp on people they don't like, and become soldiers in God's chosen army. With a big payday coming down the line from the Dream Mine. Who'd go for that line of crap, you might ask? Well, keep in mind the U. S. all-volunteer army isn't full of Rhodes scholars. Enlisted personnel, in particular. Lot of not-real-smart kids in there."

"You think Massey recruited Danny?"

"Hell, I don't know. But it's plausible."

"Fits with what his mother told me about him, the kind of kid he was. Not real smart. Very impressionable. And eager to make it big to make his daddy proud of him. But Danny didn't mention Orrin Massey to Packy."

"Maybe he hadn't met him yet," Valerie said. "Maybe he met him in the last few weeks before he disappeared."

"You guys are thinking some pretty wild stuff," I said.

"You can't buy it?" Valerie said.

"I… Who knows? Maybe. It does explain things, I'll give it that."

"If there's any truth to it, where would the base of operations be, the place where the army would be?" Muhammad asked.

"On a twenty thousand acre spread in northern Idaho."

"So, let's go look," Valerie said. "It's just up the road a piece."

I stared at her. I said, "You, me, and him? Just walk in and say we're a traveling vaudeville act looking for a place to spend the night? Valerie, walk over there and turn around and take a look at us. Stay here while you do it."

"We've got to find out."

"Find out what? Only thing we need to know is the truth. I don't think whoever's up there'll tell us. If it's what Muhammad thinks, we'll have to beat it out of them. We don't even know what Orrin Massey looks like."

"Yeah, we do," Muhammad said. "Francis got lucky."

"Good. I want to see it. And I want the Honolulu police to see it. I think we're a step or two away from scouting up north. How'd you figure on getting there, by the way?"

Valerie said, "Bonners Ferry's got a four thousand-foot airstrip in a valley at about two thousand feet. We can charter a King Air. Seats four in the cabin. Be there in two hours. Rent a truck. Off we go."

"We don't know where Massey's place is, do we?"

"Francis found it," Muhammad said. "Like you could hide twenty thousand acres."

"How many square miles is twenty thousand acres?"

"About thirty."

"I would like to see it. I think it's a mistake to invade it, but maybe we could do a flyover and take some pictures. Might be a waste of money, though. Time, too."

"We can afford it, Harry," Valerie said.

It was still morning in Utah. Barely. What the hell. "Let's go. Airborne only, though. Forget about spending an unforgettable evening in Bonners Ferry. We'll fly up, take a good look, take some pictures and fly back.

"It's a flyover," I said to the manager at the counter, from whom we arranged to charter a Beechcraft King Air C90B. "We don't expect to land. We want photos. Distance to Bonners Ferry is..." I turned to Valerie with the question and the pilot standing behind the manager said, "Five hundred ten nautical miles. The lady already put us on it. With this payload—the three of you, two pilots, minimal luggage, full fuel—that's a little less than half our range. Depending, we'll either go non-stop or refuel at someplace like Pocatello on the way back."

"Can you rent us a high-resolution digital camera?"

"Got a Canon Hi8 Camcorder with good magnification. And I can let you have an EOS SLR for stills. Zoom lens on that."

"Great. Put it on the bill. We're ready when you are."

Idaho. Aloft.

Mountains, mountains everywhere…

Big round windows. Quiet, cruising at 275 miles per hour at 18,000 feet, a steady baritone hum that was kind of soporific. Or maybe it was the synthetic air.

The cabin was nifty for normal people but Muhammad was almost too big to sit down in its 4'9" vertical clearance. He'd have to roll out into the aisle and crawl to the lavatory, but it was a nice one and worth the crawl.

We sat in the two-facing-two configuration with Valerie toe-to-toe with me so Muhammad could extend his legs to the limit. A small refrigerator with bottled water and sodas was in the rear. An electric kettle and stuff for tea and coffee was in a rack on its top. While we'd waited to board, with the manager's help, I had hustled up a half-dozen sandwiches and two quarts of ice cream. After we made altitude outside Salt Lake City, I served lunch. Cindy would have been impressed.

The cockpit was open to us and we could hear the pilots chatter with air traffic control. When they wanted to speak to us there were speakers above our heads. And there was a microphone between each seat-pair for talking to them.

Spending money is fun.

We didn't say much. I dozed and once, when I awoke, Valerie was asleep. Muhammad got acquainted with both cameras and then went on with his reading of "Under The Banner Of Heaven." I had maps, a bunch I'd picked up at the airport and others I accessed one at a time on my laptop at a great web site called TopoZone. It was good information but slightly inconvenient, hard to go a few pages back to check something you remembered seeing like you can more easily do if they're on paper. Paper maybe has a future.

I went to the cockpit with a note in my hand and said, "You guys know exactly where we're going?"

"We were just talking about it," the copilot said. "Your friend gave us an approximate but you probably don't want to wander around too much, do you?"

"No. I just found it on my laptop. It's a spread of about thirty square miles. About in the center is a place called Solomon Mountain. It's at forty-two hundred feet. 48.7908 north, 116.1078 west," I read from my note and handed it to him. "Looks like it's the highest point in the neighborhood and plateaued on the top. It's maybe as good as place as any to start. Maybe we'll find what we're looking for there."

"Which is what exactly?"

"Buildings. People."

"You think we'll be welcomed?"

"No. We might even be interfered with. Guy owns it's got enough money for at least a helicopter, maybe even something fixed-wing somewhere nearby. I'd like to come in quick and when we find the buildings that I hope are there, make a couple of passes for pictures and then hook it up. How do you handle something like this with air traffic control?"

"Place is north of Bonners Ferry, isn't it?"

"Yeah. About ten miles or so northeast of the airport."

"We'll come in at about ten thousand, tell them we're heading north into Canada. Shouldn't be a problem then to do a little sightseeing."

"How soon?"

"Fifteen, twenty minutes. We'll start our descent any time now."

"Okay. How about, when we find what we're looking for, you come in low?"

"Okay. Steep bank angle for good visibility?"

"Yeah. Enough to get the wing out of the way. Thanks. Feed us all your conversation from here on."

My TopoZone maps showed a stream called Deer Creek coming down from the north and passing to the west of the mountain at an elevation of 2,000 feet. North of the mountain, Solomon Creek branched off from Deer Creek and headed south along the eastern side of the mountain. Solomon Creek became Solomon Lake a little northeast of the mountain and then returned to creek status at the lake's southern end. The map showed "undeveloped roads" at both creek beds that wound up the mountain and joined near the top. On the map Deer Creek's bed looked flat enough for about two miles that it might have accommodated a landing strip. Whole thing had the potential to be a little slice of heaven. Or the other.

I told Valerie and Muhammad of my conversation up front and of what I'd seen on the maps and they nodded. Muhammad said, "I can handle the camcorder."

"And I can handle the EOS," Valerie said. "I've got one of my own."

"Okay. Both passes'll be on the same side. You might have to jockey around to get a view over the wing. I'll go to the back and look out from there." I picked up my mike and said into it, "Can I jack one of these in at the rear?"

"There's one back there. And an overhead speaker," came the answer.

We heard them identify themselves to the Bonners Ferry tower, say they were heading north into Canada for some hunting and would come down to five thousand and check out the scenery. Then say to us, "The airport's coming up to the right. About two o'clock right now."

Muhammad, on that side, picked up his mike and said, "I see it."

Then, as we descended steeply, I heard, "If your coordinates are correct that should be Solomon Mountain just ahead. We'll make a pass well to the west at about five thousand. Should be able to see any development from that altitude out the right side. Way I see this, right side'll get all the action."

I went to the rear and Valerie moved across the aisle and sat with Muhammad. They began to shoot.

The view was worth the trip. The forest was dense and lush, majestic and unspoiled. A herd of something, maybe elk, was grazing at the meadow beside Deer Creek and they broke off from their feeding and scurried uphill into the woods, maybe spooked by our approach. A long strip of the meadow beside the creek bed had a more manicured appearance than its surroundings. Into the mike, I said, "Could that be an air strip by the side of the creek?"

"Could be."

"Before we leave let's take a closer look."

"Okay. After we sweep the mountain or now?"

"After."

We approached the mountain about a half-mile off to our right. Its top was plateaued both by nature and by man.

There were light brown areas that appeared to have been recently cleared and darker strips that may have been paved. At the south end, there were two quonset-type buildings and a straight road led from them to a group of buildings at the north end.

A cluster of people all in the same dun-colored clothing were gathered outside the quonsets beside what looked like construction equipment. They moved in unison, coming together and perhaps looking up at us we passed them by.

From that end to the other, the top of Solomon Mountain was maybe five hundred yards long by half that wide. There was an area near the western edge that looked a little like an obstacle course for training, ropes and racks and pits and walls. I saw tree stumps and mounds of earth.

At the northern end, the road led to one large multi-story lodge and others, maybe cottages, were arrayed in a horseshoe configuration around it, several to each side. As we passed over, I saw a helicopter on a pad behind the large building. More people appeared at that end, coming out of the cottages to have a look at their company.

From above, we heard, "We're going out about five or ten miles to give the impression that we're gone. Then come back low and fast. Okay?"

"I like it."

I saw no evidence of the hand of man beyond the mountaintop as we went farther north, but in the lake there was a boat with a superstructure. No wake. Maybe fishing.

After a minute or so of heading north, I heard, "Tight turn coming up. We'll pass the mountain top on the eastern edge. Come in banked right maybe forty-five degrees. It'll seem like more. You want fast, slow, or medium?"

"Medium-slow the first time. Fast as hell the second."

"Fast as hell you'll need to run that EOS on power drive."

"I'll do that on both passes," Valerie said.

"Okay. You ready?"

"Ready."

"Medium-slow" at a forty-five degree bank angle made me wonder what my stomach would do at "fast as hell." We might have fooled them into thinking we were long gone, but they hadn't gone back inside. Three of them double-timed to the copter and those by the cottages dropped to their knees and pointed things at us. At the other end, a truck carrying what looked a lot like a mounted, large-caliber weapon emerged from one of the two quonsets. More people pointed more things. And we were gone.

The speaker said, "You were right about not being welcomed."

"Yeah. Anybody see evidence of any firing?"

I heard several responses, all negatives.

"I don't think they'll shoot," I said. "That'd be pretty crazy if they're doing what I think they're doing. They just want to scare us off. The copter'll be up though. You up for another pass?"

"Only at fast as hell."

"Wouldn't want any less."

It takes 3.6 seconds to traverse 500 yards at 285 miles per hour. My distance estimate might have been way off, because it seemed it took long enough for my clothes to go out of style. The copter hovered above the clearing, pointing in our direction as we approached. As we passed, it pivoted with us, holding point. We passed it close enough to see the gap in the pilot's front teeth. And we were gone.

We went north for a couple of minutes, which would have been ten miles if we didn't slow up. And I don't think we did. Then we turned and dove and came in five hundred feet above Deer Creek and took pictures of a single-engine, high-wing plane taxiing along a grass air strip. We were in another county before he made altitude.

Into my mike, I said, "How long you think that grass strip might be?"

"Long. Six, seven thousand easy."

• • • • •

We took our seats, buckled in, and exchanged looks as the King Air climbed sharply.

Valerie laid the back of her hand on her brow and said, "I think I just may *die* of boredom."

I used my seat mike, said, "You guys are good. Thanks."

"You're welcome."

"Hope you're not in any trouble over this."

"We were just talking about it. I don't think so. And if we are, finding an army on a mountaintop's sort of a mitigating factor. Hope you took the lens caps off."

"Even I won't kid about a thing like that."

I said to Muhammad and Valerie, "How long do you think it'll take Orrin Massey to learn that the plane that buzzed his hideout was chartered by a guy named Harry Pines with an address in Kailua?"

"With tail numbers, how long would it take you?" Muhammad answered. "Take Francis, I mean."

"Thirty minutes."

I told them of my conversation with Rafael in his car after Danny's wake, of his offer. "I think he didn't want us to be at a competitive disadvantage."

Muhammad said, "Well, now."

Valerie said, "Daddy."

I said, "I'm going to get our place protected twenty-four, seven. Let's do this. Valerie, you find out how soon we can get to Honolulu. Go on line or whatever. Ask the guys up front to help. Maybe we should have them take us someplace else to make a connection. We've got to be closer to Seattle right now than Salt Lake City. Be our travel agent. Get us home quick. Is all our luggage checked through to Honolulu on the Salt Lake City flight?"

"Except for what's here."

"Okay. Get us home. Muhammad, you find somebody at the house. It's mid-morning there. Cindy's probably your best bet. I'm going to call Rafael's guy and we'll need a contact for him at the house. If you can't find Cindy, try Richie or Sam at work." I told him how to reach them with a number I'd set up that dead-ended into a menu-driven audio directory of the phone contacts of everyone at the house. It was mostly for my benefit, to free up my memory.

I took the note from my money clip and punched the second number, putting 1-808 in front of it, and marveling again at how such things are possible. A soft voice with a faint Oriental accent said, "Yes?"

I said, "My name is Harry Pines and Rafael Sabatino gave me this number."

"How may I be of service?"

"I want my house in Kailua protected around the clock beginning immediately. I want a minimum of three men who can handle a variety of weapons, as well as themselves. Good people, too. Not thugs."

"Specify. Three or more."

"Three. Combat-trained."

"Provide their own weapons, or will you provide?"

"Provide their own."

"Very well. Address?"

I gave it to him. "How soon?" I asked.

"One hour, perhaps. No more than two. Meet you there?"

"No. I'm not there. Please hold." I turned to Muhammad who was talking on his phone.

He said to me, "It's Cindy. How soon?"

I told him an hour, maybe two, asked him to have her lock the front gate as soon as she got off the phone.

"How will she know it's them?" Muhammad asked me. "And not somebody else?"

I thought, said, "They'll know the name of the city where she was born." He nodded.

I told the guy on my phone that a woman named Cindy Rendell would meet his crew. "She'll have the front gate locked. To get in, they'll have to phone her when they arrive. She'll ask them where she was born. It's Manistique, Michigan. When your people are inside and the place is secure, have them call me at this number." I gave it to him, along with Cindy's. "Got all that? Should I repeat anything?"

"Not necessary. Will that be all?"

"For now."

"Best to you," and clicked off.

●　●　●　●　●

A little south of Bonners Ferry, at 20,000 feet, we turned right and went west to Seattle. Valerie had found a JAL flight from there to Honolulu and booked three first-class seats. We made it easily. I hadn't heard from Kailua so I called Cindy as we waited in the departure lounge. She said both she and the crew had been unable to get through to me. These cell phones suck, can't do anything with them.

Cindy said, "God, Harry, these guys are hot. I want a couple of them when you're through. Two of them are native Hawaiians, twins, Jack and Jim, and the third, Jerry, is a haole. I think he's the cutest, but it's close. They're all three built like humvees."

"Uh-huh. Do you have any sense of their competence, by the way? Forgive me for breaking your train of thought."

She chuckled. "Gotcha. Just fuckin' with you. They're doing fine. Padlocked the back gate, one of them sits on the front lanai, the other two roam. Don't worry, we're fine."

"What about the others?"

"I called them all, said you guys had stirred up a hornet's nest and thought better safe than sorry. Leanne and Richie and I are sort of excited, but I think

Sam and Teresa might spend the night in town. Law firm's got an apartment there. They weren't sure. Sam was curious, Teresa was jumpy. Where're you guys?"

"Seattle airport. Got a Japan Air flight. Should be on the ground in Honolulu about five your time. You call, or have somebody else call, if anything weird happens. Okay? Promise."

"Weird? Would a little uncomplicated three-way be weird?" She laughed again. "Okay. I promise. We're cool. Thanks for keeping an eye on us. But I wasn't lyin' about these guys. I am just tremblin' with desire. Quiverin.'"

"Take a cold shower, slut."

I remember buckling in my seat and turning to Valerie as she said something to me. Then she nudged me awake as we entered our final approach to Honolulu. I had even slept through the takeoff; usually I scream.

• • • • •

Kailua.

Muhammad and Valerie tracked down luggage while I got my Range Rover from the parking garage.

I phoned Cindy as we passed through the Pali tunnel on the windward side and came into Kailua.

"Queen of the manor," she answered.

"Hey, your royal highness. It's one of your subjects."

"Harry! You nearby?"

"Five minutes away. Thought I'd play it safe and not get shot pulling through the gate. Is the coast clear?"

"Yeah, but there's a password. If you can tell me how many boys I fucked in high school, I'll let you come in."

"All of them."

"Welcome home."

I unlocked the gate with my remote and it swung open. I pulled into the drive and Valerie said, "We got a big one."

A large white man in a dark shirt and matching shorts was standing on the lanai holding something at his side that looked like a shotgun. I put the Rover in the car port and the three of us started hustling luggage. He came down and joined us, took Valerie's load. We introduced ourselves. He said his name was Jerry. He didn't offer a last name and I didn't ask it. It said, "Security" in small gold letters on his shirt. He was formal and polite, in his early thirties. He had the bulked-up look of a firefighter, like he lifted for the strength and not the appearance.

Muhammad went to his apartment and Jerry followed Valerie and me to mine. At the front door I told Jerry to lay down his load, I'd take it from there.

"You settled in?" I asked. "Got everything you need?"

"Yes, sir, Mr. Pines. Well taken care of. Cindy and Leanne been feeding us. Richie showed us the gym in the back. Fine people, your neighbors."

"Skip the sir, Jerry. Call me Harry. And this is Valerie. And Muhammad's the one down there. Where're you guys staying?"

"Motel just down the road. Five minutes from here. Be sleepin' short shifts, workin' long ones."

"We appreciate your help with this."

"You're welcome. It's my job."

"Hope it turns out to be boring duty."

He shrugged. "Either way's okay."

"Ask the other two to come by in about ten minutes. To say hello."

We unpacked, put on shorts and t-shirts and came downstairs.

Two guys were in the front room. Identical twins. About the same size as Jerry. We introduced ourselves. They said they were Jack and Jim.

"How can I tell you apart?"

"Does it matter?"

"Are you native Hawaiian?"

"Yes, sir."

"Not an awful lot of you, are there?"

"No, sir. Not enough."

"You meet Muhammad?"

"Yes, sir. Just now."

"Skip the sir. Use first names. Got everything you need?"

"Well taken care of, thank you."

"Make yourselves at home. We're glad you're here."

"Thank you. We'll be helpful." They went to the door.

To their backs, I said, "Jack, Jim, and Jerry. Those your real names?"

They turned and smiled. One said, "Is anything real in this crazy world?"

Valerie went to the computer to download email. I picked up a voice mail message from the bartender at the Texas Paniolo saying he had "a pretty brown-haired Betsy target" and I could call him on his cell phone but not during working hours, "which is seven 'til late. Better call after ten any morning." It was 6:30, so I called and he answered and said, "Two girls. Betsy and Esther. Caucs. Betsy's got long brown hair and she's pretty. I chatted 'em up and got Esther's phone number. Didn't get Betsy's, didn't ask for it after Esther gave me hers. Didn't want to seem like, you know, a guy goes around collecting phone numbers."

"When was this?"

"Two nights ago."

"What's the number?"

"Be all right if you came by for it? Do some business?"

"That's fair. You on tonight?"

"Yeah."

"I'll be by."

I hung up. Valerie said, "He found her?"

"He thinks so. Betsy and Esther. Got Esther's phone number. He's rat-holing it. Wants a little more whip-out for it so I told him I'd come by tonight."

"I'll go with you."

She turned back to the computer and I went to the wall map and used a long clear ruler to search for the intersection of the coordinates where we had found Danny's remains. I had the coordinates in decimal equivalents from Runner's GPS notes—longitude 157.5644 degrees west, latitude 21.3354 degrees north—but the map's margins were tick-marked in degrees, minutes, and seconds, so I extrapolated. Longitude 157 degrees, 56 minutes, 26.4 seconds; latitude 21 degrees, 33 minutes, 32.4 seconds.

I circled, in yellow marker, the place where the two long pencilled lines came together. I leaned back to admire my work. Lot of good it did me.

Muhammad was on a stroll. Holoholo. He came in. Richie was with him. "Listen to this," Muhammad said.

"Cops came by yesterday," Richie said. "Said they were cops, anyhow. I was down working on the nets, patching rips. Leanne and Cindy were on the beach. Two guys came through the path, saw me, said, 'We're looking for Harry Pines. Do you know him?' 'Yes,' I said. 'You know where we can find him?' 'Who wants to know?' I said. 'Honolulu police,' one said and showed me his badge. Looked like a badge, but, you know, I didn't put a spyglass on it. Told them you were away, on the mainland. Wanted to know when you'd be back. I said I didn't know. They eyeballed the girls. 'Would they know?' 'Know what?' I said. 'When Harry Pines'll be back.' I said, 'They don't know who Harry Pines is.' And they left."

"Describe them."

"One local. Filipino, maybe. The other white. Had surfer hair, you know, shaggy and bleached out. Aloha shirts. Jeans. Medium size. Thirties. I'd sure know 'em if I saw them again."

I found Crandall's mug shot on my desk. "This one of them?"

"Yeah."

"Let's make sure."

I caught Dick Wong at his desk, told him the guy we'd identified as Wilton Crandall and a Filipino came by posing as cops while I was away. "Just to be sure we're right on the ID, you didn't send anybody over here, did you?"

"Nope. You back?"

"Yeah. See you tomorrow?"

"Make it early. About nine. It's homicide, Harry."

"Okay. I'll bring Valerie and a man I work with. Also my neighbor who saw the two guys, maybe have him look at some pictures, try to find the Filipino."

"Do that."

I hung up and said, "He says Danny was murdered and he didn't send any cops over here yesterday. Muhammad, what's going on?"

"Could be Crandall and this Filipino've gone rogue looking for the jewel. Like Packy said they might."

"Jewel?" Richie said.

"I need to talk with you. Leanne and Cindy, too."

"They're on the way," Richie said. "To welcome you back. Sam just got here, too."

After the welcome, I said, "We may be a little more threatened than I thought we were. Richie tell you about the two guys who came by yesterday? Said they were cops?"

He had told them. "They weren't cops," I said. "And they weren't even the reason I hired the security so, as you can see, we're kind of doubly threatened. And the police just confirmed Danny was murdered. This kind of stuff doesn't come with your lease. I think it'd be best if you moved out for a while. Not long. Wouldn't think it'd be more than a week or so. We'll pay for it. All of it. And welcome you back when it's over."

Richie said, "Not me. I'm gonna get a piece of this, lend a hand."

"No, you're not."

"Hear me out. You guys need an information manager. You're gonna be digging stuff up. Feed it to me and I'll keep a database. Interactive. Searchable. It'll be cool and it'll help."

Leanne said, "Harry, I don't want to leave. I'm not afraid. I'll sign something that lets you off the hook for my safety if you want. Legally. You can still keep an eye on me. Which you will. So will Muhammad. And now we've got Jack and Jim and Jerry, too."

"And Richie. And maybe Sam." Cindy said. "Six or seven guys looking out for me. You think I'm walking away from that, you're nuts." I think Richie may have levitated.

"Yeah," Leanne said. "Sweet of you to offer, but I'm staying."

"Suppose I insist?"

"I'll resist," Leanne said.

"Me, too," Cindy said. "And we'll win. One thing, though. Tell us what's going on. Can you do that?"

"Sam?"

"I'd like to hear about what's going on before I decide, but we're leaning to staying in the firm's apartment for a few days. Teresa's there now. Expectant parents need to be cautious."

"Okay," I said. "Here's the story."

Leanne raised her hand, said, "Hold it. Cindy and I've got seafood gumbo ready in the kitchen. Made it special for your coming home supper. We'll serve it up and we'll all eat while we talk."

"Great," I said. "But let's eat at the table in the main room."

Everybody scurried, setting the table, fixing drinks, opening wine and pouring beer, and sitting down to a rich, brown gumbo over white rice with crusty bread.

Richie asked if I'd mind if he ran a tape recorder and I said I didn't. I went back to my time at TI with Danny's father, followed the story chronologically from Valerie's arrival. The mystery of his disappearance, the green car, the girlfriend at Texas Paniolo, the house in Manoa, the Princess Leilani.

Muhammad and Valerie picked up threads along the way and gave me time to eat. It was fabulous gumbo, full of shrimp and mussels and even sausage.

I came to the jewel, to the threats to Danny, and of his admitting to his father his involvement in the theft ring. Muhammad told the religious history lesson and the likely family of Orrin Massey. And I told them what we'd found atop Solomon Mountain. "That's when I decided to hire the security. I figure they must've made note of our plane's tail numbers and it wouldn't be all that hard to trace the charter back to me right here.

"I've got the stuff we shot up there, Richie. I'd like to have it rendered as a map. If you want to help, I think that's the way." I knew he had been hobbying with his camera and computer graphics, fooling with photoshopping images that he was emailing to Curtis back in Indianapolis. "If you think you're up to it, it'd be a big help."

"Be happy to try, Harry. But that's pretty high end stuff."

Sam said, "Let Richie do the database. We've got a guy on staff at the firm who does this kind of thing for trial exhibits. He's got the hardware and software Richie probably doesn't have. Let that be my contribution. And we'll turn it around quick."

"Okay. Great."

"Leanne and I want to help. Anything we can do?" Cindy asked.

I started to say no, but Valerie jumped in. "There maybe is something. It's … Oh, God, it's so boring. And maybe nothing will come of it, but it has to be done. It absolutely *has* to be done."

"We talked about it in the kitchen," Leanne said. "And we agreed we want to help in any way we can."

"Okay. It's in Harry's office. I'll get it." And started for the door.

Sam said, "Hey, Valerie. Get that stuff you shot today, will you? I need to go back to Teresa."

Muhammad said, "Harry, let's bus this table. Show these people how professionals do it." Richie and Sam helped and it was done just as Valerie came back with Danny's bible and the media for Sam.

"This is his bible," she said. "My nephew's. A bible doesn't seem like something Danny would have, so Harry and I have been taking turns going through it page-by-page, looking for any kind of note in the margin, or something circled or underlined that might give us another way to look at it. It's … well, boring. We're …" She opened it. "Up to page 672. Out of almost 2,000. Want to do it? Take turns? It works like a sleeping pill. You'll drop right off."

Richie was fooling with his recorder as he listened. He took on a tiny smile. Leanne said, "Richie, if you say 'women's work' I'll cut your fucking throat from ear to ear with a linoleum knife. I swear to God I will."

"I was gonna say," he said, "that I'd do it myself, but I don't think I'm … meticulous enough. Not smart enough, either. Or patient enough. Or …"

"That'll do," she said.

"We're on it, Valerie. Happy to do it," Cindy said. She went to her and hugged her and said, "This is my first chance to tell you how much my own heart hurts for what you've gone through. God bless your nephew. And you, too. And let's catch the dirty rotten motherfuckers that did it." She took the bible and a glass of wine to a sofa. Leanne followed and they turned and curtsied. "Junior G-Women," Leanne said. "At your service." And they plopped down and opened the bible.

I asked Muhammad to brief Jim, Jack, and Jerry while Valerie and I went bar-hopping.

· · · · ·

"You say anything to them about the missing soldier?" I asked the bartender at the Texas Paniolo.

"Not a peep. I played it like I was on the hustle."

I gave him a matched pair of hundreds and he gave me a piece of paper with a phone number on it.

I looked at it. "This her handwriting? Esther's?"

"Yeah."

"You make a copy of it for yourself?"

"No. I would have if it'd been Betsy's, though. She's table grade."

"Describe her."

"Long light brown hair. Very hot. Maybe twenty-five. Medium size."

"Mission accomplished. Thanks."

"My pleasure. You need anything more, you know where to find me. Buy you a beer?"

"Don't have time. Another time, though. Thanks."

On the way back, Valerie said, "I'll call Esther. That woman-to-woman thing."

"Okay, but why don't we have Francis take a quick look at her first."

"Okey-dokey. But tell him to hustle. I'm starting to get traction."

"You'll need to have something to say when she asks how you got her number."

"I'll think of something."

"You need to get us an appointment to see the green Toyota, too."

"I'm on it, skipper. What about the soldier on the boat?"

"I think I'll give that to the police."

"I'm getting kind of excited. Are you?"

"My blood's up."

"Let's run over a varmint in this big fucker. Squash the life out of him. Then climb straight up that hill over there."

"Jesus."

• • • • •

Cindy and Leanne were waiting for us at the dining table with the open bible, looking smug.

Leanne said, "Cindy said, 'Why don't we start with the Book of Daniel? That's his name.' So we did. And here's what we found."

She spun the book and pointed to a passage that was carefully underlined in black ink, likely by a straight edge. She turned it back and read, "Today we dare not even open our mouths, shame and dishonor are the lot of those who serve and worship You.

"And this," she said, turning a few pages farther on to another passage underlined the same way. She read, "Daniel was released from the pit and found to be quite unhurt, because he had trusted in his God. The king sent for the men who had accused Daniel and had them thrown into the lion pit, they, their wives and their children: and they had not reached the floor of the pit before the lions had seized them and crushed their bones to pieces."

"Well," I said. I couldn't think of anything else to say.

"Let me see the citations," Valerie said. She turned back to the first. "Chapter three, line thirty-three." She flipped to the second. "Chapter six, lines twenty-four and twenty-five." She looked at me.

"That explains everything," I said.

"Don't act smart," Valerie said.

"That was smart? I meant to act stupid."

Richie and Muhammad walked in. I said, "Rich, put this in your database." I explained what they had found, but I must have made it sound useless when I meant to make myself sound useless.

"Harry," Leanne said, in a little-girl-hurt tone. "Don't hurt our feelings."

"No, forgive me. I don't mean to. It's great because it means something. But I don't know what. No, I'm grateful. Really. You guys are terrific. I'm just confused."

"What's the context of this first one?" Richie asked.

"Well, you probably didn't know this," Leanne said, squirming a little in her chair like she'd rather be at a blackboard with a pointer, "but there were four Jews, Israelites, I mean, taken to the court of King Nebuchadnezzar after he conquered Babylon. Or maybe Babylonia. Daniel was one of them. They were thought to be special, wise, like prophets. The king renamed them. Daniel was called..." She spun the book so she could read it and went back a page. "Belteshazzar. And the other three were renamed..."

"Shadrach, Meshach, and Abednego," Muhammad said.

"Yeah," Leanne said, impressed. "Very good, Muhammad. And one day the king thought they screwed up a prophecy, some kind of dream analysis, so he threw them into a pit of fire. The deal was if they died, that proved they were wrong, but if they lived, they were right. This line is part of what Abednego prayed when they tossed him in. See, he and the other three believed in their own God, so they prayed to him to save them. When he says, 'Today we dare not even open our mouths, shame and dishonor are the lot of those who serve and worship You,' he's talking to his God. That's why the 'You' is capitalized."

"Did they live?" Richie asked.

"Yes," Muhammad said. "But all the people standing around died because the fire was so hot."

"And the context of the other one is pretty obvious," Cindy said. "Later on, they threw Daniel in the lion's den to test another prophecy. And he passed."

"Tough job, prophet," I said.

"Didn't he get swallowed by a whale, too?" Richie asked.

We all looked at him, grateful for something said that was dumber than we felt. But not by much.

"Oh, yeah," he said. "That was Jonah."

ELEVEN
Thursday, March 20

Valerie and I were up early, still on mainland time, so I walked down to Muhammad's apartment thinking he might be up and knocked quietly. He opened the door. He must have been standing there. He was in khaki shorts and a brown knit shirt that said "Serena's. Chicago." on the left chest side. It always surprised me to see him out of his suit and tie uniform. It made him look bigger, but less imposing.

"Bet you already called home," I said.

"I have."

"Let's sit and talk."

"Here?"

"Valerie's up. We got coffee."

We sat in the front room, Valerie in her chair, Muhammad on the sofa, and I in the rocker.

"Any thoughts on the bible stuff?" I asked.

"Not a one."

"Valerie thinks it has nothing to do with the words. Thinks it's all about the citation."

"Three, thirty-three. Six, twenty-four and twenty-five," she said.

"Okay," Muhammad said.

"That's it," she said. "I don't know more than that. I just don't think he read the bible for inspiration, so he looked up those citations for where they were, not for what they said."

"The numbers mean something."

"That's what I think."

"No way to disagree with you."

"I know," she said. "I just want us to think about the numbers and not the messages of the passages."

"Okay."

"And, Muhammad," I said. "I'm somewhere else. These people have seen Valerie. They've seen me. I don't want them to see you as part of us."

"Meaning?"

"We'll all go see Dick Wong, take Richie to ID some mug shots on the

Filipino. Then you and Richie come back here. Valerie and I'll go to the green Toyota guy Valerie found in Pearl, then go see Esther…"

"Francis found her?"

"Name, rank, and serial number. She looks like the Virgin Mary. Works at the Polynesian Cultural Center, lives out that way. Oh, and Francis also found out that the victims in Massey's court martial for assault were homosexuals. When they got to the trial, they were nowhere to be found."

"Kind of a Fundamentalist thing to do. By the way, you know who established the Polynesian Cultural Center, still operates it?"

"No."

"Mormon church. There's a Brigham Young campus out there, too. And the Mormon Hawaiian temple. Probably doesn't mean anything. Just thought I'd say so to give you a headache. So, I'm undercover. Okay."

"I've got something in mind for you. Are you carrying?"

"Yes. Are you?"

"No, but I'm going to take care of that."

"I am, too," Valerie said.

"'Too' what?"

"Carrying."

We stared at her. "Wait right here," she said. She went upstairs two steps at a time and came down slowly about sixty seconds later with a gun in her hand. "Ever see one of these? This is the Beretta Tomcat. Seven point six five millimeter, seven shots in the magazine." She showed a magazine and slid it in and chambered a round. "Weighs about a pound. Cute little thing, isn't it? Muhammad could probably hide it in his hand. A professional taught me how to use it. I've fired it more than a thousand times. And every time I was aiming at something. I wouldn't be surprised if both of you are better shots than I am. In fact, I hope you are. But if you are, you're pretty damn good. Because so am I."

"You've kept that up there all this time?"

"Not always. Sometimes I've had it with me."

"You're just a bundle of surprises."

"You ain't seen nothin' yet."

I turned to Muhammad. "Think about a way we can use you to get a line on the helicopter the boat uses. Maybe some way to turn you into one of those special people they fly out on it. Try to get to the top of the stack. You might even run into Orrin Massey."

"Let me think about it for a few minutes." He left.

• • • • •

Muhammad was back in an hour. Valerie was upstairs.

He said, "I'll let myself be seen as a man with a big bankroll and a big itch to play with it. I'll work Waikiki, the hotels, in a limousine. I'll be carrying my wad in a briefcase. A lot of cash, maybe a hundred thousand. I'll take a couple of our guys. One to drive, one to ride shotgun. Make me look more serious and give me even more protection. I'll push whoever contacts me to take me to the top man. I'll tell him I can only make a late departure. I can sell it."

I called the number Rafael had given me.

The same soft voice said, "Yes?"

"My name is Harry Pines and Rafael Sabatino gave me this number."

"Are you satisfied with our service to date?"

"Yes. I need additional supplies. I have a list."

"Proceed."

I talked for five minutes. Twice I asked him if he was keeping up. Both times he said, "Certainly."

When I was finished, I said, "We clear?"

"Quite. Will that be all?"

"For now. Can you have all that delivered by noon today?"

"Same address?"

"Yes. A very large black man will meet them. He will say his name is Muhammad Ali."

"Best to you." He hung up.

• • • • •

"Here's what we got," Dick Wong said, after I introduced Muhammad and he sent Richie off with another cop to work with Orchid. Bobby Bentley was there, too.

"As I said, it's a homicide. Not a doubt.

"We stumbled on to an electronic homing device in his canteen. It was magnetic. Attached that way, I mean. A little button thing somebody had dropped in there. Picked up the signal by accident, one of our guys was testing another one and picked up the signal coming from the canteen. Dumb luck. Which is my specialty. So very good chance Danny was tracked up there. He was definitely trackable.

"No prints on the button. But two sets of prints on the outside of the canteen, the metal interior part. One was Danny's. Ran the other one against NCIC. Got nothing. Called a guy at Schofield owes me a favor and got access to their database. The other print matched former Corporal Michael T. Sheffield, who said, 'So what?' when Bobby talked to him, said lots of guys share lots of guy's canteens. Bobby said bullshit, he hadn't been in the army for two months, how'd he get his hands on Danny's canteen. He said he and Danny did some hiking on Danny's days off. He's got solid alibis for all his time from Danny's disappearance up through the next several days. So solid it makes you wonder if he knew what was coming. Still holding on to seeing Danny the day he disappeared, though. So all we can do for now is make him nervous. Which we are.

"One blood sample was Danny's. The other matched a soldier who was here until he was mustered out in January. Name is Roland Collins. And he's fallen off the face of the earth. Mother's dead. Father, back in Murfreesboro, Tennessee, said he hasn't heard from him in months. No other relatives."

"Which blood sample was Danny's?" I asked.

"One on the tree. Okay? Moving on. Skull showed signs of blunt force, enough to knock him out. Slight fracture in the left tibia. None of the other bones were broken, which suggests he didn't take the full fall from the clearing to the stream. Maybe hurt himself going down there to get away. Another guess. Actually, some of the thinner bones did show fractures but the ME believes that was from the chewing action of the predators, mongooses and pigs. Anyhow, he took a bad fall at some point but that didn't kill him. And neither did the blow on the head."

He paused to sip his coffee and I said, "Anything on the time of death?"

"Getting to that. Approximate time of death, very approximate, Monday, March 4th, in the afternoon. From his watch. We confirmed with his roommate that it was his watch. It was an inexpensive little thing powered by a battery that the manufacturer says will stop about ninety-six hours after the watch stops moving. So, time of death, say, 4:00 pm, March 4th, the Monday after the Wednesday when he disappeared from his platoon exercise. That's what we're going with. Actually, it could have been sooner if the animals had been, uh, moving the watch around while they fed, and that would not be surprising. But not likely later. Who knows? I'd hate to have to withstand a cross-examination on all that, but there it is. Only good thing is, it's not inconsistent with anything else. That's the window of time Sheffield's covered for. Wednesday through Monday."

Valerie said, "How convenient."

He smiled at her and said, "Isn't it? Odds and ends. We've got the hiker, Runner, up there on Thursday, March 13th. Showed up here the next day. He said he turned the shirt inside out, or rather outside in, when he found it, to check the name. Then turned it back and put a rock on it so it wouldn't go away."

I said, "What Runner did with that shirt is weird. Don't you think so, Detective?"

"Yes," Bentley said. "But he's a weird guy."

Wong said. "Other than it's a little strange to do that, there's no reason to doubt it. He's meticulous in the extreme, so it's the kind of thing he might have done. His notebook's an amazing document. He recorded everything that went into or out of his body every day he was on the hike; volume, weight, description. Everything. In both directions. How about that for strange? Read his own pulse and recorded it about ten times a day. Wrote down a description of everything he encountered, including a rusty old helmet and a length of barbed wire. Wrote down his location, the GPS coordinates, about ten times a day. Handwriting so small you almost need a glass to read it. So being kind of tidy with the shirt fits."

"Do you have Runner's address?" I asked.

"Somewhere around here," Wong said. "I'll get it for you. Just mauka of Waikiki."

"I thought you said Haleiwa."

"What Haleiwa? When did I say that?"

I scratched my head. "Well, you didn't, I guess. He did. He said he came down with the skull and hitchhiked to Haleiwa and called his wife to pick him up. Why would he go to Haleiwa if he lived in Waikiki?"

"Not a bad question, Harry. Bobby, you know anything about that?"

"Yes, sir. I caught that, too. He said he went to Haleiwa because there's a little park there where his wife was supposed to pick him up anyway. Plus, he felt like he didn't want to go into town with the skull, thought he'd rather put it in the trunk of his car somewhere where nobody'd be likely to see him. And maybe he was just rattled, took the first ride he could get, no matter which way it was going."

"I keep wondering about the belt," I said. "Did Runner take it out of the fatigues? Or find it on the ground?"

"The latter," Wong said. "Raising the question of why it was removed. To which we have no answer."

"The t-shirt?"

"Danny's."

"The small bones I found in the lean-to. What were they?"

"Chicken."

"Some kind of chicken lives up there?"

"Supermarket chicken. Yo' mama's chicken. Fried chicken."

"Huh?"

"Sheffield said he'd been up there with Danny, said Danny used it as kind of a hideaway. Kid must have been a little unusual."

"He was a loner," Valerie said.

"And ate chicken. And we've extracted DNA from the cigarette butt. Doesn't match Danny's. We're checking wider on that. We'll run it against lots of databases, certainly the military's. Give us another few days. DNA searches take some time. By itself, it doesn't confirm another person up there when he was killed, though. Could have been left at an earlier time."

"Were Danny's pockets empty? Any cash?"

"No money. No ID. Nothing. Empty."

"I've got some stuff for you. This a good time?"

"Proceed."

"I celled with Danny's father at Terminal Island a few years back. Quite a few. He's the one who put Valerie on me. Wilton Crandall was at TI at the same time. Packy, that's Danny's dad, is back inside. Nevada state. For a burglary. I've just come from seeing him."

I took him through the story of the theft and the rumor of the Sultan's Star. I told him I believed that Packy hadn't stolen it, but that I may be the only one. I said someone in Hawaii had got the word to Packy that Danny would get hurt if Packy didn't say where he'd hidden it, so Packy had Danny pay him a visit.

I said, "Packy told him about the Sultan's Star, said it wasn't true that he'd taken it, and told him of the threat. Danny told Packy he'd met Wilton Crandall over here and Crandall asked him if he was Packy's kid and he said he was. Danny told Packy he'd lost a lot of money gambling on the boat and owed most of it to a shylock who worked with Crandall and they'd told him to work it off by stealing from the military. He was doing that and he wanted out.

"Packy told him I could help him with the threat thing and help him get out of the other. That's how my name and number ended up on a note in Danny's stuff that Crandall probably saw when he was passing himself off as his uncle. That maybe explains why Crandall and the guy Richie Cosopoulous's looking for came by looking for me.

"One more thing. Valerie and I were on the Princess Leilani last week and we saw a soldier take a bad beat at the tables. They took him to Fox who sent him into a little room. Kid came out of the room like a whipped puppy. I tagged the car the kid was in after the boat docked and it belongs to a soldier at Schofield. You want the name?"

"You bet," he said. Valerie handed him a note on which she'd written what we had. "Why didn't you give me this sooner?" he asked.

"You'd have said I needed medication."

"Maybe so."

"We've got more. I'll let Muhammad tell it."

Muhammad told him of Orrin Massey, of his ownership and funding of the Children of God, of his military experiences, of his missing twelve years, and of his possible links to Mormon Fundamentalism through his place of birth and his ancestry. And a little about the kind of people the fundamentalists are and their vision of the One Mighty and Strong and the Dream Mine.

Wong said, "So?" Drawing it out. Not with disbelief, but with confusion.

Muhammad said, "Captain, let me speculate. I don't know how Orrin Massey made his money, but I don't think it was through legitimate means. Legitimate businessmen don't disappear for twelve years. I suspect that he is not merely a fundamentalist, but a militant one. Very militant. Perhaps seeing himself as the One Mighty and Strong.

"There are four other locations of the Children of God besides the one here. Each of them is similar to the one here in three ways. They are in warm climates, there is nearby casino gambling, and there is a nearby large population of military.

"Two days ago I was chewing on a suspicion, a theory that goes like this. Massey's operation recruits runaway girls through the Children of God and converts them to prostitutes, recruits soldiers to his theft ring through gambling losses and shylocking. Then Massey gives the soldiers access to the prostitutes, and uses the materials they steal for him to equip a small army. Massey owns twenty thousand acres in northern Idaho. We flew over it yesterday and saw several dozen people in a well-developed compound on a mountaintop. They were in uniform and armed and had a helicopter that may have been armed. What we saw took my suspicion from a theory to a belief. I believe we saw Massey's base of operation and it just may be where guys like Roland Collins go when they fall off the face of the earth."

"*Flew over it yesterday?*" Like he was speaking to Martians.

"Yes. In a charter. Took video and still photos, too. We have copies for you. If we're right about all this, Massey may have been recruiting Danny MacGillicuddy to his army, and if he was and somehow learned that Danny wanted out, he may have had him killed by his soldiers. He certainly can't permit his troops to change their minds." He said we had a photo of Massey and he passed it across the desk.

I said, "There's a possibility Michael Sheffield is related to Orrin Massey. A cousin, maybe."

Wong leaned back in his chair and rubbed his face with both hands, then the back of his neck. He expelled a big breath and said, "Of all the gin joints in the world, you guys had to walk into mine. Mr. Ali… *Muhammad Ali*, is it?"

"Yes. It's a common Muslim name, Captain. I'd be pleased to say I was named after him, but he was still Cassius Clay when I was born."

"Mr. Ali, what do you do?"

"I work in a restaurant."

"Really? You seem a little overqualified for that."

"It's not easy work, Captain. My wife owns it."

"Oh. Then you're probably incompetent."

"Every day."

"Which of these two acquaintances of mine brought you here?"

"Both of them. Mr. Pines and I have worked together for many years in many ways. Whereas Ms. Sabatino and I are only recently met. But I much prefer her to him."

"No kiddin'. I shudder to ask this, but what plans do you guys have for today?"

I said, "We've got a lead on the green car Danny was seen driving. I don't think it's anything bad, but we'll let you know. And he had a girlfriend, told his dad he trusted her, and I think we've found her. I'll let you know about that, too."

"Do that, Harry. And I'll appreciate it. Talk to Bobby. It's his case. Bobby, find this soldier." He handed him the note. "Try to turn him. Scare the shit out of him. Make him one of those offers you can't refuse. And get the photo of this Massey guy on the street. Bring him in. Fox, too. And the Samoan asshole. And anybody you see spittin' on the sidewalk."

"What about Crandall and this Filipino?" I asked. "Can you arrest them?"

"Can and will. Probably lock 'em up tight for about forty minutes before justice prevails and they walk out. I hope you realize you're all in grave danger if ten percent of what you've said is true. If it's all true, you may get gunned down on the front steps walking out of here. Ms. Sabatino…"

"Valerie, Captain." she said.

"Valerie. I've felt your ire before when you think you're being patronized, but I'll risk it again. If I were your father, I'd send you to a convent until all this blows over."

"If I didn't already have a really good father, Captain, I'd ask you to adopt me. But I wouldn't go to the convent."

"No. Of course you wouldn't. Neither would the daughter I've already got." He sighed again. "Who was it said progress was all right once but it's gone on too long?"

"Ogden Nash," Valerie and I said simultaneously, like game show contestants.

"Ogden Nash. I think he had liberated women in mind." He rubbed his face and neck again. "In the meantime, in between time… Valerie, I'm a cop and your nephew was murdered on my beat and I'm real pissed off about it."

• • • • •

Muhammad waited for Richie while Valerie and I went to see a man about a car.

The owner was named Franklin Hayes and he worked civilian security at

Pearl Harbor and said Valerie could see the car there. He had been in the islands since he graduated from high school in Nutley, New Jersey, we knew from Francis's work. He was thirty, unmarried, rented an apartment in Pearl City for $850 a month, which would make it nothing special, but the roof wouldn't leak. He was in his tenth year of employment with a company the government retained to augment their own security efforts at Pearl. No negs.

On the way, I said, "I think right off the bat we should get past the pretense of wanting to buy his car. Can't think what good the hustle will do us. Did he ask you how you knew about it?"

"I told him a guy I know at Schofield told me about it. What do we want from him?"

"I don't know."

"Well, that should keep us from being disappointed."

As soon as we said hello, Valerie said, "Mr. Hayes, I owe you an apology. I don't want to buy your car. Danny MacGillicuddy was my nephew and we want to talk about him."

He got a funny little look, like a dog about to get mean.

"I know it's an imposition," I said. "But we won't take up too much of your time."

He turned to walk away.

I said, "Did you ever go to Manoa with Danny when he went to see the Children of God?"

He stopped and turned around.

"Are you a cop?"

"No, but I know one. I could have him get in touch with you."

"Mr. Hayes," Valerie said. "We told the police we were coming to see you. We're working in cooperation with them. We believe Danny was murdered. So do the police. We know you knew him well enough to ask him to sell cars for you. He was seen driving your Toyota after he went AWOL. Did you see him then? Can you give us an idea as to why he went AWOL?"

Nothing.

I took a shot. "Don't let yourself become a suspect in this, Mr. Hayes. This conversation'll be easier than the next one."

"Yes, I knew him. He sold a few cars for me. For commission. At Schofield. He was selling the one you called about when he disappeared. We weren't pals. We were doing business. I buy cars, repair them and sell them. I sold a

Wrangler to Danny. That's how I met him. I never heard of whoever you said was in Manoa. I didn't see him when he went AWOL. I don't know why he went AWOL. When I heard he was missing, I went to Schofield and picked up my car. Anything else?"

"Where did you find the car? When you went to pick it up?"

"Schofield."

"Where at Schofield?"

"In the parking lot behind the PX."

"How did you know it was there?"

"I didn't, but that's where he usually kept them."

"Do you know Michael Sheffield?"

"I've met him. Through Danny. Can't say I know him."

"Okay. Sorry we got off on the wrong foot."

"Not a problem. Keep me out of this." And he walked off.

· · · · ·

Esther Monroe worked as a guide in the Polynesian Cultural Center a few miles past Kahuku Point, not far from her favorite bar. She lived a half-mile away from her job in a rented house in the tiny seaside village of Laie. She was from Minneapolis, a graduate of Carleton College with a degree in Art History, twenty-four, single, and clean as a nun. She wasn't expecting us.

"What's your approach?" I asked Valerie as we drove.

"Straightforward's the most fun. What do you think?"

"I think what's the most fun is the way we should decide everything."

Straightforward woman-to-woman worked fine.

Valerie said, "Esther, my name is Valerie and my nephew, who is now dead, knew your friend Betsy. Maybe you, too. This is my friend, Harry. We're trying to reconstruct what happened to my nephew."

She was startled. "Was your nephew Danny MacGillicuddy?"

"Yes."

"How awful what happened. I didn't know Danny very well, just talked to him once or twice. But Betsy did. She dated him. She's really broken up about it."

"What's Betsy's last name?"

"Fielding."

"Where does she work?"

"At the Turtle Bay Resort. She's a sales rep."

"Oh, that's not far. We'll go see her."

"She's not there. She's in Honolulu today, making calls. I just talked to her a little while ago. I could give you the number... I don't know... Maybe I shouldn't."

"You're probably right. Maybe you could just call her and say we're here and would like a few minutes of her time. We could meet her somewhere."

"Okay. I'll do it."

She got Betsy Fielding on her cell phone and said, "Hey, Bets. There's a nice woman here in my office who was Danny's aunt. She wonders if she could talk to you about Danny." Pause. "I don't know." To Valerie, she said, "She wants to know what about."

"I don't know either," Valerie said. "I'm just trying... May I speak with her?"

Esther handed her the phone.

Valerie said, "Betsy? Hi. I'm Valerie. Danny was my nephew. I'm just trying to put together some of the pieces of Danny's life. I know you knew him. Could I meet you somewhere? For coffee or lunch or something?" Pause. "Sure. After work would be fine. Where?" Pause. "No, but I'm sure my boyfriend does." To me: "Honey, do you know where Blue Indigo is?"

"Chinatown?" I asked. Betsy heard me say it I guess, because Valerie nodded into the phone.

"What time's good for you?" Pause. "Five's fine. What are you wearing?" Pause. "Oh, I love Nicole Miller. I saw her new line in San Diego just last week. Can I bring Harry?" Pause. "Okay." Pause. "Sure. Can I have yours, too." And gave out her cell phone number and then recited another one and glanced at me as she said it. So I wrote it down. "Thanks so much. 'Bye." She handed the phone to Esther who signed off.

Esther, puzzled, said to her, "How'd you find me? How did you know I knew Betsy and Danny?"

Somewhat straightforwardly, Valerie said, "A friend of Danny's told us he had a girlfriend named Betsy that he thought he'd met at the Texas Paniolo. He described her. So we sort of hired the bartender to keep an eye out. When he finally ran into you guys the other night he got, I don't know, flustered maybe, and got your phone number instead of hers. He gave it to us."

"I remember that. Doesn't usually happen when I'm with Betsy. You think he kept it for himself, too?"

"Unless he's nuts," I said. "I'd've kept it." She grinned.

We left, but gratefully. Very gratefully. Women are great at being grateful to each other. But you can't rush it.

Walking to the car, I said, "You are profoundly full of shit."

"The boyfriend thing? All this time I've been sleeping with you if you don't think that makes you my boyfriend, I'll move back to the Royal Hawaiian. Or you will. You were pretty full of shit your ownself, flirting like that."

"Just thought she needed a little boost."

"Listen, *honey*, women like it when other women show up with boyfriends. If another guy comes along, there's no competition. And if another guy doesn't come along, you can flirt with the boyfriend. You can't expect to be a world class sleuth until you learn how to think like a woman. Maybe you should take on a partner."

• • • • •

On the way back to Kailua, I called Bobby Bentley and told him Franklin Hayes looked okay, just a guy selling a car. And I said we'd found Danny's girlfriend and had a date to meet her at five o'clock at Blue Indigo. He said thanks for the call.

At home, I asked Jerry, who was on duty, if we'd received anything. He said look under the stairs.

Under the stairs there was a large canvas duffel bag. I unzipped it and emptied it. A Sig Blaser LRS2 magnum rifle with a scope. Three five-round magazines with .300 caliber shells. Three .357 Glocks. Three silencers. Six magazines, thirteen rounds each. Several holsters, belt and ankle. Three Benelli over-under shotguns. Several boxes of tight pattern loads. A Magellan Meridian GPS receiver. Three pairs of night vision goggles. Two combat knives in sheaths. Two boxes of disposable plastic restraining cuffs. Three C-Guard cellular jamming devices, each about the size of a box of cigars with velcro straps. Two or three other things. And a velvet pouch.

I opened the pouch and dumped a blue-green stone into Valerie's hand. I said, "The Sultan's Marble. Think it'd fool anybody?"

"Depends on who the anybody is, I guess. What've you got in mind with all this? World War Three?"

"Just covering all the bases."

"What's this thing?" She held one of the cellular jammers.

"It's a cellular jammer. Put it on a roof or a wall, turn it on, and it shuts down cellular transmission for up to two hundred meters."

I put it all back in the bag and zipped it closed.

"I hope you don't have to use any of that," she said.

"Be my preference, too. I'd like them to just surrender."

I called Francis who was five thousand miles away and asked him to take a look at Betsy Fielding, sales rep at the Turtle Bay Resort, asked him to give it priority. Then I phoned Richie who was only fifty yards away.

"You get a positive on the mug shots?" I asked.

"Yeah. His name's Melvin Villafrania."

"Which means he's got a record."

"Yeah."

"What for?"

"Armed robbery. Did four years in the state pen."

"How you doin'?"

"Good. Working on my database. Got pictures and profiles on everybody you've run into so far. It's pretty nifty."

"Valerie and I've got a five o'clock appointment on the other side with Danny's girlfriend. I'll get with you before we leave."

"Cool."

I called Francis back and gave him Melvin Villafrania, too. Just for good measure.

I called Sam Dodson and asked him what his plans were. He said they were settled on the other side and would be for a while.

"Okay. I feel bad about this."

"Don't, Harry. We're solid with you. Solid. Do your job. We're not packing up, just playing safe for a few days. I'll have your map later today. I'll bring it over or have it delivered."

"Okay. Thanks. You mind if I use your apartment, let the security guys stay there? They're good people, I think. I'll make sure everything's shipshape."

"How about putting Muhammad in our place. Put them in his. Save on the wear and tear."

"Good idea. Need anything?"

"Information. Keep in touch. I'll be on my cell. Tell Valerie and Muhammad we're on the team, pulling for all of you."

I told Valerie I thought I'd take a run on the beach. She said she'd join me. After a slow half-mile, I said, "I'm going to blow out the pipes. Do you mind if I open up a little?"

"Let's go," she said, and we set off at about a six-minute mile clip. She stayed with me for a few minutes and then slowed. "Jog," I said. "I'll turn around in ten minutes and pick you up on the way back."

When I turned, I saw her in the distance heading back toward home. It made me uneasy, seeing her so far away from my protection. I decided not to tell her that though, out of stark fear she'd cut my balls off. I closed on her and when she heard me coming she picked up her pace. I drew even and we sprinted the last few hundred yards and ran full tilt into the surf.

We showered and she said she thought she'd take a nap. I joined her but when I realized she actually wanted to take a nap, I got up quietly and went downstairs.

I went online and found email from Francis, reports on Betsy Fielding and Melvin Villafrania, including photos. Melvin was just another tinhorn gun hand. From the hotel's web site, Francis had downloaded a group photo of the sales and catering team. Betsy made the rest of them invisible.

A little later, Valerie came downstairs, dressed for the cocktail hour, and I passed the printouts to her. She took the chair and read while I boiled water for gunpowder green tea and poured two mugs.

"Anything strike you about Betsy?" she asked.

"Yeah. But you go first."

"She's too hot for Danny. You can't tell too much from the group photo, but she looks pretty damn good. Too old, too. Twenty-five-year old babes don't pick up twenty-year-old soldiers in bars and go off on a fling with them. He wasn't bad looking, but nothing special. Not a babe magnet."

"Not like me, you mean?"

She snorted. "You're a matron magnet."

I let it pass. I said, "And she got kicked off the UCLA cheerleading squad for reasons unknown. But not likely good behavior."

"How about the Filipino?"

"Just something you'd scrape off the sidewalk."

I called Richie and said I was forwarding the emails from Francis to his computer. I told him who Betsy Fielding was and asked him to work with the photo to get a larger image of her. I asked him to tell Muhammad what we had when he got home, said ask him to move into Sam and Teresa's, and tell him I'd be on my cell phone, but not to expect us back until maybe ten or so, thinking we'd have dinner out. I asked him to insist that Jerry, Jack, and Jim move into Muhammad's apartment after he'd cleared out. I hung up.

"You look fabulous," I said to Valerie, in a rare moment of complete candor. She was wearing some kind of nubby silk pantsuit, somewhere between beige and lemon and a loose, sleeveless brown blouse. And brown medium-high heels with a sling back. Take my word for it. "And I look like shit. Let me see if I can find something to wear that won't embarrass you." And went upstairs to change.

When I came back down, not looking all that much better by any standards, to say nothing of compared to her, I found her in the office, looking at the wall maps.

"Harry," she said, turning to me. "Do I look like a genius?"

"No. Not my first notion, no. You look like somebody who might *be* a genius, but a normal guy wouldn't be able to think about how smart you are until after he got you in bed."

"You are so sweet. I think I've figured out this bible thing. If Danny wanted to record the coordinates of a place up there near where he was killed, say a place where he hid something, he wouldn't have to use all of it. He could get by with just the second digit of the minutes and both digits of the seconds. Maybe just the seconds if it was real close. I mean it's all longitude one fifty-seven, fiftyish. Latitude twenty-one, thirtyish. And if he didn't want to store the coordinates in his GPS where somebody might look for it, he could have gone to the Book of Daniel in the bible and underlined the passages that matched the numbers, the last numbers of the location. Like this."

She then wrote the full coordinates of the clearing on two post-it notes and pinned them to the map on the wall. One read 21, 33, 32 and the other read 157, 56, 26. Then, below the first, she wrote the first of the bible citations—3, 33—lining it up flush right with the final numerals. On the other note she wrote both citations—6, 24 and 6, 25—lining up both numbers flush right, also.

"Now, I happen to know, because I looked into it, that at the equator one minute of longitude equals one mile. So, one second, one sixtieth of a minute is eighty-eight feet. Which is the result of dividing 5,280 by sixty. It's less as the altitude rises and less as the distance from the equator increases. But we're pretty far south and the elevation in question is only about 2,000 feet so let's just stay with the basic proposition. If I'm right, then these bible notations indicate a location approximately eighty-eight feet north and one hundred thirty-two feet east of the clearing. One hundred thirty-two because he underlined two citations so my guess is he meant to split the distance. Up," she pointed, "and over."

I was mute, dumbstruck.

She said, "Want to go up there after dinner? See what's there?"

"Maybe tomorrow. Let's go meet Betsy."

• • • • •

Blue Indigo is a busy after-work spot. Mock pagoda architecture on the downtown side of Chinatown. Tasty appetizers—"pupus" in the local patois—and fair drink prices. And Boodles, to boot.

We got there ten minutes early and seated ourselves at an open-air table with a view of the street. Twenty minutes later, a black Porsche Boxster with the top down cruised by slowly. A car pulled out of its parking space just in front and the Boxster, driven by a beautiful woman with shoulder-length, light brown hair, slid into the empty spot. She was wearing an expensive-looking linen skirtsuit and heels not made for walking. She hurried up and paused at the entrance.

Valerie went to her and greeted her like she was truly happy to meet her, which she was. She brought her to the table and I stood for my introduction.

I pulled out a chair for her and helped her remove her jacket. She wore a loose flower-print blouse that wasn't loose enough to hide an impressive rack, and a strand of pearls.

"I'm so glad you could come," Valerie said. She was a little overeager, but I decided to let it play out.

Betsy glanced at her watch. "I don't have an awful lot of time," she said.

"Then let me go to the bar and get you a drink. That'll save time."

She asked for a Campari and soda and I went for it. It took a few minutes which gave the matrons at the bar a chance to ogle me. The babes looked away. Back at the table, Valerie said to me, "Betsy and Danny were fixed up. Isn't that nice?"

Not according to the guy who was with Danny when he met her.

"Did you ever go on the boat with him?" I asked. "The Princess Leilani? I heard he liked to gamble. From his father. I'm an old friend of his," I explained. "That's how we met." Indicating Valerie and me. "In prison. Not Valerie and me. Danny's daddy and me." I was playing the fool, maybe not playing, just sort of tossing chum over the side, seeing if any of it would attract attention. "So, did you? Go on the boat?"

"Sure. Lots of times."

"Esther told us you're in sales with the Turtle Bay Resort. I bet the Princess Leilani is a real asset, isn't it? A sales feature, I mean."

"Yes, it is. It's kind of far from where we are, but some of our guests access it by helicopter. The boat has one and so does the hotel."

"How was Danny? I mean before he disappeared. Was anything bothering him?"

She looked down, said, "Not that I could tell. Not a care in the world."

"Did he ever tell you about something he had was, I don't know, worth some money?"

She shook her head. She was quiet, fiddled with a pretty pearl ring on her index finger.

"Did you know Danny's friend Mike Sheffield?"

"Uh-huh. That's who introduced us."

"How about another guy he knew. Eric Fox."

She blinked. "Uh, no. Don't think so."

"He works on the boat. Big, dark, good-looking guy. Thought maybe you ran into him there."

"No. Can't say I did." She looked at her watch. It was about seven minutes later than the last time she looked. "Listen, I'm really on short time. Valerie, let's keep in touch. Call me anytime. I just feel terrible about Danny. I know how you must feel. Just call anytime." She took the last half of her drink in one gulp and excused herself. Drove off in her Boxster.

"I was nervous," Valerie said.

"You smelled she wasn't right."

"I did. She's a lying little bitch."

"With a better lifestyle than you'd expect from a hotel sales rep. She must be good at her job. Question is, 'Which job?'"

Valerie's phone chirped. She answered. "Oh. Hi." Pause. "Yes. That's him." Pause. "Okay." And handed me the phone, saying, "It's Betsy. Wants to talk with you."

Into the phone, I said, "Betsy?"

"I, uh, I need to, uh, talk with you."

"Okay."

"Someplace else. Not there."

"Okay."

"Do you know Punchbowl? How it's laid out?"

"Pretty much. I've been there."

"My, uh… Section O. Can you find that?"

"Sure."

"Fifteen minutes?"

"We'll be there." I closed the phone. "She wants to talk. Place not far from here. Let's go."

Punchbowl Crater is the site of the National Memorial Cemetery of the Pacific. Tens of thousands of veterans and their families are buried there in neat rows marked with white crosses. It's a smaller version of Arlington National. Centuries ago, to appease the gods, humans were sacrificed in the volcano at the crater's center. It was called Puowaina, which translates to Hill of Sacrifice. Now, it's Punchbowl and it's dormant and in a place, overlooking the Pacific and the city, that would be chilling even if its purpose wasn't.

It's just mauka of downtown. We took the Pali until it crossed Lunalilo, then a quick right on Iolani to intersect with the access road that wraps around Punchbowl and enters it on the high side. A map of the layout at the entrance indicated Section O off to the left. I drove in that direction until we saw Betsy's car and parked beside it. We got out and saw her fifty yards away, up a rise, standing at a grave.

She said, "This is my grandfather's grave. He was killed in Korea. I never knew him. Of course." Her cheeks were tear-streaked. She looked at me. "Danny told me about you. Told me his daddy said you were somebody who could help him. I guess you couldn't, could you?"

"I didn't get the chance. He didn't call me."

"Can you help me?"

"Yes. Can and will."

"I don't know…where to begin."

"Just blurt it out."

"I used Danny. For Eric. Eric Fox. I was in love with him. With Eric, not Danny. He hurt me…used me… broke my heart. He has…a way with women. Sure, he does. He's a fucking pimp! They're all good with women. Stupid women, especially. I got so…messed up. I'm so embarrassed." She cried. Valerie went to her and held her, wrapped her up tight, cooed to her, and she wailed, broke into deep, stomach-wrenching sobs.

"It's all right, Betsy," Valerie said. "It's all right. It's going to be fine from now on. It is. It really is. You're going to be fine. You've found friends now. We'll help."

There was a bench, just a marble slab, and Valerie walked her to it and sat down beside her with her arm around her shoulders. I sat on the grass at their feet with my legs folded. Valerie took a clump of tissues from her purse and dabbed Betsy's cheeks. She took the tissues and blew her nose into them, straightened up.

She said, "You shouldn't help me. You should hate me."

I said, "We were getting ready to hate you. But then you called. Now we don't hate you. Now we love you."

She small smiled, but not for long. She crunched her face up and said, "Please believe I had no idea what was going to happen to Danny. Ooooh. That's not true, either. I just didn't know how bad it would be. I knew they were angry with him. But God! They killed him! I know they did and I didn't know *that* would happen. I don't know… maybe I just didn't think about it, didn't *want* to think about it."

I said, "Fox and Sheffield told you to make Danny fall in love with you. Is that right?"

"Yes."

"And to get him to confide in you."

"Yes."

"And he did?"

"Yes."

"He told you he was stealing for them and he told you he wanted out and you told them."

"Yes."

"Did he tell you somebody was threatening him about a jewel?"

"Yes. The jewel was what it was all about in the beginning. That was my job, to get him to talk about the jewel. I really couldn't without coming right out and asking him about it and if I did that he'd know I wasn't…what I seemed to be. So I tried to string him along, said things like maybe we could be happy together if he had more money." She dabbed her nose. "Nice girl, huh? He didn't say anything about it until the day he came back from seeing his daddy. Then he told me. And he said he didn't know anything about it and neither did his daddy. But when I told Eric he didn't believe it."

"Did Danny hide something in the mountains?"

"I don't know. He went up there a lot on his own. He could have, I guess. He didn't say anything to me about it, though."

"Have you met Orrin Massey?"

"Yes. He's the most dreadful man. He made my skin crawl. He's big and he has these crazy eyes, real close together, and he giggles. He told me he was destined to change the world. He called himself the 'one mighty and strong.' Like it was his name or something. He's the one behind all this. He's awful. They're all awful, but he's the worst. And that's saying something."

"Did Orrin Massey try to hire Danny?"

"Yes. He wanted him to come to work with him when he got out. He was about to get out. Danny told him yes, said he would, told me he was going to make a lot of money. Then one night Danny came to me and just broke down." She sobbed. "Valerie, Danny was the sweetest boy who ever lived. Wouldn't swat a fly." She took a deep breath. "Danny said he'd found out they were killers. He thought it was some kind of security job but he found out Orrin Massey is some kind of religious fanatic. The job wasn't security. It was some kind of crazy army. Killing Massey's enemies. People he didn't even know. People who, I don't know, just got in his way, I guess. Danny said he'd found out they had killed that bunch of homeless people the night before. For practice."

"And you told Eric Fox what Danny said?"

She shuddered and folded up inside herself. "Yes. They're going to kill me now. When they find out I've talked to you."

"No, they're not," Valerie said. "We're going to protect you. We'll take you with us. To our house. It's safe. We'll get you a very good lawyer and we'll all go to the police together. It may be hard for a while, but we'll work through it. We'll stand beside you."

"Do you think... Will I go to jail?"

I said, "I don't know, but I don't think so. We'll fight hard to keep you out. Let's go home."

We went to my Rover and Valerie climbed in the back with Betsy. I took her keys and closed the top of the Boxster and locked it. We drove off.

Betsy blew her nose again and said, "I'm gonna need a lawyer."

Valerie said, "Betsy, we've got lawyers runnin' out our ears."

"What about clothes? I don't have any clothes."

"We've got clothes, too. Four women live at our house. We've got plenty clothes. And five big, strong, dangerous men to look after us. Six, if you count Harry." And Betsy laughed.

· · · · ·

There was a long black limousine backed into the carport. One of the Hawaiians was on the front porch.

I said to Betsy, "This is Jack. Or maybe Jim." To him, I said, "This is Betsy. Don't let anything happen to her."

He shook her hand and looked at her with unconcealed admiration. "Jack. I'm Jack. Man! The hits just keep on comin'. And to think I get paid for this."

"Where's everybody?" I asked.

"Jerry and Cindy are out back. Jim's in the big room, watching television or shooting pool."

"Where's Leanne?"

"I'm not exactly sure, but she's here. Maybe in with Jim."

"Which leaves Muhammad and Richie."

"And they're in Richie's place, I believe."

Leanne emerged from the Great Room. Valerie introduced her to Betsy, said, "Betsy's going to be staying with us for a few days. She'll need clothes."

"Cool. We got clothes. My sofa makes a bed, Betsy. We'll be roomies. Come on. I'll settle you in."

Valerie and I went to my office and I called Sam. I said, "We've got a big break on this thing. Danny's girlfriend, Betsy Fielding. She was one of the bad guys but now she's turned. We're putting her up over here for a few days to keep an eye on her. This thing's messy. She needs a real good criminal lawyer."

"Got one just down the hall. Hold on. I'll get my guy on the phone."

Muhammad came in. I said, "How'd it go?"

"It worked okay, I think. I met Massey."

"I want to hear about it soon as I'm off this call." To Valerie, I said, "Tell him where we are." They went into the front room. I said, "Hey, Valerie. Tell him what you figured out on the map."

Sam came back on, said, "Harry Pines, say hello to Walter McCall." I did. I said, "I've got a woman in my custody who's what I think you might call an unwitting accessory to a murder. And maybe a few other things. She's been a bad girl. She wants to turn state's evidence, straighten her life out. I want to call Dick Wong at HPD and tell him I've got her. But I don't want to bring her to him without you there."

"Why don't I call Wong?" he said.

"No. I want to. I owe it to him."

"Okay. Tell him we'll bring her in tomorrow. But I want to talk with her first."

"You free tonight?"

He sighed. "It's my wife's birthday."

"Bring her along. We'll put together a birthday dinner for her right here. It's a nice place. Sam knows. He lives here."

Sam said, "Harry, does this woman implicate this Massey guy?"

"Completely. And his little army. Danny MacGillicuddy told her they killed those seven homeless people."

"Walt, this is big," Sam said. "If this thing unpeels like I think it might, it'll be network news. You'll be rich and famous. And you guys haven't even seen the maps I've got. They tie it all together, Harry. Call Jamie, Walt. Teresa and I'll come along, make you feel at home. Even drive you over and drive you back."

I said, "Walt, we'll show your wife a good time, try to make her forgive you for changing plans."

"Okay."

"See you in about an hour," Sam said.

I called Bobby Bentley. I said, "Bobby, Danny's girlfriend, Betsy Fielding, wasn't actually his girlfriend. She was a plant. For Sheffield and Fox and Orrin Massey. She's had enough, wants to come clean. She's here with us now. Protected. Her lawyer's on his way over here to sit down with her. We'll bring her to you tomorrow."

"What's she got to say?"

"That Fox planted her. That Danny was stealing for Fox and wanted out. That Orrin Massey tried to recruit him for his army. That Danny said okay and then came to his senses when he found out it wasn't a security job, it was a killing machine. That Danny told her Massey's guys killed those homeless people. Danny told Betsy all of it. She told Fox and Massey all of it. That enough?"

"Yeah. That's enough. Nine o'clock?"

"We'll be there."

I hustled through the front room saying to Muhammad and Valerie as I passed them, "We got a criminal lawyer for Betsy. Sam's bringing him over in about an hour to talk with her. With their wives. For a birthday party. Lawyer's wife. Help me get things started and then we'll talk."

Cindy was in the kitchen with Jerry. "Help," I said to her. "We're throwing a birthday party tonight. For the wife of Betsy's lawyer. Her name's Jamie. Can you guys throw in with Valerie and Muhammad and rustle up a meal? And a birthday cake? And a party? Be all of us, plus four more. Sam and Teresa are coming, too." As I passed them by on my way to Leanne's I heard Cindy say, "Who's Betsy?"

I knocked on Leanne's door and she opened it. Betsy was behind her. "Leanne, we need help with dinner. Get Richie, too. Big birthday party. Betsy, I just hired you a criminal lawyer. Good one. He'll be here in about an hour to talk with you. Wash your face or whatever girls do when they meet their lawyer. All you got to do is tell it all and tell it straight. We're about to turn your life around. You up for it?"

"I guess so."

• • • • •

The pace of the place got a little madcap. You couldn't walk through a room without bumping into somebody hustling a chore. They were cooking in the kitchen, cooking on the Weber, setting the table, both tables, cutting flowers and putting out vases. Even Betsy got into the act. I found her seated before a pile of buds from our garden. Wearing somebody's shorts and sleeveless shirt and no makeup, and looking like the prettiest cheerleader at UCLA.

"What are you doing?" I asked.

"Making leis."

"Oh. Got your game face on?"

She nodded and smiled and reached out her hand. I took it and she said, "Thanks, Harry. For all this. Are you my guardian angel?"

"You bet, baby. Everybody needs one and everybody's got one. I'm yours."

"Who's yours?"

"Muhammad."

On my way into the kitchen, I bumped into Valerie who stopped me and put her arms around me and gave me a huge kiss. "I lurve you, Harry Pines. I truly do. You are my hero."

"Who was that guy directed all those screwball Hollywood comedies back in the forties? People skittering around all over the place, hiding in the pantry, bumping into each other? For fifty points."

"Preston Sturges. Why?"

"I think he's behind this party."

When Sam's car pulled in, the girls rushed out and put leis on everybody's neck and sang "Happy Birthday, Jamie" to a total stranger who, for some reason, got all teary-eyed about it. Walt and Jamie were about the size of leprechauns. He was jolly and plump and she was red-haired and cute and top-heavy. But not in a bad way. If there is one. Cindy and Richie took drink orders and filled and delivered them. We toasted Jamie and I said, "Okay, everybody engage in unsupervised recreation while Walt and Betsy talk."

I took them into my office. Muhammad and Valerie and Sam followed. I said to Walt, "Muhammad and Valerie are attorneys. Not that you need them. Just wanted you to know we got a deep bench. How d'you want to handle this?"

"Who knows the most about this case? You?"

"It's a three-way tie."

"Well, Sam and I want to talk with just one of you alone and then with Betsy alone. Choose."

"Me," I said. We went into the office and he closed the door and sat at the desk and pulled out a leather-bound pad and a pen. I told him and Sam in ten minutes pretty much everything I knew. Then Sam gave me the maps, told me how to use them, and I left them alone with Betsy and joined Muhammad and Valerie.

Muhammad said, "Orrin Massey's an imposing figure. Quite large. Taller than you and wide, but not fat. Looks very solid. And eerie. He seems to teeter between compelling and daft."

He told us how he worked the Waikiki strip that day with Jack and Jim in the limo, leaving his phone number with concierges and bell captains, saying he was interested in gambling while he was on his holiday. Eventually, he got a call. The caller identified himself as "Wilton" and Muhammad agreed to meet him at the Pacific Beach Hotel at the Diamond Head end of Waikiki.

"In the lobby," Wilton said.

"No," Muhammad said. "In my car. I'll send my man in for you."

"There are financial requirements," Wilton said.

"I'm certain I can meet them."

He waited in the limousine at the Pacific Beach while Jim went in the hotel and returned with Wilton Crandall. In the back, Muhammad opened a briefcase that was packed tight with $100 bills. "There are one thousand of that denomination here. Will that be sufficient?"

Wilton made a call. "My associate will see you," he said after he hung up. "Come with me."

"Ride with us. I'll bring you back."

They drove back through Waikiki to the Ilikai, a high-rise tower overlooking the Yacht Harbor.

"I'll take you up," he said when they arrived at the main entrance.

"Gentlemen, please accompany me," Muhammad said to the men in the front.

"No, just you," Wilton said.

"No, we'll all come."

Reluctantly, he led Muhammad, carrying the briefcase, and Jack and Jim through the lobby and to the elevator which they took to the 18th floor. A Samoan, about Muhammad's size, met the elevator. He looked a little surprised at the entourage, but led them down the hall to a door that opened to a large room with a panoramic view of the ocean. Jack and Jim entered the room and moved sideways, one to each side of the door, where they stood with their backs to the wall.

A man with dark hair and a dark mustache introduced himself to Muhammad as Eric Fox.

"And you are?" he asked Muhammad.

"Ah. I am the man with a hundred thousand dollars who wishes to gamble."

"Yes. But what shall I call you?"

"Muhammad Ali."

Fox smiled. "Yes, of course. We are associated with the Princess Leilani, a beautiful ship which provides casino gambling for our selected friends. In international waters. May I examine the contents of the briefcase?"

Muhammad handed it to him. He took it to a long, white sectional sofa and opened it. Muhammad stayed with him. He took several of the bills out and examined them closely, then closed it and gave it back to Muhammad.

Another man emerged from a room to the side, making a conspicuous show of zipping his fly. "Lovely moment," he said. "Just lovely."

Muhammad recognized him as Massey. He looked at him, expecting to be introduced, but he was not. Massey said, "You're a big fellow."

Muhammad said nothing.

"I said, 'You're a big fellow.' Played football, I'll bet."

Muhammad said nothing.

"And a little rude, too. Need to learn your manners."

"I'm not the one who walked into the room with his fly open," Muhammad said.

Massey laughed, looked at Jack and Jim against the wall, said to the Samoan, "Manny, old top, think you could handle these boys."

Manny snickered. Jim said, "Not any boys here."

Fox said, "We have a new customer here, Orrin. Looking for a hundred thousand dollars worth of action."

Massey said, "In my experience, those who gamble have more money than sense. When they arrive, in any case."

Muhammad said to Fox, "Can we do business?"

"We would be pleased to have you as our guest," Fox said. "The Princess Leilani disembarks at 8:00 this evening from Honolulu Harbor."

"I prefer a later departure," Muhammad said. "My wife retires early. She won't be coming, of course. When it's convenient, perhaps tonight, perhaps tomorrow, I would like to phone and make the arrangement. But I'm sure eight o'clock will be too early. Are there other arrangements that can be made?"

As it turned out, there were. Departure, when Muhammad was ready, would be from the rooftop heliport of the Ilikai.

We spread Sam's maps out on the coffee table. They were about three-feet by four, and in color.

One was of a style called axonometric, having a three-dimensional aspect. It portrayed, from the east-looking-west view, the entire mountaintop as we'd seen it in our first low pass, with each of the structures and people seen in perspective, by way of expressing their relative heights as well as their actual positions.

The other was flat, two-dimensional, lacking the more interesting perspective and without the people, but, Sam had said, "more precise in the lateral dimensions." It indicated the clearing to be 475 yards by 250.

There were eighteen people on the axonometric map, all in the same colored clothing. Three of them were running for the helicopter, ten by the cottages, and five at the other, non-residential end of the clearing.

At the residential end, there were utilitarian-looking things that appeared to be a septic tank, a modest water tower, and a structure that perhaps enclosed a generator. The main lodge was impressive, a wooden, rambling two-and-a-half stories with many balconies and two roof-mounted satellite dishes. In front of the main building in a paved turnaround was a large SUV. There were five cottages in the horseshoe on each side of the main building and evidence of ground broken for two more. Something was stacked in front of one of them.

The thing that looked to my eye like an obstacle course as we passed still looked like that, a training field. A narrow strip of paved road branched off from the larger strip to meet the "unfinished road" at the place where it reached the mountaintop. At the other end, the vehicle that I thought carried something fixed and high-caliber now looked like a pickup truck with a large weapon on a tripod in its bed. Next to it was a bulldozer and a pickup truck with a load of something white. And off to the side, what looked like two portable toilets. And the two quonset huts.

Valerie said, "Women there, too, wouldn't you think? That's part of the deal."

"You'd think at least one for each guy," Muhammad said. "Which would make some of these cottages multi-family. Unless some stay in the big house. It's plenty big enough."

"Children, maybe?" she said.

"Most likely infants if there are," he said.

"There aren't any women there," I said. "Or children. If there were, surely some of them would have come out of the cottages to check out all the commotion. Wonder if some of the soldiers are women."

"No chance," Muhammad said. "Women aren't entitled to be soldiers with these people."

"Look closely at these cottages," I said. "No power lines connect with them. At least you can't see any. There's a generator at this end behind the quonset huts and another here behind the big house. And power lines are visible feeding from both of them to the huts and to the big house. This thing behind the big house is a water tank and this one is probably a septic tank but unless it connects to the cottages underground, which would be a big job, they don't have toilets. So nobody's living there. See this truck at the other end? That could be construction material, maybe drywall in it. And this could be a stack of drywall by this cottage. These cottages aren't finished. These people were working on them when we passed over."

"So whoever lives there is in the big house?" Valerie asked.

"Or the quonsets. Using the portable toilets. But no water tank down there."

"So, are those just construction workers?" Valerie asked.

"Not just," I said. "These are soldiers doing construction work."

"If they don't live there, where do they live?"

I shrugged. "Someplace else. Bountiful, maybe. It's not far. They may be operating this compound like a firehouse, crews work there for a couple of days, then go back to their women and other crews come in. You know, there's nothing particularly defensible about this place other than the ground itself, the high ground. No emplacements. No barriers to overcome. No fencing. What we have here is a work in progress."

The office door opened and the three of them came out, Betsy a little red-eyed, the two men looking slightly happy.

I said, to Walt, "So…You her lawyer?"

He said, "If she'll have me."

"Betsy?"

"Sure."

I said, "Betsy, is Mike Sheffield related to Orrin Massey?"

"Yes. He's his cousin. Harry…if you'd heard what I told them just now… Are you sure you want to help me?"

"Sure. We all do. Don't you want to help us?"

She sniffled and nodded. She said, "I did some pretty bad things."

"Everybody deserves another chance. You'll redeem yourself."

Walt said, "Cheer up, Betsy. There'll be some tough times to come, but we'll get through them together. You might have to go through that embarrassing booking business tomorrow. Get, you know, fingerprinted and photographed all that, but if we don't walk out of there together in the sunshine of a pretty day, you should fire me. And nobody fires Walter McCall."

"And then what?" I said.

"Well, the future is a little less clear. Against us is she's been, by any standards, an accessory to some pretty bad things. For us is she's willing to bust it all up like the rack on a pool table. Without Betsy, it'd take them 'til the cows come home to do it." He put an arm around her shoulder and said, "I'm your lawyer, Betsy. Trust me completely. Always tell me the truth and I'll be your shield. I'll stand in front of you when things get tough. Am I hired?"

"How … I don't have …"

"I have," I said. "You're hired."

"Part of my fee is you guys have to make my wife glad she came."

"Let's take a whack at it."

And we rejoined the party.

● ● ● ● ●

I don't know if we did. I think we did. You expose a not particularly outgoing woman on her birthday to a bunch of strangers who tend to treat the postman like he's George Clooney and, I don't know, it could be too much. But at least too much of a good thing.

The meal was a roasted yellow pepper soup from Richie, a crab and green tomato salad from Cindy, with Richie's leftover chilled gazpacho as a dressing, three of Leanne's oven-roasted bass stuffed with dill and red pepper and basil and other things, three three-pound hens that Richie and Cindy roasted Barbara Kafka's way—high heat and fast—a lot of blanched asparagus with chanterelles and wilted spinach from Muhammad, and a double fudge birthday cake from Valerie that said "Happy Birthday, Jamie" on top.

And a lot of wine.

Things broke up like they do, slowly at first, and then in a rush. I think first off, though it's none of my business, Cindy took Jerry away to a moment he wouldn't soon forget. Jack and Jim drew the short straws for guard duty and Leanne and Betsy sat outside with them and fed them grapes and made them laugh. Teresa told me she was proud of me and if they had a boy they were thinking of naming him Samuel Harrison and calling him Harry and I think I got a little stupid about that. I told Richie he was getting close to becoming a really attractive guy and he said fuck off, I was a latent and I hadn't even seen his database. I was sort of drunk and sort of happy. And oblivious to my life's lessons of the danger of contentment with myself.

Valerie and I walked the foursome from the other side to their car. Betsy came down from the lanai and kissed Jamie on the cheek and said to Walt, "I am so glad you think enough of me to represent me. I'm really grateful." And Walt gave her a little hug.

As they drove off, Valerie peeled off and joined the group on the front lanai. Muhammad said to me, "I've got a couple of cigars. Want one?"

"You bet."

We went out back and lit up Cohibas and he said, "You're doing good work, Harry. I'm proud of you."

A niggling feeling arose from wherever feelings are stored. I didn't want it to ruin my mood so I ignored it. I said, "Muhammad, I'd still be shufflin' around if it wasn't for you. I'm not going to tell you how many times I look at something and think, okay, what would it take here to make Muhammad proud of me."

"We've busted this thing. You have."

That was it, the memory of premature congratulations. I said, "Don't say that. Every time I reach around to pat myself on the back something bad happens."

We unlocked the back gate and went to the beach. The surf was in a friendly swooshing churn. We walked down near the water's edge, the tide rising.

"What now?" he said.

"I guess get enough from Betsy tomorrow and they'll arrest them all."

"And then?"

"Yeah. Probably all get off, won't they?"

He said, "It won't be any easy prosecution unless they turn a lot of people.

Work their way up the ladder one snitch at a time. But you didn't sign on to do anything but find out who did it. And you got that done."

"That's not exactly true. I told Danny's mother I'd hurt these cocksuckers for her. Handing them off to the judiciary's not what I think she had in mind."

"Does feel a little empty. Maybe they'll come for us. That might be fun."

"Not with all these women around. You know what's wrong with me? I'm conflicted. On the one hand, I'm softhearted. I get weepy looking at pork tenderloin in the meat market. But up against something like this, I don't want to hand it off to the man, I want to fucking waste them."

"Me, too. Difference between me and you is I stopped trying to get over it, said to myself, what the hell, I'm a conflicted man. Sometimes you work too hard on it."

"I guess I do. So… You win a little and you lose a little and you never really know if you're making a difference and then you die."

"Better than not doing it."

"Much."

"Let's go to bed."

Richie and Jack were strolling in the back yard, laughing about something, when we went in.

"Everything cool?" I said to Jack.

"Cool. Very nice evening, Harry. Thanks for letting us be part of it."

"You're welcome."

I tapped Richie's extended hand as I passed him. He said, "Good job, Harry." I nodded.

Leanne and Jim were on the front lanai. "Nice party," Jim said.

"Was. Everything buttoned down?"

"Valerie and Betsy went to the drugstore a couple of minutes ago. Soon's they get back, we'll be on cruise control."

"To the drugstore?"

"Yeah. I said I'd come along. Valerie laughed, said forget it. Took the Miata."

Something cold and mean crawled up into the pit of my stomach. Muhammad and I went to my place. The phone rang.

"Missing somebody?"

"Who's this?"

"Two pretty girls?"

"Who's this?"

"One with a bad attitude? Another just a common whore?"

"Let me talk to her."

"Here you go, honey. Boyfriend wants to hear your voice. Say, 'Hi, Harry.'"

"Harry?" She sounded sleepy.

"Valerie! I'm coming for you."

"She didn't hear that part," the man said. "I'll tell her you're coming for her. Because you are."

"What do you want?"

"Little ol' jewel called the Sultan's Star. Pretty thing, I hear. Like this pretty thing I've got here. Probably not as much fun as she is, but in the long run worth a lot more."

"I've got it. You can have it."

"I know that. The sooner the better, if you know what I mean."

"A straight trade. The girls for the jewel."

"Your hand's a little weak, cowboy. Here's the play. You don't come. The big nigger does."

"What big nigger?"

"The one we followed to your place, motherfucker. And he comes alone. To the house in Manoa. You know where it is. He knocks on the front door. He's not alone or he don't have the jewel, I get a call and both girls die. Right after we all fuck 'em. If it goes down the right way, you get a call on this phone you're holdin' right now telling you where you can pick 'em up. And, oh yeah, I almost forgot, have the nigger bring that bag of cash, too."

"Give me an hour. He'll be there."

"11:30." The call ended.

$$\cdot\ \cdot\ \cdot\ \cdot\ \cdot$$

"They went to the drugstore, for Christ's sake," I said to Muhammad. "Goddammit. To the fucking drugstore! They must have been right here. Right outside."

"They want to swap for the stone?"

"Yeah. Guy said have you bring it to Manoa. Plus the cash in the briefcase. At 11:30. Then they call me here to say where she is."

"I have to pretend to be a big nigger?"

"Yeah. Wear a disguise." I looked at my watch. 10:40. I felt myself getting calm and cold, finding focus. I said, "We'll fuckin' bring it, all right. They're not gonna be there, but we've got to shut it down anyway."

"I could just take them the cash and the rock we got. Might fool 'em. You wait here for the call."

I looked at him like he was nuts.

"Good," he said. "I was hoping you'd say that. I'd rather just go ahead and start killing them. Been a while since you were in this place, hasn't it?"

"Yeah. You, too."

"Need to be cool and hot both."

"Yeah." Rafael's words at the wake came to me. "Need to proceed with an aspect of purposeful aggression."

"Sounds like a useful mantra."

"They're gonna wish they'd French-kissed a rattlesnake instead of fuckin' with me. That's my mantra."

"I don't plan to be polite."

He reached out his mammoth fist to me and I tapped it with mine.

· · · · ·

Jerry took the duty at the front of the house and Jack and Jim came with me in the Range Rover. Jim got apologetic. I said, "Save it. Use it. Make it work for you."

Manoa's night rain was falling softly. I entered the park that backed up to Puuhoonua and then just went overland, through bushes and ditches, feeling my way, using the low fog lamps the last part. At 11:15, facing a low rising hill, I stopped, hoping it was the right hill, and we got out.

We wore black. Our faces were blacked. We put on the night vision goggles. "Fuck these things," one of them said and threw them in the car. The other one and I did, too. I reached into the glove box and took out a flashlight. "Only got one," I said. Jack said, "We both got bat vision. You keep it."

We carried Benellis and holstered Glocks with silencers in our pockets. And small backpacks with extra ammunition and plastic cuffs. Each of us had a C-Guard jammer. We had rubber-gripped, heavy-duty shears tucked in our belts. I had a combat knife in a waist sheath.

We went up the hill full tilt, sliding on the wet grass, fell to our bellies at the top, and peered over. I had missed by a couple hundred yards. I signaled to them and we went down ten yards and ran about two hundred, then back to the top and looked down on the house. There was a fifty-yard downhill slope that ended at about an eight-foot cyclone fence. A small back yard. The downstairs was lit up as were two windows on the top floor.

"Put the silencers on the Glocks," I said. "There's a sign out front that says 'Beware of Dog.' If there is a dog, that's what the silencer's for. No dog, take the silencer off. Jack, you come straight for the back door. Jim, you take the side by the garage. There's a side door there, up a couple of steps. I'm on the other side. In five minutes Muhammad's gonna walk up to the front door and knock loud enough for us to hear it. When you hear it, take a ten-count, cut the power lines. Jack, you activate the jammer. Jack comes in the back way, Jim the side. Blow the doors even if they're open. Come in strong. I'll go in the front. Muhammad'll back away and cover the front. Let's go."

We fanned out and ran down the hill, vaulted the fence, crouched, and paused. The house was ten yards away. Laughter from inside. Women's laughter. A man growled and the laughter died. Music. Maybe a television. Jack was beside the small back porch before I even saw him move. I found a cluster of power lines at the side of the house near the front. I peered around. No dog. I removed the silencer and holstered the Glock.

The van and a black SUV were in the driveway. Richie's pickup truck came down the street. It passed the house and turned in and out of a driveway across the street and parked at the curb in front of the house, aiming the way it had come. Muhammad got out, carrying the briefcase, opened the front gate, and walked up to the front door. He knocked. I counted to eight and cut a cluster of lines. The house went dark. And quiet.

I rushed up beside Muhammad and he took a step back. I blasted the door at the handle with the Benelli and heard two other blasts in close succession. I threw my shoulder to the front door and rolled in low and came up in a crouch in the darkness. A man lay on the floor, moaning, staring at his bloody, shredded arm. Two others sat on a sofa, holding beer bottles. Two young women stood, staring with gaping mouths. To my right, Jack threw the gun stock in the face of a man in a doorway and came in, stepping over him as he fell. The girls screamed and I hit one with a short punch and Jack hit the other. They fell. Down a hallway I saw the shape of Jim walking toward me.

I said to Jim, "Empty back there?" He nodded. "Stay here. Cuff everybody."
To Jack I said, "Check the rooms back there. I'll go up."

I bounded up the stairway and heard a shotgun blast behind me. At the top, I sensed four rooms, two across from me, a third to my left and a fourth to my right. I took the Glock from the holster and held it in my left hand, the shotgun in my right. I went down the hall to two facing doors. I turned, facing the way I'd come and shot one door with each gun. I kicked in first one door, then the other, saw beds and shapes in the beds in both of them. "Get up! Get out here! Get downstairs!" I shouted. I fired the Glock into the walls over the beds and the shapes scrambled. I ran down the hall to the other end and turned back the way I had come and shot both of those doors, down low, not wanting to kill one of the idiot girls who might be coming out. But I didn't care if I hurt them, so then I kicked both doors in and said, "Get out here or I'll kill you." And shot off a couple of threatening rounds.

I went to the top of the stairs and called out, "Jim!"

"Yeah!"

"I'm going to be running people down to you. Can you handle it?"

"Yeah."

"Jack busy?"

"Cleaning up."

"Send him up here soon as you can. Tell him to be noisy."

I went to the first two rooms, dragged a girl and a man from one and threw them into the hall, found two girls in the other and threw them out. I looked in both closets. They were empty. I was scurrying like a crazed bug. Back in the hall, I saw that two men and two girls were standing at the far end.

I shouted, "Are those rooms empty?" My voice was a little shrill.

The girls nodded.

"They fuckin' better be or I'll kill you for lyin'. Are they?"

"Yes," they said, together.

"Everybody downstairs! Single file! Walk slow!" and fired the Glock into the ceiling for effect, then looked up and thought, Jesus, the widow's walk, there's at least an attic up there, what the hell have I done? What if she's there?

"Where's the door to the attic?" I said, and a girl near me pointed to a door set in the ceiling and then to a pole with a hook leaning beside a small table.

Jack said from the stairs, "Harry, I'm coming up. Is it cool?"

"Come on. It's kind of crowded."

He appeared. "You handle this. I'm going up." As I reached for the door's latch above my head, I said, "I haven't cleared out those two rooms down there. If anybody's still in there, kill those two girls."

"Okay."

I hooked the latch and drew down the fold-up ladder and climbed until my head reached into the space. If the house was dark, the attic was a tomb. I swept the void with the Maglite and climbed in.

There was nobody up there. There wasn't room. There were rows and rows of steel shelves, wall-to-wall, floor-to-ceiling, and they were stocked with military-issue cartons of medical supplies. It could have been the regional warehouse for Wal-Mart Pharmacies.

I hurried back down, thinking I'd hear sirens soon. Muhammad was in the living room along with Jack and Jim and about fifteen other people in various states of attire and distress. Everybody who could move was cuffed hands and feet and lined up against a wall. I walked the guys out into the kitchen and said, "Take my truck. Meet us at the entrance to the Ilikai parking garage."

"Want me to detach the jammer?"

"No. Leave it like it is."

They went out the back. Muhammad and I went out the front, hurried to the truck and drove off to the sounds of approaching sirens. I called Bobby Bentley.

"You've got a couple of squads on their way to a disturbance at 456 Puuhoonua Street. The clubhouse of the Children of God. Before they let anybody go, have them look in the attic and in the garage. I think you'll see where the army's missing supplies've been ending up."

"Yeah?" he said. "A disturbance, huh? You the disturber?"

"Can't hear you. Must be out of range." I shut off.

To Muhammad, I said, "We kill anybody back there?"

"Not unless that guy you shot doesn't make it."

"Well, the night's young."

• • • • •

Muhammad pulled up behind the Range Rover at the curb a few yards from the entrance to the parking garage. We jumped out and went to it, got in the back.

We entered the garage and drove up the ramp. I got another magazine from my backpack and reloaded the Glock.

"We're gonna need another jammer up here. Jim, you handle it. Can't cut power up here, so come in fast and take out the phones quick. No outgoing calls. My guess is Valerie and Betsy aren't here, either. I'm thinking the boat. We bust in, break everybody up, cuff 'em as we go, check all the rooms. Then get out quick and go to the roof, get control of the copter. We'll take the stairs for that."

"What if the copter's not there?" Jim said. Nobody answered. "Forget I said that."

Jack was looking for a spot near the elevator and stairs and found one on Four.

We passed through an unlocked door and entered a short pedway to the building. It was about fifteen-feet long, a pre-fab concrete chamber. A steel door with a knob and a keycard insert blocked our way at the other end. It was locked.

I double-chambered the Benelli. I said, "The good news is the noise of this'll probably be confined to this pedway. That's also the bad news. No reason for all of us to go deaf. Go back to the garage." I pulled my shirt out of my jeans and cut a strip with the knife, made a couple of ragged ear inserts and tied a strip around my head to hold them in. Better than nothing, but not by much. They hadn't moved. "Go," I said. "That's an order."

When the door to the garage closed behind me, I fired both chambers at the lock before I could think about it. I think I may have screamed, but I couldn't have heard myself if I did. The three of them came back in and I didn't care for their expressions when they looked at me. I pointed at the door to get their minds on the matter at hand and Jack opened it.

We entered a carpeted hallway, turned left, and hurried to an elevator bank. Muhammad looked at me with concern. "I'm okay," I lied, not knowing if I was whispering or shouting. We entered an elevator and Muhammad punched "18" and, as the door closed, Jim turned to me and saluted. Jack, too. Muhammad said something and they laughed. Muhammad reached for my Benelli and when I resisted he said something with a smile. I think he said, "Give it to me. That's an order." I gave it to him and unholstered the Glock and chambered a round.

At eighteen, Muhammad and the twins took the lead. They hurried down the corridor and I had to hustle to keep up. At a double door that read "1812" in brass numerals, Muhammad fired the Benelli and Jack and Jim were inside just as the second shell hit. Muhammad followed quickly. I was last in.

Wilton Crandall and Melvin Villafrania lay dead on the floor on their backs in front of a long white sofa. Each had a hole in his forehead, oozing something.

Jim and Jack split off to the hallways to either side. Muhammad and I stood there, looking at the two corpses and each other. Jack and Jim came back shaking their heads.

Muhammad said, "They're leaving town. They don't give a shit about the jewel. These guys here did, but not Massey. Let's look at the roof. Maybe they're still there."

We went out into the hall and closed the door. Muhammad knocked on the door across the hall. A tiny and ancient Oriental man opened it immediately. He must have been standing there wondering what the hell was going on. He slowly raised his head until he got to Muhammad's. Muhammad said, "Stay inside. We'll call the police. Stay inside." He closed the door.

We double-timed it up four flights of stairs. Muhammad fell a full floor behind. In front, as I turned the last corner, I almost fell on top of Manu Tsiasopo. He lay on the stairs face-down as though he was crawling up them on his stomach. There was a hole in the back of his head and red and gray stuff was leaking out of it.

There was a door at his head, so this must be the roof. The door opened outward, its knob on the right. I climbed over dead Manny and jiggled the knob. It was unlocked.

"Let's go through here fast and low. I'm first. Muhammad, you're last. Give me the Benelli."

He looked at the shotgun and handed it to me. "I'm going to want this back," he said.

I opened the door quietly, went up four steps fast, and rolled far enough out to make room for the three of them behind me. I took a crouch and did a wide sweep with the Benelli. A large white helicopter was there, tied down. And to the left, a small, well-lit enclosure, probably a break room for the pilots. Jack and Jim ran around behind the stairwell and came around shaking their heads.

We walked quietly to the enclosure and entered. Two men in white uniforms were seated at a small table with coffee cups in front of them. They turned and stared at us. "You the pilots?" I asked. They nodded. "Anybody else take off from here recently?" They nodded. I raised the Benelli and said, "Well, I certainly would be grateful if you'd tell me who it was and when it was and where they went."

"Mr. Fox and Mr. Massey and another man. Sheffield, I think. And two women. In Mr. Massey's helicopter."

"Were the women bound?'

"Don't think so. Seemed to be hurt, maybe. Had to be helped as they walked."

"What did you two do?"

"Mr. Fox came in here and told us not to come out. We didn't. Just watched. Then Mr. Fox got in the copter and they left."

"Was Massey the pilot?"

"Uh-huh."

"When was this?"

"'Bout a half-hour ago. Maybe less." It was now 12:10.

"Which direction?"

"To sea, I think."

"To the boat?"

"In that direction."

"Get the copter ready," I told them. "Stay off the radio."

Muhammad said, "I'm going to phone this in."

I said to him, "Man, I don't like this very much."

"Not much to like. I'd say Massey's decided he's got as much out of Hawaii as he can get. Plus a bonus."

"Two women?"

"Yeah. If he'd wanted them dead, they'd be here dead. He wants to keep them. He's tearing down the snitch ladder, leaving nobody behind to talk. He wants to travel fast and light." He made a call.

The pilots had loosened the tie-downs. The engine was turning over, the props moving slowly. We got in and lifted off.

The lights of the city were receding when the co-pilot turned to Muhammad and said something. Muhammad leaned forward and spoke into his ear.

He turned to me. "He said it wouldn't be easy finding the Princess out in open waters without radio contact. I told him nothing worthwhile comes easily."

It only took ten minutes. We came in from her stern. I heard Muhammad say, "Don't fuck around with this, gentlemen. Don't hover. Set this bastard down quick."

We came in low over the stacks and the pilothouse and touched down with a bump. Before it settled, I was out my side running aft. There was a door where I expected to find one. I put three from the Glock in the handle and kicked it in. The front room was empty. I went through a door into a bedroom and there was Eric Fox, on the floor against a wall with one hole in his forehead and another in his chest. Above his head was an open and empty wall safe.

I ran outside, went beyond the copter and looked up to the pilothouse. I saw a face in the front glass pane and pointed at it, motioned it to come to me. The captain hurried down an exterior stairway.

"You know Orrin Massey?" I asked impolitely.

He nodded.

"He set down here a few minutes ago in his copter?"

He nodded.

"And didn't stay long?"

He nodded.

"You see who was with him?"

"Yes."

"*Yes*? Every sonofabitch I run into thinks this is true-false. Who?" I raised my voice somewhat.

"Mr. Massey and Eric Fox got out and they went in the cabin. Mike Sheffield came up the stairs and told me to stay where I was. He said he'd kill me if I didn't. Then he went down and in a minute he and Mr. Massey came out of the cabin and got in the copter and they lifted off. I've been up there since."

"Did you see anybody else in the copter?"

"I think there were two people in the back. I think they were women."

"How long ago?"

"Maybe twenty minutes, maybe a little more."

"Which way'd they go?"

He pointed east. "Towards Molokai."

I turned to Muhammad. He was on his phone. He closed it. "Bentley wants us to meet him at the Ilikai. I said we would." He said to the captain, "You've got a dead man in there," pointing to the cabin. "It's Eric Fox. The police are on the way. You are ordered to return to the pilothouse and hold your position."

I walked over to the bulkhead and leaned against it. I slid down until I was sitting on my butt and put my head between my knees.

TWELVE
Friday, March 21
Idaho.

We lifted off from Honolulu International in a Hawker Horizon and headed towards San Francisco into the rising sun. I was letting myself fall asleep. We were six. I thought that would be plenty.

I'd beat myself up for as long as I thought I needed it and then took a look ahead. Ahead was where I'd get back to even. After it was all over and I'd squared things, I thought I'd go off somewhere and kill myself.

$$\bullet \ \bullet \ \bullet \ \bullet \ \bullet$$

Muhammad had done most of the talking with Bentley and Wong back at the Ilikai and at HPD headquarters. I was not handling things well.

Dick Wong told me I was out of it now. "He's gone, Harry. His helicopter is at Kahului on Maui and his jet lifted off two hours ago with a flight plan to Tahiti. It's an FBI job now. It's not your problem any more. I know how you feel, but that's the way it is."

"Bullshit, Dick. He's not going to fuckin' Tahiti. He's on his way to Idaho. To his little nest. Tell the FBI that's where he is. Tell 'em to go up there with both barrels blazing. You know where it is. Tell them!"

"I'll tell them."

As soon as Wong cleared Jack and Jim, I sent them back to Kailua in my Rover and Richie's truck to round up Jerry and extra clothes and stuff for all of us. Plus the briefcase and the maps and Muhammad's laptop. And to tell the others to keep a light in the window, we'd be home soon with Betsy and Valerie.

Muhammad and I went for coffee, and to make a few calls, at an all-night café a couple of blocks from the police station. I called Rafael's friend and placed a completely new order since Muhammad had us throw all our weapons into the Pacific on the copter flight back to the Ilikai. We needed different stuff anyway. The order included the Hawker. The different stuff was in it.

I called Rafael and gave him the bad news. I told him I felt confident about how to unravel the thing and said I'd need some help at the back end of the play. He said I had his full confidence and he'd do whatever I asked. I told him what I needed.

"Do you need more men on the ground?" he asked.

"No. They do." I signed off.

My phone chirped. Bobby Bentley said, "You got room for one more?"

"One more what?"

"I just went on official leave. Told the captain I was worn out, needed a few days off. He said okay, winked at me, said he wished he could join me, he was tired too. Said to tell you that."

"What're you talking about?"

"Hey, man, don't be cute. We know where you guys are going. I want to come along. I'm handy."

A gift horse. I didn't look in its mouth.

A little before sunup, Richie delivered the boys at the airport, along with about two dozen doggy bags Cindy and Leanne had prepared from last night's feast. Each bag was labeled and sealed with a kiss. Folded, stapled, and then big, red, sticky, lip smears slapped over the crease. And a few tear stains.

Richie got down from the truck and looked at me and said, "Kill a couple of 'em for me, Harry."

"If there's any left."

"I'd give you a hug but I'm afraid you're turnin' queer."

"Just as well you don't. Might push me over the edge."

"I'll keep an eye on things." And drove off.

• • • • •

We flew to San Francisco, refueled, and then to Spokane where we picked up our ride, a black Toyota Land Cruiser. We had checked out all our gear in the plane. We crossed into Idaho on I-90 and took a left, heading north, on 95 just west of Couer D'Alene.

A little more than eight hours out now and, allowing for the time we'd lost on the clock, coming up on twilight in northern Idaho.

I'd never been in such staggering country. But for the road, there was no sense that anyone had passed this way before. We were at 3,500 feet and in a valley, mountains rising several thousand feet above us on either side, tall pines on the slopes so near to vertical they looked plumb-lined. Twilight wouldn't linger up here. Full darkness would come in a rush.

We'd didn't have much conventional luggage, but a lot of other stuff that was heavy. Still, using the roof rack, everything fit real well in this $60,000 truck which was a twin of the one Muhammad had back home, so we gave him the wheel, Jerry beside him. I was in the second row with Bobby. Jack and Jim were in the third.

Jack said, "Hey, Bobby, how come you're along on this? What's your stake?"

Bobby, who hadn't said two hundred words since we left, said, "Valerie Sabatino."

I glanced at him. Jim said, "Yeah? You figurin' on backdoorin' Harry?"

"No. Not like that. I'm happily married. Just I've watched this woman two or three times and I think she's special. My boss does, too. She's got serious guts. Worth saving. Plus, I'm a professional crime fighter."

Jerry, up front, said, "Muhammad, you drive one of these elephants back and forth from where you live to where you work? And you work in downtown Chicago? Are you nuts?"

"Yes. I am nuts. If I can't find a parking place, I just push a car up on the sidewalk and go on my way. Chicago's an aggressive town, Jerry. No place for the faint of heart. Real men in Chicago. Real women, too." He was bullshitting. He garaged his Land Cruiser, took it out only once or twice a month for tailgating or a trip. In town, he and Serena used cabs and an aging minivan.

Jerry said, "Yeah? Well, the women in Chicago can't be any realer than Cindy Rendell. That girl makes my dick harder'n Chinese arithmetic."

Jack moaned. "I hate this. Every time this motherfucker gets laid, he goes into this."

Jim said, "Well, it's only a couple times a year. He's gotta be the worst fuck in history. Last time he got invited back, he was married to her."

How the boys talk when the girls aren't around.

I was worried they wouldn't be there, that we were taking a long trip for nothing. Muhammad and I had wondered about it before we left and talked about it again on the flight. We kept coming back to the same conclusion. We had no place else to look. The other way stations were bad possibilities. Massey knew every time he put a foot on open ground with two drugged out women, he'd be running a huge risk. So we convinced ourselves this was the play. Worse, if we were right, we couldn't be sure he'd arrived yet. But he had a five hour start on us, so I put that thought to rest. If he was coming here, and I was betting a bundle he was, he'd be here by now.

We crossed Pend Oreille Lake and entered the town of Sandpoint. Bonners Ferry was thirty miles ahead.

I called out to Muhammad, loud enough for the others to hear, "Muhammad, how far you figure this place we've got rooms is from the mountain?" We didn't have any rooms. I was testing.

"You mean how long to get there?"

"Yeah. That *is* what I fucking mean. Since I have very little interest in the flight of crows."

He said to Jerry, "It's good to see him bitchy. He's good bitchy. Harry, we been flyin' and dozin' and eatin' leftovers and shit all day long and it's time we heard what you got in mind for a plan. I don't know if you want to drive up there or walk up there or drop in from the sky." He knew the plan. We'd gone over it on the plane. We were just cranking things up.

"Hell, I don't know. I hate making decisions."

Jack said, "*All right*, commander! I'll follow you anywhere."

"Okay. Here's where I am. I want to come in at night. So, I'm wondering if you guys are too tired to do it tonight. We need to be fresh."

Jerry said, "Too tired? You think I came all this way to get a good night's sleep?"

Jack said, "I cannot believe this old cocksucker's askin' us if we're fresh. Christ, only thing I'm worried about is havin' to carry him up some fuckin' hill."

Jim said, "And how 'bout that big sonofabitch drivin'? I'm totally leavin' him. Wouldn't pick him up if buzzards were circlin'."

They sounded pretty salty. "Bobby?" I asked.

"Let's dance."

"Okay. We go tonight."

Jim said, "So why do we need rooms?"

"We don't. We just booked 'em in case you needed a little nap."

I told them how I saw it playing out.

• • • • •

We finished off the doggy bags and washed it down with bottled water. We descended into a valley and entered Bonners Ferry, crossed the Kootenai

River, and stayed with 95 as it rose again and wound through the mountains and then straightened out, heading northeast. At a place called Threemile Corner we took a right on County Route 2 and drove a mile to the Boundary County Airport where we parked in the small lot.

Everybody climbed out and stretched. It was colder than I'd expected, not much above freezing. Muhammad shook hands with each of us, wished us well, and walked into the terminal. Jerry got behind the wheel and I took the seat beside him.

We followed 95 for four miles and left it where it intersected with Meadow Creek Road, a narrow two-laner with no shoulders. From here on I was betting big on the accuracy of the maps I had downloaded and printed on the plane. They were a scale of 1:25,000 and I had about twenty pages, overlapping sectors. I read them with the help of a penlite. Meadow Creek Road wound northeast for another half-dozen miles where it intersected with Deer Creek Road.

We took a small chance by stopping at the intersection in the middle of the road, but we hadn't seen another vehicle since we left 95 and there was no place to pull off. Everybody took a leak and got fully armed, including headsets and earplugs for our two-way radios. Jerry applied pitch black, handed me the tin, and got behind the wheel. I got in, applied it and passed it to Bobby. Jack and Jim put on Aloha shirts and skipped the pitch black. Jim removed the bulbs from the light rack above his head while Jack and Bobby did the same with those in the side.

We traveled Deer Creek Road for two miles, heading south. Jerry went to the fog beams. Darkness in these mountains would be diminished only by the stars and the moon and we were blessed by a full and heavy cloud cover. We were blocked from lateral observation by heavy tree cover on both sides, but I expected that to give way on our left as we came upon the low meadow where we'd found the grass airstrip. It came quickly and, as it did, Jerry shut down the fogs.

About two hundred yards ahead was the low aluminum hangar. In the dark, to which our eyes had adjusted, Jerry moved ahead and stopped behind it. Bobby and I got out and walked around the front. Solomon Mountain loomed in front of us. Bugs chirped; otherwise, it was quiet.

Bobby moved to the hangar door and fiddled with the padlock with a set of picks. It opened. He handed it to me so there'd be no rattling from it as he opened the door. He opened it no more than two feet and went in. Through the crack I saw the illumination of his Maglite. I stood motionless. In less than five minutes, he emerged and handed me two distributor caps. I'd expected only one. I looked at him. He shook his head. He quietly closed the door and I handed him the padlock. He wrapped his gloved hands around it to muffle the sound as it closed. We returned to the truck. The others were out, standing beside it.

Bobby said, quietly, "Two planes. A little high-wing thing, single engine, and a twin-engine job. Saw Cessna on it. Disabled them both."

"Good. That big one improves the chances they're up there." We were talking just above a whisper.

Jack and Jim got in the truck. Bobby, Jerry and I went back to the tree line and began our ascent up the northern side of the slope. The climb was a little more than 2,000 feet. It was an easy traverse, just trees and modest brush, not like the jungle. Noise was the problem getting through the brush, but winter hadn't yet left Idaho and the ground was moist. Nearer the top we'd have no real cover as we passed from tree to tree. We made good time, staying together until about 500 feet from the top when they each motioned to me and peeled off to the right.

Jerry would head south to arrive at the top at its southern end, by the huts. Bobby would arrive in the center near the obstacle course and make his way through and across it to narrow the width of the playing field. I would arrive at the rear of the house.

I pushed on. About thirty feet below the rim, still unseen I was sure, I sat behind a tree to await word from the other two.

In a moment, in my earpiece, I heard, "Bobby ready." Five minutes more and I heard, "Jerry ready."

I said into the mike as quietly as I could, "Truck. Go."

In my earpiece I heard, "10-4."

I crawled to the rim and looked over into the compound. I was east of the house with a line of view to the far end. I wasn't surprised to see the house well-lit from within. It was only about 8:00. The helicopter was in place. I saw no one.

Jack and Jim would drive down Deer Creek Road and cross the meadow at its far end without lights and enter the unfinished road that led up the mountain. Then they'd hit the high beams and turn on the CD player. Loud.

I guessed it to be about a ten minute trip to the top. Soon, I heard something rap that produced a deep, pulsating, relentless beat. The truck was a boom box.

I crawled fifty yards to the septic tank to improve my position. I peered around it and saw a few shapes emerge from the huts and huddle together for a moment. Several of them went behind the huts where the noise was coming from as Jack and Jim climbed the rise to the south. They'd be very close to Jerry, but he was expecting it. The truck likely wouldn't be visible for another few minutes, until it made the last turn and climbed straight up the last two hundred yards. But its lights would already be easy to see.

One of the shapes from the other end ran in my direction, coming toward the house. The house got unintelligibly noisy. I saw more shapes arrive in front of the house, meeting the shapes coming to them, then all of them going to the other end. They were carrying rifles. Or broomsticks. I figured rifles. Suddenly, the place lit up like a State Fair midway, floodlights from the hut and the house.

I rolled under the septic tank and dug out my cell phone, wrapped my body around it to muffle the sound of the number I punched in. I hit "send" and laid it on the ground. If the piece of shit worked, Muhammad would now lift off from the Bonners Ferry airport in the helicopter I'd requested from Rafael as our way out. It should take no more than ten minutes for it to arrive.

I crawled out and scanned the scene. The area behind the house was il-luminated by a pair of floods mounted high on the house. A man came out the rear porch and stared from left to right. His gaze passed over my position without notice. He went back inside.

The boom box got louder. A dozen or so men jogged into position, form-ing a loose line about twenty feet back from where Jack and Jim would arrive. They had weapons at the ready. As it climbed the hill, the truck's headlights made a hole in the penumbral edge of the compound's bright light and the men steadied and raised their rifles. The truck arrived with attitude, came up fast and heavy, powered over the edge, its front wheels lifting off and the rears grabbing for traction, and slammed to a stop ten feet from the greeting party. The boom box blared. Then Jack shut the truck down and the headlights faded and the CD quit and he and Jim stepped out in their matching Aloha shirts and stood beside their open doors and things got very quiet. Quiet enough that I heard Jack say, "Lookee here, bro. Haoles. We are pretty fuckin' lost." He spread his arms to the heavens in mock supplication.

One of the men said, "On your knees, motherfuckers! Hands behind your heads!" And I looked in Bobby's direction and saw him rise and toss a concussion grenade in a high, lazy lob towards the center of the compound. It hit and exploded and I came to one knee and took aim on the cluster of soldiers. As they turned in the direction of the deafening sound, Jack and Jim reached into the truck and each came out with an evil-looking AK-100.

Over the fading echoes, I heard their guns ratchet to the ready and Jim say, "Okay, boys. There's two very mean guns aiming at your backs. The grown-up version of the AK-47. We can kill all of you in about two seconds. Just in case you're wonderin' if I'm lyin' I want this guy on the end, the end nearest to the huts, to turn his head to the right and take a look. Go on. You know which one you are. Take a little peep. I won't shoot you."

He turned his head and then turned back.

"Okay, pal. Save your buddies from sudden death. Show them we're serious. Toss your rifle out in front of you and lie down on your face and put your hands together on the back of your head. Or you die first."

He tossed his rifle and lay down.

"See? Now the rest of you. Slow and easy. Toss the guns and assume the position and you get to live to see your grandchildren. Let's do it."

Nothing happened for what seemed about a week. Then one soldier tossed his rifle and went slowly down to his face. Then another, and two more, and more. Until only three were standing, their backs to Jack and Jim.

"Long life to come, boys, if you do this right. Steady now," Jim said.

And the three spun quickly, lowering themselves as they did, and Jack and Jim sprayed them dead in less time than it takes to remember it. I thought, this game's ours.

John D. MacDonald described Travis McGee as having "a John Wayne day" in one of his last books, "The Green Ripper." It was a day when McGee was up against all the odds and everything just went Hollywood-perfect. I thought maybe I was going to have one of those. That was fiction, of course, so probably bullshit. Plus the thing is your luck always turns. It's just a question of when.

I saw Jerry along the side of the hut in the distance. He crept forward. Two men stood outside the hut's door facing his way. Maybe they'd heard him. He turned the corner and they opened fire on him and he went down. There went the John Wayne day. I fired a long burst into them with my AR-15, aiming a little high, and Jack and Jim did, too. The two men went down.

To my right, I saw Bobby coming forward to cover the front of the house. He knelt and shot out the floods. Jack sprinted maybe two hundred yards to where Jerry lay as Jim gathered the rifles and threw them over the rim. He poured a threatening burst into the ground just in front of the men lying down. Then he turned to the house and moved slowly forward, glancing behind him every step or two to be certain those behind him were behaving.

I went behind the house. I saw two men entering the copter as a third started it up. I came up behind it on full automatic pouring shots into its cabin. One man opened the door and fell to the ground and I threw an incendiary grenade through the open door and ran for cover from the explosion. The copter went up in flames. I ran out for a clear shot and took out the two floods on the back of the house. I went to the back deck and climbed the wooden, exterior stairs. I heard heavy fire from the front, grenade explosions in the distance, and an approaching concussive thump-thump. The helicopter. The stairs led to another deck where double doors opened into a wide hallway. I kicked my way through and a man came around a corner and opened fire on me. The AR-15 overpowered him.

I didn't know how many would be here, but I thought we'd taken out close to twenty. If the boys out front were still on their feet and their prisoners secure, the odds had to be leaning our way.

The symmetry of the house had suggested a central stairway and I turned the corner where the last man had come and ran down a hall that opened at a railing on my left to a big room below. A wide stairway emptied there and, from well above, I saw Orrin Massey scurry across the entryway, pushing Valerie and Betsy before him. They were wearing long white dresses and stumbling like drunks. He jerked on a bridle-like thing that connected to their necks to bring them upright. Tape wrapped around their heads at their mouths.

Forty feet of glass panels rose above the doorway. I stood at the top of the stairs and saw clearly to the distant end of the compound. The only light came across the long reach from the two burning huts, giving back-lit shadows to Bobby and Jim that were a dozen times their height. Before them were several people down on their faces with their hands clasped over their heads and three others sprawled in the awkward, angular poses the suddenly dead assume.

In the distance, Jack, with Jerry over one shoulder and his AK-100 at the ready, trotted from the huts towards the men on the ground by the truck. The helicopter descended. It was massive. It touched down. Two men jumped out the far side and jogged towards Jack who laid Jerry gently on the ground and stood by the cluster of bodies at the truck. Muhammad stepped out of the copter. He carried an H&K shotgun with a twenty-round magazine. He came forward and stood with Jim and Bobby.

I came down the stairs and quietly walked out the door until I was ten feet behind Massey who stood on the porch with the girls tugged tight to him. He had a revolver in the hand that held the bridle and something small in the other that he raised as he said, "If I release this button, these two women die. They are strapped with explosives controlled by the release of this button. I want that helicopter. I'm going to walk to it now and you're going to let me pass. If you shoot me, we'll all die. All of us."

He went forward to the steps and I followed closely. He took one careful step down, keeping Valerie and Betsy tight to either side. The three of them made their way down to the pavement. Massey took another step forward and Bobby Bentley, ten feet away, raised his AR-15 to his waist and put a three-shot burst in his chest. He fell back and I dove over him and flailed for the button thing as it fell from his hand. From the front, Jim took one quick step and went horizontal with the same intention. We both missed. It fell to the pavement and bounced once. Bobby walked to it and smashed it with the heel of his boot.

THIRTEEN
Tuesday, March 25
Oahu.

On a low rise in Punchbowl, white crosses at parade rest in tight formation all around us, under low clouds and a steady drizzle that I thanked God for sending, we buried Jerry Sloan. He had earned this resting place through a three-year tour in the Marines and Dick Wong's insistence.

The bureaucrats had raised doubts of the propriety of the site because of the circumstances of Jerry's death, but Dick killed the question as it left their lips.

Rafael and Madeleine were there. And Belinda and Roscoe whom Rafael had picked up in Louisville before he took his plane to Chicago to fetch Serena. Everybody from Kailua. Jack and Jim, Bobby and Dick. Betsy Fielding. Jerry's ex-wife, Brenda, and their daughter. And friends of his I didn't know and hadn't bothered to meet at the visitation yesterday because I just sat there feeling angry and guilty and acting like a child.

I knew what had happened, how I'd let it all go wrong. At the party the night we met Betsy I'd let myself get swept up in praise, went aloft with self-regard. I drank too much and let my guard down.

A minister attended and spoke of the Jerry Sloan he had hardly known. And led us in prayer. A Marine color guard provided a twenty-one gun salute and presented a folded flag to a pretty six-year-old named Heather Sloan who accepted it with a trembling chin and put her head in her mother's breast. We filed past the casket and spread spoonsful of dirt on it.

And at the awkward pause that always precedes the leaving and the last exhalation, I stood at the foot of the casket and said, without warning or notice, "If there's a better place than this, Jerry Sloan is there. And it eases my pain to believe there is such a place, so I do. But I can't act as though this is anything other than a deep and unending tragedy. I knew this man not long, but very well. A few of us here shared an experience with him of such intensity that I'm sure I speak for each of them when I say we honored him with our unlimited admiration. You should all know, especially you, Heather, that he was a man of decency, integrity, and great courage. He was as good as a man can be. It is of no consolation to say that we will never forget him, but it is true. It is the least we can do and, sadly, the most. Godspeed, Jerry Sloan."

I turned away to hide my eyes, and Valerie, standing behind me, put her arms around me and buried her bruised face in my chest.

•••••

Muhammad, Jack, Jim, and Bobby had stayed behind to secure the compound and answer police questions. I left in the copter with Valerie and Betsy. Bobby asked us to leave Jerry's body behind, thought it was proper procedure and would strengthen our hand.

After carrying the girls to the copter and handing them off to the two paramedics, Muhammad asked Bobby the question on all our minds: "What made you take that chance?"

"Valerie. I looked at her as soon as she came through the door because I could see she'd taken some punches. And she locked on me. Stared at me. Then she started shifting her eyes from right to left, left to right, back and forth. Held her head steady. Her eyes went back and forth. All the way to one side, all the way to the other. Didn't stop. I thought, what the hell's this? And I caught it. She was shaking her head without shaking her head. She was saying don't believe a word he's saying, saying it was all bullshit. She stopped and looked hard at me and I got it and looked up at his hand and back to her eyes and made a big no with my mouth like it was a question. And she gave me the same look back. Touched her stomach. Nooo with a little shake of her head. I just knew that thing in his hand was a piece of shit and they weren't strapped with explosives. Didn't have a doubt. I did think for a minute maybe we should just, you know, capture him, but then I thought, fuck you, and shot him."

The flight from Solomon Mountain to the Sacred Heart Medical Center in Spokane, where Rafael had arranged for our arrival, took about forty minutes. Betsy was dazed and limp. She lay mute on a cot, strapped carefully to it. But Valerie was amped, alive with energy. She sat up, her legs crossed under her like a kid at a slumber party. She told the paramedics they'd both been drugged, but, she thought, Betsy'd been shot up recently.

"And I haven't," she said. "They stuck both of us with a hypodeemic nerdle when they snatched us and they gave me another one last night on the airplane. But when I came out of it, I figured I'd just go on acting like I was in a coma 'til Harry showed up."

"How'd you get so beat up?" I asked. "I mean why?"

"I's obstreperous. Landed a couple of punches too, baby. You'd a been proud of me. But they had what d'ya call it? Superior force. So, I thought, okay I'll behave, but my boyfriend's gonna be really pissed at you assholes."

One of the medics working over Betsy on a stretcher, asked, "Do you have any idea what it was they gave you?"

"No, sir. No idea. But I bet you could get hooked on it pretty easy. Man, did I get a good night's sleep."

He looked at me and then her and asked, "Were you raped?"

She giggled. "No. We're unclean."

"Unclean?"

"Menstruating. Both of us. Ol' Orrin said God forbids sex with an unclean woman. Talk about lucky! Wow! For him, I mean. I'd a killed him he tried anything. Ooops. I forgot. He's dead anyhow. Ooops." She giggled again.

"Came on last night. Betsy and I were sittin' on the porch, I mean the *lanai*, just talkin', gettin' a little drunk, and I thought, oh-oh, I gotta go to the drugstore and Betsy looked at me and said, 'Valerie, do you have any Tampax?'" She giggled. "Is that just a stitch? Simultaneous curse arrival. What're the odds of that? So we went to the drugstore. Jack, or Jim, said wait up, he'd come along. I just laughed at him. I mean, come on, women don't need men trackin' 'em to the drugstore." She giggled.

The medic said, "Miss, I think it would be good for you to be sedated. You've been under a lot of stress."

"No way. Wanna talk to my honey. He's Batman!"

"She's fine," I said. "Take care of Betsy."

"Yeah," Valerie said. "How's she? How's she doin'?"

"She's been sedated. She's sleeping."

"God love her. What she's gone through."

I said, "So, what happened? We found a lot of dead people along the way."

"Jesus, Harry. He's a freakin' bedbug."

"Was."

"Yeah. Good."

"So?"

"So what? God, you look great! All that black shit on your face. Come here." And grabbed me and planted a big kiss. Let go and covered her mouth.

"How's my breath?"

"Strong. Good and strong."

She giggled, pulled out the top of her dress and sniffed herself down her chest. "Do I stink? Hey," remembering something. "Everybody okay up there? All the guys?"

"Yes," I lied.

"You sure? Looked like Jerry was down."

"Fine. He's fine."

"You know I played signals with 'tective Bentley? Like code? You know that?"

"Yeah. He told us. Pretty damn smart of you. We were all impressed."

"No kiddin'? That's great! Great!" She leaned back on the stretcher, laid down and said, "Heard that boom-boom-boom comin' up the hill. Heard it! Made me smile. Said to myself, 'Harry's comin', Orrin. An' your ass is grass.'" She giggled once and her head rolled to the side and she snored.

$$• • • • •$$

On Saturday, we assembled in the room Valerie and Betsy were sharing at the hospital. The other four had driven the Land Cruiser to Spokane after long conversations with the Idaho State Police and an FBI SWAT unit that dropped in about two hours after we left.

Valerie and Betsy were propped up in bed and looking beautiful. Betsy was still subdued and it wasn't from medication. It was remorse and shame. I recognized it from my own experiences and knew it would pass neither soon nor easily. Valerie was badly bruised but full of herself, adrenalinized all over again by her company. She held court.

She winked at Bobby Bentley, said, "We did good, didn't we, Detective?"

"Bobby, please. Yes ma'am, we did. You did."

"Okay, here's what happened. Betsy and I went to the drugstore. One of these guys..." She waved at Jack and Jim. "... tried to come along, but we ran off from him, so don't blame him." Jim raised his hand. "I mean, it's only about two minutes from the front gate. So why not? But, unbeknownst to us," she smiled at the expression, "we were under surveillance." She looked at me and grinned. She was playing the moment for comic drama and knew I knew it.

"We pull into a parking place, the place is deserted, and two big ol' vehicles pull in beside us, so tight on my side I couldn't open my door. I had the top down. That was my big mistake. If I'd had the top up I could've got my gun out before they noticed and shot 'em up. But the guy on my side rolled his window down and pointed a gun at me. It was the Filipino guy. The giant asshole got out of the other vehicle and put one of those things over Betsy's face, I guess it was chloroform. You think so, Bets?" Betsy nodded. "And picked her up and put her in the back seat.

"The Filipino tells me to crawl across the seat and get out. I tried to drive off, but the big asshole reached in and took the keys. So, I had to get out. He went for my face with the rag so I kicked him in the balls like Harry had done that day. Remember?" I smiled at her. "But it didn't work as well when I did it. I don't think I had good position. You know, leverage? So he slapped me. Or maybe hit me with his fist. It hurt. Then Uncle Francis, the Wilton Crandall guy, comes around from the other vehicle and the big asshole picked me up from around my waist and I kicked Uncle Francis. Somewhere. Not in the balls, though. But somewhere because it pissed him off. Then I hit him in the jaw with a good shot. A left. They never expect you to come with a left. I don't know why that is. You got two hands, but they never expect the left." The others gave her looks at that and she caught my eye and winked. "And then the lights went out. I remember somebody rolling me over and sticking a needle in my butt and I remember somebody sticking a cell phone in my face and telling me to say hello to Harry and I think I did.

"Next thing I know we're walking down a hall and we go into somebody's apartment. Or condo. Orrin and Eric Fox and that Sheffield prick are there. The guys who snatched us are explaining what happened and next thing I know Sheffield shoots the Filipino and Orrin shoots Uncle Francis.

"Then they hustled us up some stairs and the big asshole, up front, gets to this door and Orrin shot him in the back of the head. Down he went. Then Orrin and Sheffield hustled us through the door and we were on the roof and we went to a helicopter and Eric Fox came along and off we went. I heard Eric and Orrin arguing about something and we landed on the boat and by this time Sheffield's tied Betsy and me up tight so they left us in the back and off they went to the captain's cabin, a place I am familiar with. Few minutes later, Sheffield and Orrin're back, but no Eric Fox, and off we go again, east, I think, and cross one island, maybe Molokai, and go on to, I guess, Maui. We landed just outside a hangar with an open door and they hustled us inside and put us in a private plane. They untied us then and I took a swing at Orrin and caught him good, but he's out of my weight division, so he just laughed and next thing I know I'm getting' another shot in the butt.

"I woke up when we were landing somewhere, I have no idea where, but by then I thought instead of causing any more trouble, I'd just wait for you guys to find us and kick their asses up around their shoulders.

"Which you did. Thank you so much. When I get cleaned up and presentable enough to make the moment unforgettable, I intend to give each of you the hug and kiss you deserve. I'd kiss you now but I don't feel like I look sufficiently kissable." And brought herself up short and said, "Speaking of which, where's Jerry?"

We told her and she cried. I'm sure it was the first time she cried since she'd gone to the drugstore. Betsy cried, too. So hard and long a nurse came in and put her back to sleep.

A little later we asked Valerie if she had any idea where Michael Sheffield was and she said she didn't. At the compound, she'd been locked in a room and if he'd gone somewhere, she was not aware of it.

•••••

We landed in Honolulu at about noon on Sunday. Richie met us with the maps from my wall and Danny's bible and we set off, in a HPD helicopter, to see if Valerie's theory held up. Muhammad said he'd take the girls, drive out to Betsy's place by Kahuku Point to get enough of her things for a couple more days with us, and then take them both to Kailua. Richie asked to come along on the copter trip and it was good to have him.

The copter hovered above the clearing where Danny had died. Jack, Jim, Bobby, Richie, and I lowered in. Bobby had a GPS and we set the coordinates to match those of Valerie's deduction.

The coordinates of 157.56 .24/25 and 21.33.33 took us to a tangle of growth emerging from a foul, muddy bog. When the GPS settled, I drove a stake in the soft ground and we all crawled around digging with sharp little shovels. Except for Richie. He stood back and stared.

"Look at this," he said, pointing to what appeared to be three diagonal slices in the trunk of the tree. "Wouldn't you think those are man made?"

We all stood up and examined the cuts and had to agree they were.

"So, it's at the base of this tree," I said, stupidly, and went to work on my knees with my shovel.

"What's that?" Richie said, pointing up into the tree. "That little lump up there where that branch comes out."

Bobby stood on Jim's shoulders and retrieved, from a branch ten feet up, a mini-cassette, wrapped in oilcloth and taped to the limb with duck tape.

•••••

On Monday, we sat in Dick Wong's office and listened to the tape. Walt McCall was there with Betsy. Muhammad and Valerie, too.

Dick said, "We've improved the audio." And punched a button.

A voice I didn't know said, "Danny, my boy. Good to see you. Have a seat."

Dick turned the playback off and said, "Anybody recognize that voice?"

Muhammad said, "It's Orrin Massey."

Betsy said, "Yes, it is."

Dick said, "Some chit-chat came next. We skipped over it." He punched the button again.

The voice continued. "Soldier, I believe you to be worthy of membership in the most elite and select fighting force ever assembled. The Army of God. At this time, our number is small, less than forty. But our skills and our faith and our commitment to a course that will change the history of the world are immense. In time, soon, we will rise up in a moment of universal Armageddon and lead the holy ones in a conflict with evil that will be swift and decisive. Untold power and riches await that moment, but power and riches pale before our greater goal, the fulfillment of the work of God Almighty. Do you consider yourself to be worthy?" His voice rose with the challenge of the question.

"Yes, sir," responded another voice I didn't know. It lacked conviction, I thought. "What exactly will my job be?"

"Your job will be to participate, with your comrades in arms, in the systematic destruction of our enemies. And who are these enemies? They are the weak and the wasteful, the mongrel class, the apostates, and those who refuse to join with us in their elimination. In these early days, our work will go unrecognized, as it did last night. But as our numbers grow, and as the social order continues its pathetic deterioration, we will slowly rise to the surface. And those who believe in our cause will see us as their shield, as their sword, and as their salvation."

"Last night?" asked the other voice.

"Last night a small squad of our army executed seven degenerates. Homeless drug addicts. The scum of the earth. Here in Hawaii. Swiftly and silently and completely. And disappeared without a trace. A training exercise, if you will. You'll have similar opportunities in the months ahead, opportunities for which your skills and your faith make you singularly qualified."

Dick pushed the button. "It goes on for another few minutes, but you've heard the big bang. I'm going to advance it to bring it to the best part." He stared at the recorder as he held a button down. He released it and punched the play command.

The other voice said, "My name is Daniel Aloysius MacGillicuddy. I am a Specialist Fourth Class in the U. S. Army stationed at Schofield Barracks on the island of Oahu in the state of Hawaii. What you have heard on this tape is a conversation I had last night, um, let me see, last night was Monday, twenty-four February. I, uh, recorded it to, uh, show anyone who is listening what is happening. The man speaking on the tape is named Orrin Massey. I met him after I became involved in illegal activities here in Hawaii. I have been stealing from the army as part of a group of other soldiers. I was deeply in debt to, uh, people who, uh, as it turned out worked for Orrin Massey and I agreed to steal the supplies to pay off my debt. I know now no matter how much I stole I wouldn't ever get away from these people.

"I didn't know that these people who I owed money to worked for Orrin Massey. He offered me a job after I left the army working for him in his security business. And I thought it would give me a clean break. He told me he knew I owed money to these other people and he told me if I went to work for him I wouldn't have to worry about it anymore, he'd pay it off. So I said yes. And then I got even more worried. I don't know why exactly. Some things about it just didn't make sense. And, uh, I talked to my daddy and he said, just told me things that, uh, made me suspicious. So, last night, when Orrin Massey asked me to meet with him, I taped my recorder under my shirt and now, uh, I'm going to get this tape to, I don't know, the authorities, I guess.

"I told my girlfriend, Betsy Fielding, all this last night after I left Orrin Massey, so if anything happens to me, you can ask her. She, uh, works at the Turtle Bay Resort.

"For now, though, I'm, uh, well, I'm not sure what's next. But … That's all. I'm Spec Four Daniel MacGillicuddy and it's now, uh, oh-eight-thirty hours on Tuesday, twenty-five February. Signing off."

FOURTEEN
Thursday, March 27
Kailua.

Near normal…

For the four days she was here, Serena forced five or six meals a day on all of us. I hated to see her go but it was either that or have my clothes let out.

Richie and the girls took Roscoe and Belinda fishing in the whaler, but they passed on the canoe.

Rafael suggested a way I could turn my failing fish pond into an interesting fountain, said he had a design in mind he thought I might like and he'd send me the plans.

Madeleine tried to persuade Valerie that she might benefit from a nice recuperation in Monaco, but couldn't sell it.

This morning, they all left. Even Muhammad. In Rafael's plane.

Bobby Bentley called. He said, "If I told you that one of the guys we killed on the mountain was a former Schofield soldier named Roland Collins and he was from Murfreesboro, Tennessee, would that be good news or ho-hum news?"

"Depends. Which one was he?"

"One of them in the helicopter."

"That would be good news. Sort of fulfills a promise I made to Danny's mother."

"How about another one up there, captured but still alive, whose DNA matches the cigarette butt we found in the clearing?"

"The 'still alive' part sort of mitigates my glee."

"It's an imperfect world."

"Yes. It is. Saturday about three?"

"See you then."

Bobby and his wife, Jeanette, and their two pre-teen daughters whom we had not yet met, were coming over to join Valerie and me, and probably Richie, in fishing for our dinner. And then cooking and eating it.

Rafael, no surprise, had been generous.

Yesterday I drove him to Brenda Sloan's house in Hawaii Kai. He told her he would like to provide for Heather's education. "Anywhere she wants to go, for so long as she wants to go. Tuition. Room and board. Books. Walking around money. All of it. And I want her to keep in touch with me. Write and call. You, too, for that matter. But I want a chance to tell … to suggest to Heather how to handle her education."

On the way back I said, "What'll you tell her?"

"To stay in school as long as she can. It's life's last great vacation."

He tried to force all the cash in the briefcase on me but I declined. The $40,000 was plenty, I told him.

He graced Jack and Jim—John and James Kanae—with a leisurely tour through Tahiti, Fiji, and a couple other South Sea ports of call and enough cash to make themselves popular when they got there. They left yesterday, taking Cindy and Leanne with them. Taking Cindy was Leanne's suggestion. She knew Cindy needed to get away for a while and she sold it to the twins. Taking Leanne, too, who was on spring break, was the boys' idea.

They began by asking Cindy and she resisted. "You guys. I'll just cramp your style."

"Cindy, if you don't come, there won't be any style to cramp," one of them said.

"What if both of you get the hots for me?"

"What do you mean *if*?"

"I hate it when men fight over me. It's the story of my life."

"Okay, we'll take Leanne, too."

"I like that better. What if we decide neither of you is our type?"

"We'll be in Tahiti with our pockets full of money and our hearts full of love. Maybe we'll get lucky."

Off they went. I was almost jealous.

After the funeral Betsy was arrested and booked. Dick Wong saw to it that the procedure was as decent and humane as possible. "A search is a search," he said. "Can't make it pleasant. It's humiliating. But she'll be treated as well as possible considering what we have to do."

She and Walter McCall had an appointment next week with the state's attorney to discuss her testimony. Dick was prepared to endorse an agreement that the state would ask for five years' probation, no time to be served. She was arraigned as soon as the booking was completed and Valerie and I made her $50,000 bail on the spot.

Throughout the procedure Valerie and I stayed with her as much as we were permitted. While we waited, Valerie said, "Harry, you're going to have to help her through all this. You're the guy who saved her life. Twice. She's going to throw herself at you as soon as she gets a chance. It's all she knows right now, letting a man use her to get by. Trading herself for favors from men is her haven. You're going to have to handle it very carefully. A lot's at stake for her."

"It doesn't seem fair."

"What doesn't?"

"That I have to turn her down for her sake."

She hit me again.

· · · · ·

I sat in the rocker tooting on my beautiful Selmer Signature clarinet. Valerie was in her chair reading—re-reading, actually—Larry McMurtry's "Lonesome Dove" which we had discovered we both considered our favorite novel.

I was past novice with the clarinet, but still a long way from good. Good enough, though, to find most of the notes I had in my head. Just not yet real deft.

"See if you know what this is," I said, interrupting her reading. She smiled, as if to an annoying child.

I picked at the simple, repetitive, but lovely rhythm of the introduction to "Someone To Watch Over Me". I made my way through it once and she said, "Sure. I know that. Play it again, Harry. Take it from the top."

And she sang it as I played it, all the way through. Finished, I said, "Could be a cabaret act developing here. Pines and Sabatino."

"Or conversely. Harry, it's nice being in love, isn't it?"

"Quite."

"I think we'll last forever."

"Me, too."

"I don't want to get married. You don't either, do you?"

"No. Not exactly."

"And I don't think we have to live together to stay in love. Do you?"

"Do I what? Agree? Yes, I agree."

"So… In a few days, I think I'll go to New York."

"New York? Why?"

"Why not?"

"Good point."

"And let the future take care of itself."

"Like we have another choice?"

"Exactly. I'd like for you to come with me. For, you know, a week or two. Maybe a little longer. R&R. Take in some shows, shop a little, hang out. Have some fun."

"Can we go to Mario Batali's restaurants?"

"I suppose. But you've been putting on weight."

"I'll just eat appetizers."

Mike Sheffield ripped open the screen door, taking it half off its hinges, and took two steps into the room with a gun in his hand.

"Looks like I get the last laugh," he said.

Over his shoulder I saw Richie arrive in the open doorway. Blood streamed down his cheek from an ugly gash above his eye. He held my big kitchen knife, the twelve-inch blade we use on Thanksgiving turkeys. He said, "Hey," and Sheffield half-turned in his direction. Richie took one step forward and drove the blade into Sheffield's side just above his waist with such force I thought I saw the tip come out the other side. Richie withdrew the blade and Sheffield went down slowly, like a melting snowman, like a bad soufflé.

Richie said, "How's *that* feel? Asshole."

The End

Harry's next adventure takes him to Chicago in December. His job is to uncover the truth of the murder of a beautiful woman for which a friend of Muhammad is wrongly charged and imprisoned. Along the way, Harry too sees the inside of a cell. Enjoy this excerpt from the soon-to-be-published "Big Shoulders Shiver."

Muhammad drove the big Land Cruiser, Valerie rode beside him, and I sat in the back stretching my legs and making calls. The snow had accumulated, crowding a foot, but the Land Cruiser ate it up.

Francis answered, said, "Free at last, free at last. Hope you didn't get butt-fucked."

"Highest priority. On the night Erica Conway was killed, Monday, November third, I checked into the O'Hare Radisson about five o'clock. Used American Express. Had dinner in one of their restaurants, one just off the main lobby. Charged it to my room. Also, I think I made a call to my place in Kailua from my room. Used the room phone. Get into the bill. Check the times of the transactions. Get word to Muhammad on his cell phone at the speed of light. Got it?"

"Get off the phone. You're slowing me down."

I called Vangie and told her what was coming down. She said, "Jesus! Never walk into a police station without your lawyer, for Christ's sake. Don't say one word until I get there. Not one! Agreed?"

"How long'll it take you?"

"Ten minutes."

I shut the phone and chewed on my situation while Muhammad and Valerie chatted up front.

I thought, one day I'll lose it and if I don't see it coming it'll kill me.

If I do see it coming, I may choose to push my luck and dare it to happen. Might be fun. But if that's what I choose, it still will happen. Maybe not the first time or the second but inevitably, if I go on living this life, I will one day die by better hands. Or maybe I'll see it coming and I'll decide I want to grow old with Valerie if she'll let me and we'll have a kid to spoil and I'll just lower the shades and finally get serious about cooking and reading and a few other important things.

Either way, it'll be my choice.

But only if I see it coming. And I want to. I don't want to go out blind. Or stupid.

Until I come up with a better one, the test I give myself is how much time am I spending thinking about something after I've passed the point where thinking isn't helping. Pile up a lot of those minutes, the ones where

I'm thinking and getting nowhere and the other guy's making moves and it's a very bad sign. I was there now, on the verge of failing the test.

A woman was paying me to get her husband out of jail if he deserved it. And he did. The people who were guilty didn't seem like they'd have a change of heart and give themselves up. Every move I made bit me in the ass, every step I took amused invisible others. I couldn't keep track of my clothes or my shit and I was sleeping in more beds than Goldilocks. Outsmarting me was turning into a parlor game for the perceptually handicapped.

Easy for me to say I hadn't lost it yet, but I was about the only one.

There was a copy of the Sun-Times in the seat and I picked it up absently, flipping through the pages. I came to the obituaries and thought I'd check to see if anybody important had died recently in the world at large. A face in the listings leapt out at me. It was Marie O'Brien, the woman who lived across the hall from Erica Conway. The obit read like it was a heart attack, encouraged contributions to the American Heart Association.

I leaned into the front seat and said, "The woman who lived across the hall from Erica Conway died on Tuesday. She looked pretty healthy on Monday."

I called Laurie. I said, "Today's Sun-Times obituaries list a woman named Marie O'Brien. Shows her picture. She's the lady lived across the hall from Erica Conway. I talked to her on Monday and she looked pretty healthy to me. Is that interesting?"

"Yes. I'll look into it. You on the way?"

"Yeah. See you."

Muhammad got a call. He listened, said, "Great work, Francis," and signed off. He said, "You signed for dinner at the Radisson at 7:17 pm on Monday, the third. Made a call to Kailua a half-hour later."

I said, "Let's fuck with Fenlon on this. Lead him on. Play a little rope-a-dope."

Muhammad turned off Division onto Larrabee and went past the station house to the parking lot beside it. The snow was coming in sideways.

Vangie was waiting for us at the head of the stairs in the station house. We shook out our snow at the door and I walked to the interview room with my arm around Vangie, said quietly into her ear, "While Erica Conway was getting killed and Jack Netherland shot, I was having dinner at the O'Hare Radisson. Then made a call to Hawaii from my room. We have confirmation. Hotel receipts. I want to hold that information until Fenlon gets all the way out on the plank. There's more to this than just keeping me from getting arrested. Although that also would be greatly appreciated. You cool with it?"

"You better be goddamn sure."

"I am."

We crowded the small room. A stenographer was there seated before a stenotype device and a tape recorder. Larry Fenlon and a suit sat beside her. Vangie and I sat and Muhammad and Valerie stood against a wall.

Fenlon looked at the crowd, said, "Who're all these people?"

"My legal team. I'm all lawyered up."

Laurie and Reggie came in, closed the door, and leaned on it. Fenlon said, "Thanks for setting this up, guys, but we don't need you in here."

Reggie said, "It's my job to be here."

"How's this investigation get to be your job?"

"Your partner made it my job when she came to me."

He glared at Laurie and said, "You bitch." Mumbling the noun.

Vangie said, "Detective, I don't even know why *you're* here. My client is here voluntarily to give a statement detailing all his activities of the past week, as well as of any other time frame of interest. All we need is someone to swear him in and someone to take his statement. Maybe you could quit cursing and act like a man and get on with it."

My phone chirped. I looked at it, the calling number was blocked. I said, "Excuse me a moment," and went out into the hall. I answered and a man said, "Mr. Pines, we haven't met. But it's time we did. I'm with your two friends. Here, the gentleman wants a word with you." A pause and Francis' choked voice said, "Harry, who are these assholes?" The other voice returned, said, "I don't want them, Mr. Pines. I want you. If you want to save them, come here immediately. Alone. If anyone comes with you, I'll kill them both. And whomever comes with you. And make you watch."

I said, "Twenty minutes. I'll be there."

I went back into the room and said to Muhammad, "I left something in your truck. Give me the keys." He looked a little suspicious but handed them over. I left the room and hurried through the station house. Laurie caught up with me as I was going down the steps to the street.

She said, "What the hell are you doing?"

I double-timed. She kept up. She grabbed my sleeve and slowed me down. I pulled away from her and broke into a sprint, grabbing for traction in the snow and slipping. She made up the ground and as I entered the gate in the cyclone fence of the parking lot, she grabbed both my arms from behind and added her weight to mine. I slid to a stop and turned to face her. I don't think she was especially comfortable with my expression because she put two open-handed slaps on my face, a left and a right, hard and serious. Loosened a little snot. "I'm a fucking cop, Harry. Don't fuck with me! Where are you going? What was that call about?"

"I don't have time to argue with you, Laurie. If you want to arrest me for ignoring you, take your best hold."

She shook my shoulders, said, "Get your head out of your ass!" She pulled a Glock from a shoulder holster, held it pointing down, to let me see it. "Answer me or I'll shoot you in the fucking foot for resisting arrest. I swear I will."

I took an overquick breath, a gasp, said, "The bad guy, the guy who's been doing all this's got two of my friends. I've gotta go there. He wants me, not them."

"Let's go. I'm coming with you."

"No! He said… You know what he said. Come alone or he'll kill them. And you, too."

"Harry, there's not an ass in this town I can't kick."

"I'm taking Muhammad's truck. There's a gun in there. I'm going to use it."

"Let's go. I'll have to bust you for an unlicensed firearm but that'll come later."

She put the gun away and as we hurried to the truck we passed two uniforms emerging from a squad car. She said, almost in a girlish lilt, "Hey, guys, you got a body vest in the trunk of that thing in maybe a medium? I'm going to a costume party."

"Sure, Laurie. It'll screw up your line though. You goin' as a bull dyke?"

She just laughed. The cop opened the trunk and took out a kevlar vest and handed it to her. She thanked him with a little hug and we went to the truck.

I fired it up and she got in the other side. As I pulled out and turned north on Larrabee, she made a cell call. I heard her say, "Reggie, something's come up. Harry's got a problem and I'm gonna help him with it." Pause. "I can't hear you. These goddamn phones!" And hung up.

I said, "Do you know what you're doing?"

"Making decisions."

"Make this one. There's a gun in the glove box. Give it to me. Become my accessory."

She got it out. It was the Walther. She checked the load. She said, "I think I'll take all the bullets out." And laughed. She chambered a round and handed it to me. I took it from her and put it in my jacket pocket.

She said, "How do we get in this place where we're going? I mean, get in sneaky. And quiet." She took off her leather jacket and her shoulder holster, put on the kevlar, adjusted the straps of the Glock rig, and put it back on. She checked the load in her gun, chambered one and slipped it in, put her jacket back on.

"There's only one way in." I thought about that. "Maybe not. Can you climb a wall? Fifty feet of painted brick?"

"With what? My fingernails?"

"A telephone pole."

She looked at me and grinned and said, "I love this shit. Love it! I just hope you can keep up."

• • • • •

On the way, I told her, "There's at least two of them. At least two bad guys. Two good guys, too. The good guys are a little guy with a full black beard and a Spanish woman. Kind of spectacular looking. Don't shoot them. Shoot all the other ones."

"Okay."

"This guy's a professional killer, Laurie."

"Me, too."

"He's not alone."

"Me, neither."

I parked the truck a block south of Goethe and we walked quickly through the snow, but didn't run, no need to raise a ruckus just yet.

I said, "I hate having you here but it makes me feel good. What's that mean?"

"You're probably falling in love with me. I hope so 'cause then I can break your heart."

At the alley I stopped and said, "See that utility pole?" pointing to the one that broke the wall's expanse about halfway along. "That's your way up to the roof."

"What?"

"If you can get up there, you can come in from above them. They're on the second floor. It's got no windows on this side so they can't see you coming. Up there, there'll be skylights, so be careful. I think they'll show through the snow cover. Maybe the heat of the room'll have melted some on them. Don't step on them. In the middle of the roof there's an elevator housing and a door next to it that leads to a down stairway. A spiral stairway. Understand?"

"No. You might as well be speaking Swahili. Let's go."

We hurried to the pole. I said, "When I was a kid I used to do this. You wedge yourself between the wall and the pole and walk up backwards, back on the wall, feet on the pole, pushing yourself with your hands. At the top you'll just have to feel for the ledge and push yourself over backwards. Snow cover ought to muffle your fall."

"If you could do it, I can do it."

"I'll come in from the front. I'll have to." I took the Walther out. "Here. Take mine, too. He'll get it off me if you don't. We'll figure something out." She stuck it in her jacket pocket.

She looked the problem over, then leaned her back and hands flat against the brick wall, braced her feet against the pole, grabbing it on either side with the rubber soles of her shoes, and shoved herself up. Her soles were wet and that didn't help, but the rough cut wood of the pole squeeged them some and she rose a couple of inches and grinned at me. She said, "Bet your girlfriend couldn't do this."

I said, "Just keep going. Trust the process."

I walked to the front, willing myself not to look back. I turned the corner and went to the door. I rang the bell to bring on the dogs thinking their noise and the distraction couldn't do Laurie's arrival on the roof any harm. After they stopped snarling, a voice from the box beside me said, "Identify yourself."

"It's me. Pines." I heard him ask Francis how to get the door open. I ended the charade by pressing the three times and the voice said, "It's open now." I went in the tiny room and the outer door closed behind me. The voice said, "Are you armed, Mr. Pines?"

"No."

"Naturally, I don't believe you. Take your clothes off."

I got out of my jacket and raised my arms.

"All of your clothes."

I stripped to my pants and took my shoes off. I heard the lift lowering to the garage.

"Now your trousers."

I complied. Down to my Ralphs and my socks and taking a slight chill.

"I suppose that will do. Wait just a moment." I heard the lift settle and stop and its door open and then another scratchy conversation. He said, "Please come in, Mr. Pines. My associate is waiting for you. If you think she's only a girl and you can handle her, this will end rather abruptly."

The LED panel glowed and I opened the door. The babe stood just inside. She was out of the red dress now, in all black, assassin attire, her hair tucked into a watch cap and aiming a mean little pistol at my bare, shivering tummy. Black gloves. She looked me over and smiled, said, "Not bad. Drop your skivvies. Just slide them down so I can get a good look."

I said, "Okay. But you might just switch sides."

I did it and she smiled. She said, "Turn around and bend over." I did and she said, "Okay. Pull them back up." I guess it wasn't enough. I'd probably have to resort to force.

She waved the gun slightly in the direction of the lift and said, "Off we go." At the lift she said, "Go to the back. Face the rear." I did. I heard the door close and we started rising. I trembled from the cold. She said, "If you turn around, I'll shoot you. It's gonna happen pretty soon anyhow, so here'll work just fine."

The lift stopped and the door opened and she said, "Don't turn. Back out. Slowly."

I backed out into the warmth of the room and appreciated it. I had in mind that I needed to get near the center of the room, to the lift and stairway Laurie would use, before I let them try to bind me somehow. I'd let them try but I wouldn't let it happen. That's when I'd make a play. That was my plan. I almost laughed aloud at the thought.

The babe put the barrel of her gun in my back and marched me into the room. Francis and Miranda were in their office chairs. They were duck-taped up like you could hand them off to UPS. Arms and hands bound on the chair arms, torsos taped to the backs, legs and feet snugged up tight and black bags loosely draped over their heads. A man stood behind them. He was a little taller than me and, I guessed, a little older, but not much. Lean. Leathery. Empty eyes. Steel gray hair cut close to his skull. A little smile. I didn't take comfort from the smile. He fit the picture I anticipated. Killing was his life's work. He wore black also. A long sleeved turtleneck and jeans. No jacket. A shoulder rig with a gun in it. And gloves. The babe came around from behind me and walked over and stood near him. She held the pistol steady on me. I took a long slow look around the room as a way of stealing a glance at the elevator and saw nothing.

He said, "Just us, Mr. Pines. Just we four. Five now."

I said, "Let me see them."

"Certainly." He raised one of the bags and the babe the other, holding them above the heads of Miranda and Francis. There were small pieces of tape over their mouths. They looked frightened. No, maybe not. The tape job might've fooled me. On second thought, I thought they looked pissed. I found each of them by the eyes and they gave little nods. They dropped the bags back down.

"Make your play," I said.

He laughed. "My play? How melodramatic. My play is that of a journalist. A reporter. My play is to interview you. Chat you up a bit. We've built a small fire in the hearth. To bring a little warmth to our task. Let's go sit by it, shall we?"

Hmm. Built a little fire? Had to go to the roof to get logs for that. Probably brought them down in the lift. I would have. Wonder if they walked up to check things out and rode down with their little hands full. I would have if I was in a strange place and wanted to see it all. I made a bet Laurie would use the stairs. Which meant if she was stealthy—I love that word—she could get halfway down before being seen from the fireplace side of the room.

"Leave them here," I said, nodding at my pals. I didn't want him to. If he did, he'd leave the babe over here with them and she could see Laurie as she came down. I wanted everybody across the room by the fireplace.

"Not bad, Mr. Pines. Looking for a handle on things, aren't you? Any kind of hold. It is kind of an unending struggle to get a purchase, no matter how slight. Life, I mean. Death, too. No, we'll bring them along. Let them watch."

Point for me, motherfucker.

"You take the gentleman first. Roll him over there. I'll come along with you. Then, we'll come back for the lady. Step lively." He removed his gun.

I did. I rolled Francis to the edge of the rug, let the wheels catch and tangle so I could act clumsy. I backed him out and turned around to lift him up and wheel him backwards. As I did, I watched what was happening back in the office area. Nothing. I rolled Francis across the rug, the first of the two, passing the stairs and lift on the way. The man followed us. I settled Francis by the fireplace, between the Eames chair and a leather sofa. The man, said, "Now the lady."

I turned back and, as I passed the stairs I felt a sudden chill, nothing much, a small downdraft, easier for a man in his underwear to notice than a clothed one.

I stumbled deliberately and he nudged me with the pistol and I said, "Give me a minute to get her across the room, too. I'm going as fast as I can." Talking to Laurie, I hoped she knew. If she heard. The babe passed us by, on her way to tend Francis and I said, "The two of you are good. She seems to read your mind." Jesus, could I get away with this crap? I'd have to.

I went to Miranda and wrestled her chair.

In another moment, the five of us were cozied up by the fire. The babe got a ladder-back chair from the sidewall and dragged it over. A stronger jolt of chill hit me and I struggled not to shiver. He tensed, catlike. The chill passed. He relaxed.

I said, slightly overloud, hoping I'd sound nervous, "What do you want me to do now? Sit in that chair while you tie me up? I'd rather not." I stood between them. I faced the stairwell and they were turned in my direction. An edge of Laurie appeared on the stairs, coming clear of the lift housing. The man's eyes, on me, narrowed and his gun came out and he whirled and fired and the woman did too. Laurie caught two shots square in the chest and she fell over the railing and went ten feet to the floor on her back.

• • • • •

I can't swear to the details of the rest of it.

I remember swinging my left in a wide arc without looking and catching the woman with full force flush in the face with the meaty heel of my closed fist. I felt bones give, at least her nose and maybe the cheek beneath her eye, and she went back and fell hard. The man's gun arm recoiled in my direction like a cable snapping and I went for it at the forearm, grabbing with both hands and twisting to get the gun out of his hand. His left hand grabbed my head with fingers like steel pipes. I saw a lot of purple then and things got hazy.

I think I held tight to his gun arm and drove away from the pressure coming from the back of my head. Just before I thought his wrist would break, the gun fell and I spun him around in a whip arc to free my head. It didn't work. We went down together, crashing through Miranda, or maybe Francis, and bringing the three of us to the floor. His right hand found my head, joining with the left, and he probed it with those pistons like he was trying to drive ten holes in my skull. I drove myself on top of him and pounded his stomach with both fists until I felt the pressure loosen. I drove both his hands away from my head with my arms and hit his face over and over until, suddenly as I remember, I was lifted off and flipped high and far across the room where I landed on my back. He was on me as I hit and I rolled into a fetal ball and forced myself to my feet and returned to pounding his midsection. I drove him across the room, clearing out a tall, free-standing, lily-like aluminum sculpture, tearing the points of it into both of us as we fell with it. Like a nose tackle, I drove my body into his and lifted him up on my shoulders and powered him and we ended up on the bottom steps of the stairs. He got the grip on my head again and I drove into him moving up the stairs with each blow. On his back he slid up and away from me and I drove my fists into his balls over and over and heard him moan. I think he closed his legs and I think I just carried him up the stairs and through the door onto the roof and put him on his back in the snow. I remember my shorts and my socks were gone by then, remember thinking the snow wasn't cold at all, was kind of comfortable. He flipped me again and I landed beside a skylight. He was on me and I forced myself back up and just put him in a bear hug and hurled him down hard on the skylight. He broke through like it was the surface of a pond and, if he hadn't taken my head with him, I'd have had him right then. But I went down and through with him, on top thank God. I saw the counter where we had eaten two nights ago coming up fast and the last thing I remember is that my face was heading for what looked like a poached salmon filet studded with chives and capers.

On letting Harry do all the talking

"An Ice Cold Paradise" is fiction, fictitious, wholly imaginary, populated exclusively by people who don't exist, and never did.

It is inspired, if that's not too grand a word, by the work of those whose tales of crime and adventure are told in the first person by the adventurer as it "happened" to him. There is no view and no voice other than his, other than, here, Harry's. Others speak, of course, but you don't hear them; you only hear what Harry heard.

As a reader, I've always liked the use of the unforgiving 'I' for the way it puts me in the hide of the hunter who never knows when a car or a bullet or a woman will come hurtling at him. As a writer, it's a little more work, which may explain why some use the first person until they get stuck and then go to the third person to rescue themselves. Explains it, but doesn't justify it. If you pick up a book that does this, put it down.

Terry Holland

Terry Holland has worked as an advertorialist, as a farm hand, as a political consultant, as a fishmonger, and as a geodemographic targeter. And a few other things. He lives in Louisville.

Printed in the United States
130154LV00003B/1-99/P